# SHADOWBORN SECRETS

## SHADOWS OF THE LOESS HILLS

2

# SHADOWBORN SECRETS

SHADOWS OF THE LOESS HILLS

2

Visit Mandi Oyster online at
www.MandiOyster.com

Facebook: https://www.facebook.com/MandiOysterAuthor
Instagram: https://www.instagram.com/MandiOyster/

# Trigger Warnings

*This book contains themes and descriptions
of past child abuse, abusive parents,
encounters with demons,
references to possible sacrifice,
and alcohol abuse.*

*Reader discretion is advised.*

# Subtitles

In Shadowborn Sorceress, Schmendrick felt inclined to let people
know how he feels about their intelligence. In Shadowborn Secrets,
he wanted to remind people what the world would be like without
cats. The chapter titles are courtesy of him.

# *Prologue*

*"The only escape from the miseries of life are music and cats..."*
*~Albert Einstein*

$S$chmendrick knew that Molly thought he spent his days sleeping, and even though that wasn't the case at all, it didn't bother him. He had taken the form of a house cat after all, and cats slept seventeen hours a day.

The fact was his actions intentionally encouraged her belief. There was no point in worrying her. She didn't need to know what he actually did, so he always made sure to be back in her house, lounging about when she returned from work or whatever activity had taken her from him.

It had started when she was a child, but somehow, he still felt the need to protect and maybe even coddle her a bit, which was odd in itself. He'd never felt the inclination with any of his other charges.

However, on that day, he wasn't sure he would have the chance to return to her. For on that most fateful of days, Schmendrick had mistakenly awoken a dragon, and even an immortal kitty like Schmendrick could be eaten.

He transformed into his true self, but a dragon was still a formidable foe.

# Chapter 1



"Schmendrick," I hollered up the steps. "I'm going to be late for my date." My knees weakened, and I clutched the door handle to keep from tipping over. I hadn't seen Jayden since the morning after I'd found out that he was my mate.

Rubbing my chest, I tried to slow my breathing. My stomach fluttered, and my heart raced at the thought of spending time alone with Jayden. We'd only known each other for a few weeks, and somehow, he could tell that I was his mate. What if he was wrong? What if he was wrong for me? My keys clattered against the stand with a dull thunk. With them in my pocket, it was too tempting to hop in my car and drive off, to leave everything behind.

It wouldn't be the first time. I'd done it before. Ran away and not looked back, not for four years. Not until Mom was kidnapped and Caelan stepped into Harvest Moon Café, where I worked, and thought I'd been hidden from the cabal's sight.

There was no denying that I liked Jayden and wanted to get to know him better, but I'd only been on two dates in my lifetime. A lifelong commitment wasn't something I was prepared for. My chest tightened at the thought of forever.

Why did my sperm donor have to announce that Jayden was my mate? Why couldn't he have left well enough alone, given me the chance to move slow enough to figure things out in my own time?

My thoughts turned to Malachai, and I shook my head. I didn't have time to think about the demon who'd spawned me and his offer of training. Instead, I focused on my after-work ritual, tucking the day's tips beneath the silk roses by the door and kicking my boots off with an overly dramatic sigh. My feet hadn't been comfortable since Caelan came strolling back into my life eons ago. (Had it really only been a couple of weeks? It felt like ages.) Sorcerers wore hard-soled shoes to help channel magic, but my feet were made for the cushy insoles tucked inside a pair of sneakers.

"Schmendrick, come get your treats." Hanging my coat up, I started up the stairs. "Schmendrick?" A lead weight seemed to settle in my stomach, slowing my steps and making my breath catch in my throat. It was normal for him to ignore me. He was a cat after all, but I couldn't remember the last time he'd ignored treats.

A crash shook the house, coming from my bedroom, and was immediately followed by the faintest mewling sound. Taking the remaining stairs two at a time, I rushed for the door, looking through a cloud of dust and debris into my bedroom.

If I didn't know any better, I would have said a tornado had touched down right in the center of my room before rising back into the sky.

Standing in the doorway, taking in the destruction, I wondered what had happened. My queen-sized bed was split in the middle. The wooden frame had been snapped in half, and springs jutted out from the mattress.

Tip-toeing through the mess, I inched toward the bed. Schmendrick lay in the center of the destruction. His eyes were closed, and his black fur was dull. Blood spilled from the corner of his mouth.

Fear clutched my heart, keeping it from beating. All the noises in the house seemed to narrow to a point before being sucked into a vacuum. Blood pulsed through my veins, and my heart started again. The only things I could hear came from within me, and the only thing I could see was Schmendrick lying limply on my bed.

Dropping to my knees beside him, I stared at his chest. "Breathe, Buddy."

My hand hovered in the air above his still body, afraid to touch him, to move him, to hurt him more. I didn't know what I should do. He'd never been to a vet. As far as I could remember, he'd never been sick or injured. He'd always seemed indestructible. Unbreakable.

He may have looked like a cat, but he was something else. Something more. But what exactly that was, I didn't have the slightest clue. He'd never shown me his true form. Never called himself anything but a cat. Though more than once, he'd hinted at being a god. (But, in all honesty, what cat didn't?)

His chest shuddered, and a sob caught in my throat.

"Oh, Schmenny, what happened?" My mind shuffled through everyone I knew and everyone who knew Schmendrick was more than a cat. Then I remembered the day I met Jayden and how he'd casually told me that Schmendrick was fae. Picking up my phone, I pressed the call button next to Jayden's image.

"A little eager for our date?" To anyone else, Jayden would have sounded upbeat, but I could hear the undertone of fear that tinged his voice, the worry that I was calling to cancel. "I'm almost there."

Holding the phone next to my ear, I tried to tell him what happened, tried to say anything, but the words caught in my throat, and my mouth floundered until a guttural sob tore from me.

"Molly?" All traces of his earlier optimism disappeared behind a growl. "Are you okay?"

Hoping to hold my tears back, I wrapped my arm around my stomach and pressed my eyes closed. "It's Schmenny. Hurry."

Hours or maybe minutes later, a hand clamped down on my shoulder. A startled scream escaped me as I jumped up. Ready to fight off whoever had hold of me, I turned but collapsed into Jayden's arms instead. Words fled, and I sobbed, my tears escaping before I could stop them.

His clean-shaven cheek brushed against mine as he leaned down. "What happened, Molly?" His voice was soft and right next to my ear.

"I—" Sucking in a deep breath, I pulled away from him and glanced over my shoulder at Schmendrick. "I don't know. He… he didn't come down for treats. There was a crash." I waved my arm at the bed. "And I found him like this."

Jayden slid his hands from my shoulders to my fingers, then stepped back, letting go of me. Before I'd even realized what he was doing, he'd pulled his t-shirt off and thrown it into the hall away from the debris. When he reached for the button on his dark jeans, one of his thick, blond eyebrows shot up in a challenge.

Turning my back on him, I focused on Schmendrick's chest. Nothing. I sank to my knees, inching closer but afraid to touch him.

There. His chest rose ever so slightly.

I was so caught up in watching for it again that I didn't notice Jayden had shifted until he nudged me out of the way.

In his human form, Jayden towered over me. As a wolf, he stood almost as tall as my chest. Light brown fur, which was only slightly darker than his hair, covered his body. Brown undertones blended in, adding depth to his coat. His eyes, though, were the same amber color in either form. The same soul hid behind them.

He bent his head toward Schmendrick, sniffing the cat from head to toe. Then he turned and walked past me.

Following his movements, I looked over my shoulder and wished that he could talk to me when he was the wolf. The fur covering his body disappeared, and facing away from me, he lifted onto his hind legs. The edges of his body shimmered as he transformed into the man.

My mate. If I accepted him.

The thought sent my pulse racing, and for a moment, my thoughts were pulled from Schmendrick's predicament.

Scars crisscrossed Jayden's back. Reminders of an abusive past he'd yet to tell me about. His body (what I'd seen of it) was sculpted perfection. All lean muscle, like a wolf. My gaze dropped lower while he pulled his jeans on and reached for his shirt.

When he turned around, I was still staring at him. He tipped his head to the side, covering his smug look as he yanked his tee on. He tucked it in as he strode toward me. "This is going to sound weird." He combed his fingers through his hair, starting at the top and stopping at the end of his long, wavy strands. "But I'm pretty sure Schmendrick was attacked by a dragon."

# Chapter 2



"A... a dragon?" My vision locked on Jayden, fighting the pull to check on Schmendrick. "Where? How? And how do you know?" My voice trembled, caught somewhere between fear and disbelief.

His amber eyes darkened, and a muscle in his jaw ticked. "Suffice it to say, my old alpha's a dick." He stared over my shoulder, clenching and unclenching his fists while slowly breathing in and out. "Do you know any fae?"

"My coworker, Simone." For the past four years, I'd worked with her, thanked her for helping me with things, and only recently found out that she wasn't human. Luckily, since I hadn't known about her fae heritage, she couldn't hold my thanks against me, but now that I knew…

"Do you trust her?"

Lifting my shoulder in a half-shrug, I flipped my hands up. "As much as I trust anyone, I guess."

"Call her. See if she can help Schmendrick, but whatever you do—" he grabbed my arm and made sure I was looking him in the eye "—don't bargain with her."

Pulling my cell phone out of my back pocket, I scrolled through my contacts, unsure whether Simone and I had ever traded numbers. We'd always been civil to each other, but friends were the last thing I'd wanted when I moved to Glenwood. I'd been hiding from my past and my future, afraid to move forward, and afraid to look back.

"Well, this is a surprise." Of course, Simone didn't answer like a normal person would. I pictured her tossing her long blonde hair over her shoulder with her perfectly manicured fingers. "You've never called me before."

A nervous chuckle escaped me. "No, to be honest, I was a little surprised to find your number in my phone."

"I put it there when you weren't looking." There was a nervous edge to Simone's voice, a waver that made me wonder if she worried she'd overstepped her boundaries. "A little sorceress out on her own... I figured you might need a friend or just someone to talk to, and now you do. So what's up?"

"Jayden thinks Schmendrick's been attacked by a dragon." My heart thrummed in my chest. My gaze was pulled back to the demolished bed and the cat lying in the center of the destruction. He had to be okay. He just had to. "He thinks Schmendrick is a fae. Can you help?"

There was a long pause. "Schmendrick? The cat you talk about. You think he's a fae?"

"Well, honestly, I don't know what he is, but Jayden thinks he's a fae." I glanced at Jayden, wanting his reassurance that he still believed that.

He reached for my hand, squeezing my fingers with his, and nodded.

"Well, he is a wolf." She said that as if it made perfect sense to her, but I held my phone out and looked at the screen like it held the answers.

Jayden tapped his nose and mouthed, "I can smell it."

"I don't know if I'll be able to help." There was a long pause as if Simone was gathering herself, psyching herself up to succeed. "But I'll see what I can do. I'm here. Come let me in."

"That was quick." My eyes widened, and my head flinched back.

She snorted before laughing. "It's so cute how you seem to forget that we're magic."

A flush crept up my neck and onto my cheeks. There was a time when magic had been instinctual, but I'd suppressed it for so long. It was amazing how quickly it had faded from memory. "I'll be right down." As I pressed the end button on my phone, I took a step toward the door.

Jayden didn't let go of my hand, clutching it tighter, preventing me from leaving. I tried to pull my fingers free, but he wouldn't let go.

The glare I tossed over my shoulder didn't even begin to faze him. "What are you doing? Schmendrick needs help!"

"No bargains." He brushed his thumb over mine before dropping my hand.

With an unconvincing nod, I raced down the steps and threw the front door open so hard that it bounced against the doorstop.

"And don't thank her!"

If I hadn't been about to do just that, I might have been a little annoyed by his comment.

Simone stood on the cement stoop. She looked perfectly put together. Her unnatural-looking aqua eyes glowed brighter than normal. Before I'd known she was fae, I'd assumed they were the product of colored contacts, but like my purple hair, I imagined they were one part of her true self that she let shine through.

With a smile, I waved her in. "I appreciate you coming here. He's upstairs." When we stood outside my door, I stepped to the side so she could take in the whole scene. The dust had settled, leaving a thick coat on everything in the room.

"What happened here?" She stopped in the hallway, her lip curled up at the mess.

Turning toward her, my entire body slumped forward. Schmendrick had come into my life to protect me, but I should have done the same. I should have kept him safe. "I don't know, but Schmendrick's in the middle of it."

"What will you give me for healing this cat of yours?" She stood with one hand on her hip and the other held in front of her, staring at her fingernails, acting as if none of this mattered to her.

I looked toward the bed, unable to see Schmendrick lying there. My heart fractured, knowing he was suffering and that I couldn't do anything to help him. "Any—"

"No bargains, Molly." Jayden's words came out on a low growl that led me to believe he was close to transforming.

Simone laughed, a tinkling sound that reminded me of wind chimes. "A little overprotective, don't you think?" She strode toward the bed without disturbing the dust on the floor, without even leaving footprints in it. She knelt next to Schmendrick and reached for his head. Her fingers skimmed his fur, the briefest of touches, before she jerked them back with a gasp. "You named him Schmendrick?" She glared at me. "Fool? You think he's a fool?"

"No—"

"This is no mere kitty." Her glamour melted away, sharpening her canines along with most of her features. "Have you no respect?"

Hoping to calm her a little, I held my hands up in front of me. "I was five. I didn't know what it meant. I just loved the movie *The Last Unicorn*." My focus turned to him. "He says he likes the name because it's like calling a giant Tiny."

She softened a little and placed her hands on him again. "You owe me nothing for healing *Aracondo*. I would give my life that he may live."

"Th—" Sucking in a breath and shaking my head, I tried to envision the glimpse of fae that she'd given me. All sharp angles and even sharper teeth, pointed ears, and wings. Except for when she'd taken offense earlier, her glamour hid it so well that it was hard to remember the danger that she hid beneath the surface. "I appreciate your help. I don't know what I'd do without him."

"You'd be lost." Schmendrick's voice was so quiet I almost didn't hear it.

Rushing to Simone's side, I dropped onto the ground next to her. Schmendrick's fur shone like black satin, and his green eyes were slitted with what seemed to be exhaustion. "Schmen, what happened?"

"Nothing for you to worry about." He popped up and trotted toward the door, wobbling a bit as he did. "Are you coming, Molly? My treats won't serve themselves."

## Chapter 3

*"I've found that the way a person feels about cats—and the way they feel about him or her in return—is usually an excellent gauge by which to measure a person's character." -P.C. Cast*

Schmendrick led the way downstairs. His tail dragged over the carpet, and his steps wobbled, but he refused to let me carry him.

With more effort than it usually took, he jumped onto his chair, and I walked to the cabinets. My hands trembled as I grabbed his silver dish and piled extra treats on it. Taking a deep breath, I set his snack on the table in front of him while still holding the treats.

"You almost died, Buddy." The words tightened my chest, and I clutched the container, clinging to it like a lifeline.

He extended his claws and hooked a morsel on one. "It would take more than a silly lizard to kill me."

"Lizard?" The container slipped, but I caught it before it hit the floor. "So you were attacked by a dragon?"

Jayden took the jar out of my hands and put it in the cabinet, locking the treats away. "Did you doubt my nose?"

"I don't know." My fingers curled around the edge of the countertop behind me, and I leaned against it. "I suppose I did. I thought dragons were extinct." Images of the Abyssal Drake and Hydra flashed through my mind. "Well… on this realm anyway."

Simone stood next to Schmendrick. As soon as he glanced at her, she bowed. "*Aracondo.*"

"You called him that before." My eyes flicked between the two of them. "What does that mean?"

Schmendrick narrowed his eyes at Simone, and she seemed to shrivel in on herself a bit. "It means Noble Prince in Elvish." Schmendrick snagged another treat and stared at her. Something passed between the two of them.

Simone inched back a step and folded her hands together in front of her. "Fairy cats are sacred to my court."

Fae couldn't lie, but something told me I wasn't getting the whole truth from her. A glance between the two of them made me realize neither would tell me more. "You're seriously not going to let me know why my room looks like a bomb blew up in it or what happened to you."

"No." Schmendrick finished the last of his treats. His lips pinched together as he stared at the platter. Then, as if coming to terms with it, he licked his paw and rubbed it over his ear. "You're late for a date."

Jayden looked at Schmendrick, then me. "You heard the sacred kitty." (Somehow, he managed not to smirk or sound sarcastic or anything.) "You're late for our date."

Grabbing the towel off the counter, I smacked Jayden with it on my way past. "I need a shower, so you might as well have a seat."

When I left, the werewolf, the fae barista, and the immortal cat were sitting at my table, and I couldn't help but wonder what the punchline of that joke would be.

Standing in my doorway, I stared at the disaster and wished I knew how to animate brooms and mops to clean up the mess. But, unfortunately, I didn't even have any mice or birds to help me out with my chores either. The kobolds would most likely help me if I asked, but Schmendrick hated them for some unknown reason.

Tiptoeing across the room to my dresser, avoiding as much of the dust and debris as I could, I gathered my clothes, and for the first time since moving to Glenwood, I went to the guest bathroom to shower. The steamy water pelted my shoulders, releasing some of the tension, but leaving more behind than I would've liked.

Ever since Caelan had stepped through the door of Harvest Moon and told me that Mom had been kidnapped, my life had been a whirlwind. First, I'd broken my vow and returned to Ravenwood Estates. Then, I'd traveled to the Abyss and met my father. And after all that, my cat had been terrifyingly close to being killed by a dragon.

"What next?" As soon as the words came out of my mouth, I regretted them. (If you ever want the universe to show you what can go wrong, just ask, and it will.)

While rinsing the conditioner out of my hair, I tried to figure out where one would even find a dragon. We'd seen them in the Abyss while rescuing Mom, but those things didn't exist on Earth. Did they? Where would they hide? How could they have remained unnoticed all this time?

With a sigh (I'd miss the hot water cascading over my tense muscles), I shut the water off and wrapped a towel around my hair and another around my body. One thing had become abundantly clear to me. When I returned from my date, Schmendrick and I were going to have a long heart-to-heart.

Not wanting to keep Jayden waiting too long, I dried my hair with the towel, then finger-combed it with some gel on my hands. Even though I had no intention of Jayden seeing them, I wore my sexiest bra and panties, black lace. Then I slipped on a vintage teal satin blouse with long sleeves and a V-neck that showed off the amethyst pendant that I always wore tucked beneath my t-shirts. The blouse contrasted with my hair, making my locks look lustrous. Next, I stepped into my favorite pair of black jeans. They hugged my curves but moved with my body instead of constricting it.

Standing in front of the mirror, I assessed my outfit. Turning, I looked over my shoulder and gave myself an appreciative nod before walking into the spare bedroom and tugging on my boots. With only a dusting of snow so far this year, I wasn't concerned about the three-inch heels being hazardous.

I sashayed into the dining room, knowing Jayden wouldn't mind if I'd worn a ratty t-shirt and sweats—but something told me he'd like this a lot more.

His gaze roved over me, stopping at the pear-cut amethyst nestled between my breasts that shimmered with all the shades of my hair, before traveling back up to meet mine. He scooted his chair back and stood, striding toward me without looking away from my eyes. He brushed the back of his knuckles along my cheek. "You look more beautiful than ever." His voice was husky.

"That's my cue to leave." Simone bowed to Schmendrick, her hair falling over her shoulder, before pushing her chair in. She flicked the blonde strands back and smiled at me. "I'll see you at work, Molly."

With some difficulty, I pulled my gaze from Jayden's. "Th—" I shook my head. "Good grief. You didn't have to come to Schmendrick's rescue. You didn't know he was a special kitty, but I appreciate it more than you know. Have a good evening."

Simone didn't walk to the door. With a little finger wave, she vanished. Like the Cheshire Cat, her eyes were the last thing to disappear.

Jayden slid his hand down my arm and twined his fingers through mine, then turned to Schmendrick. "Stay fur away from the dragon while we're gone."

"Don't you have a stick to fetch?" Schmendrick jumped down and rubbed against my leg on his way upstairs.

Grabbing my dressier-looking coat, I watched his tail flick as he trotted up the steps. "Be safe, Buddy."

"You too, Molly." He glanced over his shoulder at me. His green eyes met mine. "Stay out of trouble tonight."

Jayden led me outside and to his truck. He opened the passenger door, closing it once I was settled. Then he strode to his side. When he was behind the wheel, he turned toward me. "I was going to take you to Classic Café in Malvern, but now"— his eyes roved over me again—"I'm wondering if I should take you somewhere nicer."

"Classic sounds fine." I pressed the button for the seat heater and settled back. "I've heard good things about them."

His head turned toward me so quickly that I wondered if he gave himself whiplash. "You've heard they're good? You've never eaten there?" He took my hand in his and pulled out of my driveway. "Oh, Molly, you've been missing out. They have the best burgers and different specials every night."

"Okay, then." Laughter spilled out of me, relief and nervousness exiting my body the only way they knew how to. "It sounds like I made the right choice."

## Chapter 4



Jayden parked on the street in front of Classic Café. The
sign in the window said NOPE. "They're not open." Disappointment settled in my gut as I turned to him. "I guess we'll
have to go somewhere else."

"Nah, they open at 5:00." He was out of the truck before I
could reply, coming around to my side like he always did.

After the first time we went out, I realized that I might as
well let him be the gentleman. It could have been a wolf thing
or a Jayden thing, but either way, it made him happy.

He opened my door and reached up, taking hold of my
hand and helping me out. Like most small towns in Iowa, the
buildings on the main street were brick businesses that connect-

ed. Classic Café was in the same stretch of buildings as a mechanic, the fire station, and a gym.

We walked past the little wrought-iron fence that created patio seating, and the sign in the window flashed from NOPE to OPEN. A lady strode past us, unlocked the door, and held it open. "Go ahead and seat yourself. One of us will be with you in just a moment."

My boots clacked across the weathered-looking wood laminate flooring as I followed Jayden to a booth against the back wall. He slid across the bench, leaving room for me to sit next to him.

While waiting for our menus, I took in the restaurant. The ceilings were high. The walls were brick and plaster, and paintings covered them. Some were on canvas and some on the walls themselves. The ceiling above the restrooms was lower than the rest of the restaurant, creating a shelf with a bike and a picket fence standing on top of it.

A waitress with long gray hair strode over to our table. "Welcome to Classic. Our specials tonight are Chicken Alfredo, Southwest Chicken Pasta, Chicken Parmesan, and Beef Stroganoff. Can I get you something to drink?"

My eyebrows pulled together. "Dr. Pepper?"

"Mr. Pibb?"

"Sure."

"Corona with a lime, please, and an order of cheese curds."

When she walked away, I focused on the menu. "What do you recommend?"

"The bacon cheeseburger, the Philly, the gyro, a wrap, one of the specials." He flipped his menu over. "Everything here is good."

The waitress returned with our drinks and cheese curds, then took our orders. When she walked away, I leaned closer to Jayden. "What do you know about dragons? Do I need to worry about Schmendrick?"

When Jayden was with me, he softened, losing some of the stern appearance of the Beta. His muscles relaxed, and he turned from a formidable foe into a teddy bear. At my question, darkness spread over his face, and his body tensed.

"Hey." I slid my hand over his. "We don't need to talk about this now."

He squeezed my fingers before slipping his hand out from under mine. Then he draped his arm over my shoulders and pulled me closer. Leaning down so his breath caressed my ear, he said, "I don't want to scare you away, Molly." He rubbed my arm. "It wouldn't be right for you to accept me without knowing about my past, but this isn't the right place to talk about it."

"Okay." I tried to pull away so that I could look him in the eyes, but he held onto me. "I have to go to Ravenwood tonight, and I work tomorrow morning. Maybe after that?"

He kissed my ear, sending shivers racing through my body. "Call me when you're done or come to the castle." He inched away, taking his warmth with him. He plucked up a curd, dipped it in ranch, and popped it in his mouth. Even though he smiled at me, darkness still lingered in his eyes.

Regret clotted in my throat. Why had I brought it up? Why did I have to make a mess out of everything?

I wanted the easygoing Jayden back for our date, not the one haunted by his past. When a tall girl with her hair pulled into a messy bun brought our burgers to us, I was saved from coming up with another topic of conversation. I put lettuce and tomato on mine, then ate all my pickles, pretending not to notice Jayden watching as I took a bite.

"Well?" He bumped his arm against mine.

Nodding, I covered my mouth with my fingers. "Best burger ever." I wasn't even saying it to placate him.

He loaded all of his toppings onto his burger, added ketchup and mustard, and took a bite. His shoulders relaxed a little, and I was glad I hadn't ruined the whole evening.

The half-eaten burger sat on my plate, tempting me to take another bite, but I threw my napkin over it and pushed my plate away. "That was really good but really filling."

"Yeah." He laughed before shoving the last bite of his burger into his mouth. "They give you a lot of food here."

The waitress came back with a box for me and the bill. Jayden snatched it up before I could grab it. "Are you ready?" He picked up his beer and swallowed the last swig of it.

"Yeah." I scooted out and pulled on my leather coat.

Jayden waited for me before walking to the counter and paying for our dinner. As we walked outside, his hand settled on my lower back. Night had fallen while we'd eaten, and it was noticeably cooler. Across the street from where Jayden parked, white lights decorated a metal tree, giving the area a touch of whimsy.

Jayden opened my door for me, pulling me against him before I could climb inside, and pressed a kiss to the top of my head. He drove along Main Street, tapping his thumbs against the steering wheel, glancing at me, then back at the road, and then at me again. "My old alpha used the entire pack as weapons."

"You don't have to do this now." Reaching across the console, I settled my hand on his leg. It twitched beneath my touch, a small, involuntary reaction.

He didn't say anything else until we were on Highway 34. There were no street lights between Malvern and Glenwood, and his headlights seemed to be sucked into the stygian November evening. Even when Jayden turned on the brights, the night swallowed them. The intimacy of the dark cab was the perfect place to divulge secrets. "He always wanted more. More power. More land. More wealth."

"Sounds like a real douche."

"Yeah." He grabbed my hand, squeezing my fingers. "In his search for power, he sent me to another pack. I wasn't strong enough to defy his control yet." He let go of me, dragging his hand through his hair before grabbing the steering wheel. "I need you to understand that I had no choice."

"I saw that when I was at the castle and Garrett commanded you." The dim lighting of the dashboard did little to illuminate him. If I had been human, I wouldn't have seen the pain written all over his face. The grief and the torment. And maybe even a bit of fear. But I wasn't, and I could see it all. "He said you were strong enough to ignore him."

"I am now." His gaze flicked to me before returning to the road. "I wasn't then."

"Okay."

He wrung his hands on the steering wheel, refusing to look at me. "I killed them." His Adam's apple bobbed when he swallowed. "Every man and woman. I tried to save the pups, but Phelan found out. He put me and the pups in the arena and forbade me to transform. Then he released the dragons." His words came out hushed and broken, and I imagined he was reliving every pain-filled moment. "They'd been starved for so long. Madness had overtaken them." Oncoming headlights caught a tear as it raced down his cheek, making it glisten. "I did everything I could to save the pups, but I wasn't enough."

When I reached for his hand, he jerked away from me. Heat surged to my cheeks, and my fingers lingered in the air, unsure. The silence in the cab grew until I thought it would suffocate me. Nothing I said would matter. He was trapped in the gruesome visions of his past.

When he pulled into my driveway, I unbuckled my seatbelt. Lifting the console, I scooted across the seat and brushed his tears away. Then I cupped his cheek in my hand and turned his face to me, holding his gaze. His amber eyes were more wolf than human. "You are enough, Jayden. You're more than enough." I remembered him telling me that part of his duties was to keep the other wolves in line when a full moon was nearing. "You tried. That's more than most would've done in your situation."

"But I failed." He lifted my hand from his face and set it in my lap. "I wear the scars to remind me of what happened because I wasn't strong enough."

## Chapter 5

*"Perhaps one reason we are fascinated by cats is because such a small animal can contain so much independence, dignity, and freedom of spirit. Unlike the dog, the cat's personality is never bet on a human's. He demands acceptance on his own terms." -Lloyd Alexander*

Jayden got out of the truck and walked around to my side. Without looking at me, he opened my door and helped me down. As soon as my feet were on the ground, he dropped my hand like it had burned him and stepped back. "Now that you know my secret, I understand if you want nothing to do with me."

I moved toward him, intending to wrap my arms around his waist, to comfort him and let him know that I didn't blame him, but he held his hand up in a stop motion. Then he strode to the driver's door and climbed behind the wheel. He sped around the corner before I stepped inside my house.

"Give him time." Schmendrick hopped onto the stand by the door. "He needs to lick his wounds."

With a roll of my eyes, I headed upstairs. When I reached the top of the steps, I remembered that my room was a disaster. "Schmen—"

"Don't worry about me." He rubbed against my legs. "I'm fine." He trotted into my room and turned in a circle. It almost looked like he was smiling.

Following him, I turned my light on. My hand hung in the air while I tried to figure out what I was seeing. I flipped the switch down, then up again. "What happened?"

"Never let it be said that I am incapable of cleaning up after myself." Schmendrick hopped up onto my bed, walked in several circles, and fluffed the comforter before lying down. "Cat-tastrophe averted."

I scratched behind his ears. "Thanks, Buddy."

"You'd better get going, or you'll be late." He curled his tail around his body and closed his green eyes.

After the day I'd had, going to Ravenwood Estates was the last thing I wanted to do, but if I didn't show up, Mom would come looking for me (or at least send someone to bring me back). In exchange for my freedom, I'd agreed to continue training.

Exhaustion—the bone-deep kind that had nothing to do with sleep deprivation—clung to me, but I changed into my workout clothes and grabbed my swords. "Are you coming with me, Schmen?"

"Not tonight, Molly." He managed to lift his head a fraction before it sagged back onto his paws. "Tonight, I must rest."

Climbing into my Equinox, I backed out of my garage. In the dark, brooding silence of my vehicle, Jayden's pain settled deep inside of me. I couldn't shake his guilt or remorse. Thinking back, I tried to remember if I'd ever felt somebody else's pain so deeply, but I hadn't. His agony felt like my own, and despite just finding out about it, my heart ached for the wolf pups he hadn't been able to save.

Blinking back my tears, I saw dragons descending upon him, saw him try to protect them, and watched as his back was shredded.

The images felt so real, like I was seeing his memories, reliving them with him.

Could it have something to do with the bond? Had I accepted it when I'd shouted at Malachai that Jayden was mine? Were our souls entwined, whether I was ready for them to be or not?

Or was my imagination playing with me, recreating that fateful day?

Turning the radio up, I hoped to drown out the thoughts, the visions, and the heartache, but the music disappeared beneath everything echoing through my mind. I glanced at the passenger seat, wishing Schmendrick had come along, missing his snarky comments and his company.

The thirty-minute drive felt never-ending. As much as I dreaded going back to the cabal, I let out a relieved sigh when I saw the entrance to the hidden neighborhood.

Magic pressed down on me as I pulled into Ravenwood Estates. The air was thick with it. Parking in front of the citadel, I stared up at the guardians. In the daylight, they looked like benevolent creatures, but at night, lights shone on them, casting shadows across their faces and making them appear malevolent.

Being there alone made the shadows more sinister, like they were hiding monsters within them. Schmendrick's snarky comments typically kept my mind off my memories, and in the short time I'd known him, Jayden's company had comforted me more than I was willing to admit to him.

The car door slammed behind me as I broke into a run for the doors, heart thudding in my chest. Bright blue light emanated from the runes as soon as I touched the handle. It spread from the top of the frame and down the wood to the Ravenwood crest that was carved on the doors' surface. My likeness appeared. With a sword in my hand, I stood face to face with a massive dragon. Its wings were tucked tight against its body, and a plume of smoke rose from its mouth.

Desperate to outrun the image, I shoved the door open and raced inside, but after everything that had happened that day, I needed to know what it meant—whether it was a premonition or fear brought on by Schmendrick's near-death experience and Jayden's past.

# Chapter 6



$\mathcal{A}$s I raced through the corridor toward the great hall,
the shadows writhed along the walls, sprouting wings and jagged teeth, transforming into massive, hulking dragons. Their
talons clawed the stone as they stalked me, waiting for the
perfect moment to strike. My lungs burned. Sweat slicked my
palms. Seizing the door handle with both hands, I jerked it open
and stumbled inside, breath ragged, heart pounding, still looking over my shoulder.

"You're late." Caius' smug voice filled the hall, echoing
through the vast open chamber.

Shuffling sounded behind me, either from the dais or the
guardians standing in front of it, but I refused to turn my back

on the door until it closed. The feeling of being watched had been too intense, too real, even if it was irrational.

"Turn around, Mahlia." His voice was a low snarl that used to send shivers crawling up my spine, but since I left the cabal, it no longer held the same power over me.

Grabbing my phone out of my hoodie's pouch, I glanced at the time, then sucked in several deep breaths, releasing each of them slowly before turning around. "Well, Cai, I am not late." Swallowing the anger that threatened to spill, I stared into his hate-filled eyes, letting him know he no longer intimidated me. "I was told to be here at 7:00, and it's 6:58."

"Early is on time, and on time is late."

With one last look over my shoulder, I took my place next to the other guardians. "I guess it's a good thing I was early then."

Caelan glanced at me and shook his head. The motion cost him his balance, and he staggered forward a step.

As soon as the clock struck 7:00, Mom stepped from the shadows at the edge of the dais. The light caught the rich, midnight hue of her long-sleeve gown, making it twinkle like the night sky as she glided in front of the council members. The dress hugged her figure before flaring out delicately.

With each graceful step, a daring slit in the side revealed her toned leg from hip to ankle. The neckline plunged to her navel, revealing the sapphire and diamond necklace that she never went without. (One wrong move would be a wardrobe malfunction that I didn't want to see.) The gown swayed and sparkled, drawing everyone's focus.

Just as I was certain she had planned.

The center of attention was exactly where she wanted to be, and she owned it. With her perfectly coiffed blonde hair and classy makeup, she looked more like a twenty-something runway model than the forty-three-year-old sorceress that she was.

Captivating, sophisticated, and everything I would never be, she positioned herself on the throne like a queen, careful not to wrinkle her dress.

Once she was seated, the council members followed.

After a moment's pause, Siobhan rose and stepped to the center of the dais. Her copper-colored pantsuit matched the highlights in her auburn hair and shimmered nearly as much as Mom's, almost making me feel grungy for showing up in leggings and a hoodie with my short sword and stiletto strapped to my sides. Almost.

She lifted her arms at her sides with her palms facing up and tilted her head back ever so slightly. "Let the ancient wisdom and energy of Ravenwood Citadel fill the Arcane Council and this chamber as we convene." Siobhan's voice carried power, banishing the darkness from the room and allowing me to relax slightly. "Let us focus our hearts, minds, and spirits. May our deliberations be guided by the light of understanding and the strength of unity. This meeting of the Arcane Council is now officially in session."

As Siobhan took her seat, Mom stood. She sashayed (really, there was no other word for it) in front of the other council members. As she passed Caius, her fingers brushed over his hand. When she reached the end of the platform, she pivoted, then glided to the other side. Waiting, making sure she had everyone's attention, she stopped, planting a hand on her hip. "Kur awoke this morning."

"Wait." Caelan took a step, intending to move toward the dais, but he teetered to one side and then the other. Finally, he stumbled forward. "Kur, like the Su-Su—" He caught himself before staggering into the platform.

My stomach dropped. This was my fault. I watched him wave his hand through the air as if he were searching for his words, and I wished I hadn't broken him, wished he could go back to the way he was before finding out that I was Jayden's mate.

My thoughts turned to the past, wondering if this was how he'd been when I left the cabal. A dull, throbbing pain gripped my heart as hollowness spread through me. I should've given him a choice. I shouldn't have expected him to understand. How would I have felt if he had done the same to me?

Mentally shaking myself, I focused on the present. There was nothing I could do about the past, but I could try to help him get through this.

"Uh, Ssu—" He tried again but got no further.

Waving my hand at him, I pulled the alcohol from his body. It pooled on the midnight runner beneath his feet, darkening the rug until it was almost black.

"Thank you," Siobhan mouthed to me.

Caelan spun around, narrowly avoiding tumbling to the ground as he regained his balance, but he caught himself. "The Sumerian dragon, the first dragon, the one slayed by Enki?"

*Ah, shit.* There was no way this was a coincidence. Had Schmendrick been the one to awaken him? We definitely needed to have a talk.

"Enki didn't kill the dragon." Mom's blue eyes narrowed on Caelan, and her lips pinched together. "Kur cannot be killed." She resumed pacing. Her heels clicked with each step, echoing through the hall. "If he is, the Primordial Waters will no longer be contained. They will rise, and calamity will ensue. So Enki put Kur to sleep. For at least 5,000 years, Kur has slumbered, holding the Waters at bay and protecting all of us."

"Then why say he was dead?" Lorelei's black eyebrows squished together, and she fiddled with her ring before tucking a strand of white-blonde hair behind her ear.

Mom stopped and glared at all of us. I was sure that she had an entire speech prepared and didn't like being interrupted before she could finish. Her fingers drummed on her exposed thigh. "Because, dear, gods didn't become gods by letting dragons live, so the stories were exaggerated and embellished as myths and legends often are. And now Kur is awake."

"Sounds like a bloody nightmare." Storm's blue-gray eyes sparkled, and a grin tugged at his lips.

Of course, he would be excited.

"We don't know how it happened or who woke him." Mom touched her necklace. She'd never told me what type of protection it granted her, or if it did, but I doubted she wore it for sentimental reasons. "This is a priority. It will take all of you to put him back to sleep. If we don't, he will loose the cosmic ocean and destroy the world."

Mom sat on her throne and crossed her legs. She looked down her nose at me. "Molly, I expect you to dress nicer when you stand in front of the council."

"And, I expected sword training, not to be stuck in a meeting." I tipped my head to the side.

Her eyes rolled back into her head so hard that I swore I could hear them. "You won't have time for that tonight. You need to go to Malachai immediately and find out what he knows."

"You"—I pointed at her and then at me—"want me to go back to the Abyss?" I shook my head. This was some power trip she was on. She kept a photo of Malachai in her office. She used it like a phone to communicate with him. "Why don't you ask his picture? You know. The one you keep in your desk."

Without showing even a flicker of surprise that I knew about the image, Seraphina drummed her manicured fingers on the armrest, her lips pressed into a thin, bloodless line. When she finally spoke, her voice was honey-coated venom.

"You, my dearest Mahlia, agreed to the terms when you became a guardian. That means you follow orders—*my orders*." Her hand swept toward the others with a dismissive flick. "Ours, collectively, if that makes you feel better."

Somehow, she managed to sit taller, her presence filling the space. "You will go to the Abyss. You will speak with Malachai and discover what he knows of Kur. You will determine if there's a way to return the dragon to sleep." Her words landed like a gavel with each *you will*, making me flinch despite my attempt at being as stony as her.

"You will report back to us—" she let the words hang for a moment, fingertips steepled "—and we will determine how to proceed. In the meantime, your fellow guardians will consult the library for alternatives—in case you fail."

Leaning forward, she kept her narrowed eyes trained on me, unblinking, unyielding. "Do I make myself clear?"

## Chapter 7



"Yes, Mother." Sarcasm dripped from my words, and I dropped into the lowest bow I could manage. My mind raced. Who could I trust? My father was a demon, but my mother… Staging her own kidnapping to bring me back into this world seemed like something she would do without even batting an eye.

When I straightened, her lip was lifted in disgust. "And you will dress appropriately next time you're here."

Spinning on my heel, I took a step toward the door and the freedom that awaited at the end of the runner.

"My dearest Mahlia." Caius' voice was sickeningly sweet. "Where do you think you're going? This meeting isn't over."

My hand settled on my stiletto's hilt without me even thinking about it. I clutched the cool metal before letting go and dropping my hands to my sides. Then I slowly turned. "Well, Cai, maybe you weren't listening, but I am to *immediately* go to the Abyss. My understanding of the English language makes me believe that means now, so if you don't mind."

"Immediately means as soon as you are dismissed." Alden's gray eyes narrowed on me, his smirk daring me to argue, and somehow I managed to resist the urge to tell him that an entire meal clung to his beard.

Returning to my spot, I stared at the floor of the dais, refusing to meet anyone's eyes or be goaded further. If I didn't find a way out of the guardians soon, I would end up killing one of the council members… or worse, start acting like one of them.

No sooner had I returned to my spot than Siobhan's voice filled the great hall. "Thank you, Ravenwood Citadel, for imparting your eternal wisdom and bestowing your strength upon us. May the choices we make shape the future and echo through the ages. May our hearts be filled with clarity, devotion, and unity. Let us depart in harmony, guided by the light of compassion. Until we meet again, may our journeys be blessed with achievements and success. The Arcane Council is now adjourned."

When the other guardians turned to leave, I followed them. Storm stopped until I was beside him. Then he fell into step beside me, dragging a hand through his light brown hair, leaving it a little more tousled than normal. "Not sure what ya did to get your mum's knickers in a twist, but don't take it ta heart."

From behind us, Ember Sinclair snorted. "You really think she's wearing knickers?" Her voice was as dry as the desert wind. She twisted her neck around to look behind her, and her long, black hair flipped across the shaved side of her head. When she turned back, light glistened off the small silver ring in her nose.

Storm froze mid-step, eyes wide as if he'd forgotten how to form words.

She lightly punched him in the arm. "The answer's no, by the way." Her combat boots scuffed against the tiles as she jogged the few steps to catch up to Willa and Lorelei.

Ember slung her arms over their shoulders, tattoos covering every inch of her dark skin. In green cargo pants and a sleeveless black shirt, she radiated strength and confidence. She wasn't dressed any better than me, and that thought brought me back to my conversation with Storm.

I glanced up at him. "It's hard not to take it to heart, what with all the unity and compassion B.S. that they talk about."

He patted my shoulder, and I stumbled forward with the unexpected force of it. "There's a lot goin' on with Kur. Stuff she can't control, but you—" he gave me the once over "—for some reason, she reckons she can control ya, so she's takin' it out on ya." A roguish grin lifted his lips. "I reckon you're the only one who's got control over you."

"Thanks, Storm." My eyes felt hot, but I wouldn't cry. Not there, not then. It had been a rough day, and I would get through it. "Nothing I say or do is right in her eyes, and whenever I'm around her, my guard goes up instantly." The heavy, dull pain in my body intensified with each word. I thought it would feel good to put it out there, but instead, I felt smaller, broken. "It shouldn't be like that, should it?"

He rubbed his jaw and kept sneaking glances at me as we walked down the hallway. "Yeah, I reckon there's a part of every kid that feels that way, and maybe it gets a bit stronger as ya get older. Who knows? Maybe ya'll grow outta it, or maybe ya'll grow apart." We had almost reached the door when he stopped. "Ya gonna be a'ight goin' on yer own?"

"To the Abyss?" Closing my eyes, I sucked in a deep belly breath. "Yeah, I have a standing invitation, but before I can go, I need to figure out how to find Azaroth."

The mirth that usually danced in his stormy eyes was gone, replaced by worry. "I dinnit mean gettin' there; I meant bein' there."

"Thanks." My heart clenched, and I needed a second to gather myself. Even though I didn't know Storm well at all—we'd made one (invisible and silent) trip to the Abyss together—he seemed genuinely concerned for me. "I think I will be okay." I patted his upper arm. "You'd better go to the library with the others, so she doesn't decide to try to control you."

Leaving me standing at the door, he took off after the others. He only made it a few steps before he looked over his shoulder. "Take yer wolf with ya."

My stomach dropped. The way Jayden had left me standing outside after our date hadn't left me with a warm, fuzzy feeling. I didn't know if he would go with me, and if he did, I wasn't sure he would make things easier.

Caelan turned and glared at both of us. Lifting my hands in the air, I shook my head. His negativity, or jealousy, or whatever it was, wasn't wanted or needed. (Honestly, after the day I'd had, all I needed was to go home and go to bed.)

Stepping outside, I tucked my hands into my hoodie's pouch and kept an eye on the shadows, making sure nothing or nobody hid within them. Then I hustled to my car, threw my swords in the back seat, and locked the doors as soon as I was positioned behind the wheel.

*Schmendrick.*

*Yes, Molly.* His voice came back to me more tired than I could ever remember it sounding.

Pinching my eyes closed, I hoped some of my fear would dissipate if I only focused on Schmendrick. *Mom is sending me to the Abyss.*

"Why?" His voice wasn't in my head this time.

My eyes snapped open for me to discover him walking in circles on the passenger seat. "To see if Malachai knows a way for me to stop Kur." While he curled into a ball, tucking his tail around himself, I explained everything that had happened in the meeting and my conversation with Storm after it to him.

"Jayden will go with you." Schmendrick opened one eye and peeked at me. "He will. Just ask him." He flicked his tail over his eyes. "If you don't, it will create a rift that will only get wider and wider until it cannot be crossed."

"Fine." Leaning my head back, I picked up my phone and tried to prepare myself for the disappointment that I knew was about to come. "I'll text him, but before you decide to leave, how do I contact Azaroth?"

Schmendrick stretched his front legs forward and arched his back. "He'll be waiting for you at the Black Angel." Without another word, he disappeared, leaving me to figure out how to ask Jayden to join me.

## Chapter 8

*"Cats seem to go on the principle that it never does any harm to ask for what you want." –Joseph Wood Krutch*

*G*ot a sec? Before hitting send, I stared at my phone for several seconds.

Three dots popped up on my messenger app before disappearing. Then they popped up again. Hoping a message would come through, I waited a few seconds, but nothing.

*Going to the Abyss.* My finger hovered over the send button for a second before clicking it, and before it showed that it went through, I followed it with, *Will you come?*

My phone rang, and I jumped, coming close to hitting my head on the ceiling. "Hello."

"Why? When?" Jayden's voice was rough with the wolf.

I explained everything to him. "I'll be okay on my own if you aren't ready to see me yet."

"Oh, Molly." A door closed in the background, then his engine revved. "I never meant for you to feel like that." There was a long pause, but I let it linger, knowing he had more to say. "That's a time of my life that I'm not proud of, and I haven't moved past it. I don't know how to move past it. Me leaving tonight…" While I waited for him to find the words he wanted to say, I listened to his blinker click. "Me leaving was about me, not about you. I can't forgive myself for what happened, and I don't know how you can bear to look at me."

My throat ached as I forced back my tears. A thousand responses flew through my mind, but none of them would take away his pain. "It's easier to look at you than it is to be away from you."

"Yeah." The word came out on a humorless laugh, and I could imagine the self-loathing in his eyes. "I'm a monster, Molly. I know it. You know it. I should have told you from the beginning. I shouldn't have allowed you to get close to me."

"You're not a monster, Jayden." I remembered the way Garrett had controlled him. How he'd stopped Jayden's transformation with a single command. "You can't even blame the dragons for that, not if they were starved. This is all on your old alpha."

Silence met my words. It lasted so long that I began to wonder if he'd lost his signal. "Am I meeting you at the Black Angel?"

"Yeah." From the change in subject, I knew we weren't done with this conversation yet. It would come up again. "I'll go there now."

"Don't go in without me." He sounded withdrawn. "Drive safe."

"You, too." Before the words were out of my mouth, he'd hung up.

I parked on the street and looked up at the Black Angel. Darkness swathed her like a beloved blanket, but with my demon ancestry, I had no problem seeing every detail of her. One hand hung at her side, and the other held a bowl. Her expression was somber as she stood, guarding the entrance to the Abyss.

Headlights shone in my eyes when a vehicle rounded the corner. The make and model were hidden by the darkness, but the way my stomach tightened and my heart rate increased, I knew it had to be Jayden. While he turned around so he could park behind me, I grabbed my swords out of the back and tried to strap them on. My hands trembled, and the butterflies in my stomach flapped their wings like they were fighting hurricane-force gales.

When Jayden walked over, I was still fighting with the buckle. He watched me for a few seconds, then settled his hands over mine. His palms and fingers were calloused from hard work, but his touch was tender. Warmth and strength flowed into me. "Here. Let me." When he finished, he slid his hands to my hips. "Forgive me?" His amber eyes burned into mine, and I could feel his remorse.

"Yes." The word caught on its way out, making it indecipherable. Clearing my throat, I tried again. "Yes."

Inching closer, he left only a thin layer of air separating us. The heat from his body chased away the chill of the night. Slipping his finger under my chin, he tipped my head back. "I forgot something earlier." His mouth crashed down on mine, and the tension fled from me as I responded.

Wrapping my arms around his neck, I threaded my fingers through his hair. The night blanketed us, hiding us from the rest of the world. Heat pooled in my belly, and my nerve endings tingled.

Jayden tugged me closer until our bodies melded together, and a moan slipped out of me when he nipped my lip.

"Azaroth bes goings to the Abyss." Azaroth's high-pitched voice doused the fire inside of me as if he'd dumped a bucket of cold water on my head. At the same time, it made my toes curl inside my sneakers. "Is the peoples comings or not?"

I stepped back, but Jayden didn't let go. Something about his expression made me think of a puppy that had been reprimanded. I squeezed his biceps. "I'm glad you remembered."

With those simple words, I could picture his ears perking up and his tail wagging. As I gazed into his eyes, I couldn't help but wonder if I was seeing the spirit of his wolf.

"Me too." Jayden brushed his finger along my cheek, then tucked a strand of hair behind my ear. "I'm sorry."

"I know." I focused on Azaroth. The short demon was a mashup of comical and menacing. *I can do anything except reach the top shelf* was scrawled across his neon green shirt. The color made his celadon skin an even more sickly pallor. His curved talons clacked against the sidewalk as he tapped his foot.

"Schmenny says Azaroth must bes here." He narrowed his yellow eyes and pinched his lips together until they disappeared into a thin line. "And Azaroth gets no nothings for guiding peoples. *No nothings.*"

The last time Azaroth had taken me to the Abyss, he was supposed to receive *MaunDagnir*, a dagger made from a corrupted unicorn's horn and the bone of a sacrificed virgin. That had been foiled when I stepped on sigils carved into the floor and became visible to Malachai, my demon father. Until I remembered he was a lesser demon and no good could come from him having it, I'd almost felt sorry for the little fella.

"Unless you can show me how to do it myself, Jayden and I need you to take us into the Abyss. Then I can portal to Taras Mor." The black granite castle was the only thing in the Abyss that wasn't crumbling apart. It was majestic with its intricately carved buttresses and graceful towers, and it was Malachai's domain.

Azaroth snorted before he turned and led the way to the Black Angel. Like a little kid, he was careful not to step on the cracks in the sidewalk. When he reached the statue, he climbed into the shallow pool. Both times we'd been here, it had been empty.

"Azaroth," my voice cut through the stillness of the night, "how would this work if the fountain was running?"

He glared at me. "Don't yous bes worrying. Azaroth knows what hes bes doings. He bes doings this since statue bes putted here." He sliced a claw across his palm and strode around the interior rim, dripping his blood and chanting something inde-cipherable.

When he reached the starting point, black flames burst from the ground in a blinding flash. The angel's wings snapped open with a boom. She bent her knee in a superhero pose before springing into the air. The statue had to weigh at least a thousand pounds, but she flew as gracefully as a trumpeter swan.

Beneath where she'd been standing, a stone stairway led into the darkness. Using my phone's flashlight, I followed Azaroth without hesitation. Being able to see my foot and where I was placing it made it easier than last time.

320 steps later, we reached the bottom. Jayden and I stood in the center of a circular stone room while Azaroth walked the perimeter, spilling his blood. When he was about to complete his circle, I closed my eyes and covered them with my hand. After a bright flash, I opened them and waited while a stairway extended from the wall.

The demon guardian flew off his pedestal, opening the entrance to the Abyss. As we climbed the spiral staircase, the acrid smell grew stronger, stinging my nose. The heavy thunk of the demon statue flapping its wings covered every other sound. Knowing what types of creatures filled the Abyss, as soon as I stood on the jagged, rocky ground, I immediately opened a portal to Taras Mor.

# Chapter 9



*"Never trust a man who hates cats." -Jane Pauley*

$\mathcal{A}$ shimmering portal appeared in front of us. Malachai's throne room glimmered on the other side of it. Jayden and I stepped through, our bodies moving at immense speed to traverse the distance in a heartbeat. My ears popped, and my vision spun. I closed my eyes while the world settled around me.

Before the portal closed, several statues came to life, an army of gargoyles surrounding Jayden and me. Animal heads, some with horns or antlers, connected to humanoid bodies with batlike wings. Each of them gripped a weapon of some sort in taloned fingers.

"I'm here to see Malachai." Somehow, I managed to keep my voice from trembling.

The gargoyle nearest me lowered his weapon and bowed. The tips of his long horns touched the floor. The rest of them followed, sounding like a rockslide crashing down a mountain slope. "Welcome back to Taras Mor, Princess," the first one said in a deep, gravelly voice.

The statues straightened, and all but the first one retreated to their posts. He stood with his spear held loosely in his hand, but even at ease, his size and strength made him impossible to ignore. He towered over us with horns that easily spanned eight feet. His face was that of a wild boar with fangs jutting out of his mouth.

Reaching behind me, I took hold of Jayden's hand. His fingers tightened around mine, and the surge of comfort that I felt startled me, spreading warmth through my chest. I tried not to react, but I knew Jayden, and possibly the gargoyles, would be able to scent my emotions.

The gargoyle turned his head, focusing on something beyond me. Turning, I took in my surroundings. Archways curved around the edge of the room, with stone guardians standing beneath each of them. On the far side of the chamber sat an obsidian dais covered in carved sigils that flickered like the embers of a dying fire.

Black gemstones twinkled on an empty throne, reminding me of the stars I'd gazed at the night that Caelan found me. Two massive outstretched wings tipped with black jewels in the shapes of talons made up the backrest.

"Ah, Mahlia." Malachai's voice boomed across the chamber, drawing my gaze away from the throne and to the demon entering through a door hidden amongst the statues. "Your return to Taras Mor fills me with joy." With his long, spiraling horns, upturned nostrils, and muscled body, he looked like one of the gargoyles. Blood-red eyes were the only thing that made him stand out from them.

His focus slid to Jayden, and he tipped his head back, inhaling deeply. "And I see you brought your mate along, even though you haven't bonded yet."

Jayden clutched my hand a little tighter but said nothing. Wondering if he knew what Malachai meant, I looked into Jayden's amber eyes. When he didn't meet my gaze, I realized we were going to have to talk about the mate thing when life settled down. Obviously, there was more to it than me accepting him, and if Jayden wouldn't come clean, I would ask Schmendrick.

Morphing from the imposing demon to the beautiful man, Malachai strode toward us. Instead of wearing a kilt like last time, he was dressed in black slacks with a black button-down shirt, and his long, ebony hair was pulled into a low ponytail. Stopping in front of me, he took my hand in his and kissed the back of it. "Have you come to train?"

My mind whirled with a thousand comments, but all of them jammed in my mouth while I tried to reconcile the man in front of me with the images that had been placed in my mind throughout my childhood. Yes, he was a demon, but he was also more. The light danced in his gray eyes, making them shine with amusement and an almost childlike wonder. "No." I shook my head. "Kur has awakened."

"After nigh on 5,000 years." He rubbed his jaw. "Someone extremely powerful must have gone looking for things best forgotten."

My head tipped to the side. *Had Schmendrick been searching for something?* That seemed more logical than him stumbling upon an ancient dragon by accident.

"Mom sent me to find out what you know about Kur and how to put him back to sleep." I shifted from foot to foot.

Malachai waved his hand, and a black leather couch and recliner appeared next to us. Then a coffee table with a hodge-podge of snacks covering the surface showed up. Chips and dips, nachos, nuts, cookies, and cupcakes, along with a pitcher of ice water and one of lemonade. "Why send you when she could have contacted me herself?"

"I asked that." My shoulder lifted as my head tipped to the opposite side. "She likes being in charge."

"Sit, please." Malachai settled in the recliner and snapped his fingers. A glass filled with liquor appeared in his hand. He held it up and raised his eyebrow. The question was clear.

"No thanks." I dipped a chip as I sat next to Jayden.

Jayden nodded, and a glass appeared in his hand. "Thank you."

"So… the wicked witch wants my help." Malachai slammed his drink back, and the glass refilled instantly.

Jayden nodded. "Cool trick."

"One of the handier ones." He downed that drink, then set his glass on the arm of his chair. "Kur kidnapped Ereshkigal and dragged her to the underworld. Enki sailed after them and was believed to have killed Kur, one of his greatest feats." He pulled some nachos off the plate and ate them. "As I am sure you've realized by now, Enki didn't kill Kur, and he didn't put him to sleep either. Ereshkigal was one of the strongest deities of her time. She didn't need to be rescued. She saved herself."

Movement helped me think, so I stood, pacing between the couch and the coffee table, stepping over Jayden's feet as I passed him. "How many versions of this story are there?"

"Several." Malachai laughed. "But this one's the truth."

Raking my hand through my hair, I scraped my fingernails along my scalp, making the skin tingle. "How can you be so certain? And how does it help me?"

"Ereshkigal was a bit put out, to say the least, when Enki's followers spread the lie. Of course, her worshipers never believed it." He chuckled again. It was so full of life. Happy. Genuine. And I felt a pang of sadness that I'd missed having that sound in my life. Having him in my life. What would things have been like to have had a father who laughed?

Was it possible that the demon before me was less of a monster than the sorcerer who sat on the Arcane Council? Had I been misled all my life?

## Chapter 10



Jayden snatched my hand, holding it between his. "What is it, Molly?" His eyebrows pinched together, and I could feel his concern in more than his touch. It was a thrumming pulse inside of me. Foreign, but at the same time, comforting.

"Nothing." I shook my head. "No matter how hard I try, I can't seem to put this all together. It's like I'm using six different puzzles, so the pieces aren't lining up."

Rubbing my forehead, I plopped down next to Jayden. "Okay, so how did Ereshkigal put Kur to sleep, and where is she now?" Realizing the solution could be a simple one, I sat up straighter. "Will she do it again?"

Malachai patted the air with his hands in a gesture that clearly said to calm down. "Like all gods, Erie lost a lot of her power when her followers diminished. She no longer has the ability to put a dragon as fierce and timeless as Kur to sleep. These days, it takes all her strength to make sure the dead do not return to Earth."

My shoulders slumped, and I bowed my head. "Okay." Determined not to let this get me down, I sucked in a deep breath. Replaying his words, I tipped my head toward my shoulder. "Erie?" The nickname made it sound like they were more than acquaintances. "So you know her?"

"Of course, I know her." He grabbed a pink frosted cupcake off the coffee table and pulled the wrapper down before shoving the whole thing in his mouth. He licked his lips, then eyed the tray like he was considering eating another. "She's the goddess of the Underworld." He waved his hands. "The Abyss and the Underworld are tied together, two sides of the same coin. Demons inhabit one side and the spirits of the dead the other."

Jayden leaned forward with his elbows on his knees. "So, it's like Fae and Earth, two realms separated by a thin veil?"

"Yes. Erie and I are able to see through to the other side." He stared at something beyond me.

Following his gaze over my shoulder, all I could see were gargoyles standing at attention and the black stone walls and floor of Taras Mor.

"Thousands, nay millions of souls. They travel through the seven gates, losing their possessions, then standing before Ereshkigal as they were born, naked and humbled. Their names are written on the great scroll, and Ereshkigal watches over them, making sure they never escape." Malachai's focus lingered over my shoulder for several more seconds before he focused on me again. "She is as trapped there as the spirits of the dead, but her love for the world is unending, which was why she sang Kur to sleep."

The words made my head spin. Talking about gods was one thing, but hearing someone speak of them like old acquaintances was surreal. It was as if I were standing on the edge of a myth and realizing it wasn't a story at all.

Malachai smacked his hands together and stood. "While you're here, let me show you something of our magic."

My alarm had gone off before the sun considered rising, and the day had been unending, but the opportunity to learn something that could help me was too hard to resist. Knowledge was power, and I was going to need all that I could get.

As soon as I nodded, Malachai stood. With a wave of his hand, his chair and the coffee table disappeared. The room filled with shadows. They crept across the floor, stretching and reaching. Darker than any I'd seen before.

They slithered toward Jayden and me. Inky tendrils stalking their prey. I lifted my feet onto the couch, earning a hearty chuckle from Malachai.

"You, Mahlia, can manipulate shadows." With a wave of his hand, shadow ropes wrapped around Jayden's arms and legs, holding him in place.

"What the hell?" Jayden fought against his binds, but they wove tighter.

Malachai lifted one shoulder toward his ear. "Sorry, wolf, but I need you to sit this one out." He stepped into a shadow and disappeared.

Darkness crept over the room, coiling around the statues, making them more ominous. Jayden's low growl added to the eerie setting. My heartbeat accelerated, and icy fingers of dread crept up my spine.

Glancing all around me, I studied the throne room, searching every nook and cranny for Malachai. The shadows pressed in, obscuring the gargoyles beneath the archways until they were little more than shapes in the gloom. Rising from the couch, I turned in a slow circle, scanning the room, but he was gone.

One tentative step forward, then another. The thick air pressed down on me, and I shivered, not from a chill but from the feeling of being watched, hunted.

The floor creaked behind me.

I spun around and screamed.

# Chapter 11

*"One can't teach a cat not to catch birds." ~Albert Einstein*

Malachai towered over me in his demon form, my gaze even with his six-pack. Tipping my head up, I took a step back. His red eyes glowed, diffused by the shadows that surrounded him like a streetlight in the fog. Palms the size of my head pressed on my shoulders, preventing me from darting away.

"You must take your demon form to walk from shadow to shadow." His velvety voice was in total contrast with his rock-hard muscles and formidable appearance. "You can step into any shadow, anywhere, and use it as a portal to wherever you desire, including alternate realms."

My racing heart calmed as I listened to him. "So, I can use this to come here and to return to Earth? Without pestering Azaroth?"

I didn't know what the demon did when he wasn't transporting people to the Abyss. (And, in all honesty, I wasn't sure that I wanted to know.) But the longer I could go without hearing his annoying voice, the better off I'd be.

Malachai morphed back into his human-looking guise and gazed down at his feet. His confidence seemed to melt away, leaving behind an insecure man. "If, uh—" looking anywhere but at me, he rubbed the back of his neck "—if you're only willing to, uh, embrace your demon half."

Standing in front of me was the horrible, terrifying monster that I'd been warned about my entire life, but had I been lied to?

Shaking my head, I thought about Caius. All the times he'd punished me for being the spawn of a demon. How Mom had been blind to his actions. The more time I spent with Malachai, the more I wondered why he'd been taken from my life, why Mom didn't want me to know my father.

Was this who Malachai truly was, or did he hide the vile monster from me?

Reaching for his hands, I let the demon inside of me out. By the time his fingers settled against mine, the transformation was complete.

He sucked in a breath as his gaze traveled from the tips of my spiraling horns to the end of my tail. "You are even more stunning in this form, Mahlia."

"Thank you." Heat rose to my cheeks, and I hoped that beneath my rich brown skin, he couldn't see my embarrassment.

"You must embrace your demon nature, the strength, the speed, all the gifts my blood bestowed upon you." His gray eyes stared into mine. "Take them. Accept them. Make them yours."

Shaking my head, I staggered back a step. "I–I can't." The first time I'd come to the Abyss, I'd been confronted by my demon self. The part of me that embraced the darkness and turned its back on the light. Nothing scared me more than that side of me.

"Why not, Molly?" His head tipped to the side, and his thick, black eyebrows scrunched together. "They are part of you already. Accept them. Draw on them. Claim them."

Lifting my hand, I started to drag it through my hair, but my fingers rammed into my horn. For the last four years, I'd foolishly thought I'd been using a glamour. How could I have been so stupid? How had I not realized I'd shapeshifted? Glamours only hid the truth. They didn't change them. My horns, my tail, all of it still would've been there the entire time I'd hidden in Glenwood. Things like this would've happened daily.

But I hadn't known I could shapeshift, so I'd never even considered it as a possibility.

"I can't." Dropping my hand to my side, I let my shoulders slump. "I can't let the darkness take me over. I can't become evil."

"Evil?" Malachai staggered back a step as if my words had struck him in the chest. The usual sharp glint in his eyes dulled, replaced by something raw and wounded. He shook his head wearily, more to himself than me. "Is that what you think?"

"Yes." My voice was soft and unsteady. "That's what I've been told my entire life. Caius and the others reminded me of it every chance they got."

Malachai stilled, every muscle in his body rigid. "*Caius.*" He spat the name as though it left as bad a taste in his mouth as it did in mine. "I can't believe Seraphina let you believe that about yourself." His voice was low and dangerous, the rumbling of distant thunder, the warning of a coming storm. "She knows better." Rage burned in his eyes. With his hands curled into fists at his sides, he turned slightly, as if trying to redirect the tempest of emotion threatening to tear free.

My breath hitched. The fury radiating off him—I'd unleashed this, the *monster* I'd been warned about all my life.

"Molly, breathe." Jayden's voice cut through the tension in the air, in my body. "He's not angry at you. He's not Caius."

Malachai's head snapped toward me, and his expression darkened further. His hands flexed, claws protruding from his fingertips before he closed them into fists again.

I staggered back, watching as shadows coiled near his feet, rising like vipers waiting to be unleashed.

His gaze softened ever so slightly at my reaction. It still burned, but beneath it, sorrow and something fierce and protective shone through. "Someday, I will find a way around your mother's command, and I will tear his spine from his body."

My hand trembled as I stretched it out and inched toward him. My gaze darted from the fire burning in his eyes to the serpentine shadows. "Caius is all bark and no bite these days." My fingers settled on his thick arm.

*Maybe.* I didn't say it out loud. Malachai didn't need to know that somebody wanted me dead. Not yet, anyway. First, I needed to figure out who it was.

Malachai placed his hand on top of mine. His touch was gentle, but fury lingered in his voice. "Some demons are evil, but as you've experienced, some sorcerers are, too."

"So, you're saying part of me isn't evil?" I tried to pull my hand away, but he held onto it.

A surprised chuckle escaped Malachai. "No. I'm not saying that." He patted my shoulder. "There can be no shadows without light. Everyone harbors both inside of them. You become whichever you nurture."

"Schmendrick told me I am a blend of magic and darkness, shadow and light." When I turned away from Malachai, he let go of me. "I thought he meant sorceress and demon. I thought he meant one was good, and one was bad." I plopped down onto the couch next to Jayden, jumping up again when I sat on my tail. Embarrassment clung to me like a shroud. Until I was eighteen, I'd navigated life with a tail, and I'd known how to sit without hurting myself. Gritting my teeth, I stared at Jayden, still bound by Malachai's shadows. "Can you let him go already?"

Malachai shook his head. "If you want your mate free, release him yourself."

"Stop. Calling. Him. That!" Heat surged through my veins, and I embraced my anger, letting it replace my embarrassment. "His name is Jayden, not wolf, not your mate. Jayden."

Jayden's lips curled into a smirk, and he shook his head. "I've been called worse."

"Maybe you have, but you're more than a wolf, more than my mate." I stabbed my finger through the air, pointing it at Malachai. "And he needs to understand that."

"Duly noted." He arched an eyebrow, the corner of his mouth twitching—not in amusement, but in something closer to reluctant approval. He looked between me and Jayden, then gave a slow nod, the movement stiff but deliberate.

As the fight drained out of me, exhaustion set in. "I need him free. I need to go home and sleep."

"I told you. You can control shadows." Malachai raised his eyebrow, and the challenge was clear.

Glancing from Malachai to Jayden and back again, I sucked in a deep breath. He wasn't going to let me out of this the easy way. "How?"

"You can manipulate shadows in either form, but it might be easier at first as your true self." His gaze darted away from me before landing on me again.

"Well—" I waved my hands in front of me, thinking it was quite obvious that I was in my demon form.

Malachai closed the distance between us, wrapping his arms around my shoulders, pulling me against his side, and chuckled. "My daughter is so impatient."

"Your daughter is tired and ready to go home and collapse in bed for a few hours before getting up to go to work." Crossing my arms over my chest, I tapped my foot against the black granite floor.

He ruffled my hair, then scooted away from me. "Shadow manipulation can be done in two ways. The easiest one is to embrace the darkness, but since you don't want to give in to that side of yourself, you need to call on the light and angle it, making the shadows lengthen. Then bend them to your will."

Light slipped through my fingertips, but I didn't listen to Malachai. The easiest way to disperse shadows was to shine light upon them. "Close your eyes, Jayden." As soon as he did, a bright ray covered him, shrinking the shadows until they were nothing but memory.

Jayden stood and rubbed his arms while shaking his legs out. "Enough for tonight." He nodded at me. "She needs sleep before going to work tomorrow."

"You know you needn't want for anything, don't you, Molly?" Malachai stepped toward me. "As one of the guardians, the cabal should be paying you, and I will gladly give you anything you need."

I walked to Jayden and slid my hand in his. "I work because I enjoy it, but I will ask Caelan when I get paid." I nodded at the shadow. "So, how do I do this?"

"Conjure an image of where you'd like to go, hold it in your mind, and step into the shadow. Your destination awaits on the other side." He stepped to the side, disappearing in the darkness that stretched across the floor, and reappeared right in front of me. "You might want to try a short distance first."

Shaking my head, I imagined the area right behind the Black Angel Statue. It would be hidden from any prying eyes. "Thank you for the information and for training me, but I want to go home." Stepping into the shadow, I pulled Jayden with me, grateful when he didn't resist, that he trusted me enough to follow.

## Chapter 12



*D*arkness enveloped us for a fraction of a second before chill night air caressed my face. Unlike portal travel, there was no disorientation, no ear popping. It felt like I'd just taken a step.

"Well, that oughta come in handy." Jayden pulled his phone out of his back pocket and tapped the screen. "2:03." He lifted his hand, fingers hovering inches from my cheek, the heat of his skin brushing mine without contact. "Gonna skip work so you can get some sleep."

I covered my yawn with my fingers. My body wanted to agree with him, curl up and let the world fade, but guilt tightened my chest. "No, I can't do that to Viv, but if we're slow, I might see about skipping out early."

As we walked to our vehicles, the weight of the day pressed down on me—Schmendrick crashing onto my bed, my date, learning about Jayden's violent past, the council meeting debacle, my trip to the Abyss. Too many pieces crammed into too few hours. I swallowed hard, but with Jayden next to me, it felt survivable. "Thank you for going with me."

"Always, Molly." He lifted my hand to his lips and kissed the back of it. "Thank you for not being so pissed off at me that you didn't ask."

I stopped walking, and he faltered beside me, stiffening as if I'd stepped over some invisible line he didn't know how to cross. The silence between us stretched, heavy and awkward.

Unable to meet his eyes, I stared at our joined fingers. "I wasn't mad at you. I thought you were mad at me for bringing it up." Chewing on my bottom lip, I turned toward him. "I didn't think you'd come. Storm and Schmendrick told me to ask. Schmenny said you'd be upset if I didn't."

"Oh, Molly." Jayden rubbed the back of his neck, dropping his gaze. He studied the sidewalk like he'd never seen one before, shifting from foot to foot, fingers flexing restlessly at his sides. When he looked up, his jaw was clenched, but his eyes were soft with regret. "I never meant to make you feel that way." He lifted his hand to the side of my face.

This time, I leaned into his touch, not allowing him to pull away. He brushed his thumb along my cheek. "I was never upset with you. I will always be there for you as long as I can."

Closing my eyes, I allowed the warmth of his hand to soothe me and his words to settle my fears.

Standing behind the counter at Harvest Moon, my eyelids drooped. The regulars had come and gone, their orders served less enthusiastically than normal.

"How's Schmendrick?" Simone handed me a cup of hot cocoa with the lid off.

Holding it beneath my nose, I breathed in the rich sweetness of it and smiled at her. "He seems to be his normal, snarky self. He gobbled up his treats like he hadn't eaten in a week or more." Taking a sip of my salted caramel, extra marshmallow hot chocolate, I sighed. "So good," I said in lieu of thank you.

"I'm grateful that you trusted me enough to call me for help with him." Her aqua eyes were soft and shimmered faintly. Lifting her hand to her headset, she walked away from me. "Welcome to Harvest Moon. How can I help you?"

With each sip of cocoa, I felt a little more awake, a little more prepared to take on the day. Surprisingly, I even felt like I could handle going back to Ravenwood to face the council. When the door opened, making the bell ring, my shoulders didn't slump as they had all morning. Instead, I bopped up to the counter. "Welcome to Harvest Moon. What can I get for you today?"

"Well, aren't you rather chipper this morning?" The gray-haired woman's lips rose into a smile that lit up her entire face. "Can I get an Iced White Chocolate Peppermint Mocha, please?"

"Coming right up." My steps bounced, and my hips swayed to the music on the radio as I made her order. Snapping the lid on her cup, I beamed at her as I turned around. "Have a great day!"

While I watched her walk out the door, I reached for my cocoa. The sweet and salty mix hit my tongue, and I closed my eyes as I savored the flavor. Realization sank in, and my eyes sprang open. I rounded on Simone. "What did you put in my drink?"

Simone's polished mask faltered for the briefest second. She took a half-step back, almost imperceptible, but enough to betray her instinct to retreat. Her lips parted in a silent inhale. One hand tightened on the edge of the counter while the other hovered midair. She blinked once. Slowly. "Just… ah, a vitality herb to help you wake up."

"You thanked me for trusting you; then you slipped me a Mickey?" My voice rose sharper than I intended, but betrayal stung like salt in an open wound. I got that she was a fairy, and they didn't play by the same rules as humans, but she should've known better. Shouldn't she? "That might be okay where you're from, but it's not here."

Simone flinched, a flicker in her expression as the words struck something soft beneath the surface. Her eyes dropped to the floor, as if searching for an excuse hidden in the wood grain. Her mouth opened slightly, then closed. Her lips pressed into a thin, uncertain line.

Forcing my anger to dissipate, I sucked in a deep breath. "I appreciate the thought. I really do." My throat ached with words I didn't say. It was so hard for me to trust people, and

I thought I could trust Simone. I'd wanted to trust her. "Next time, ask first."

Her gaze lifted enough to meet mine, not any further. "I only wanted to help, and I was afraid you'd say no."

"I might have, Simone." My shoulders sagged ever so slightly as the fight drained out of me. "But then it would have been my choice." I reached for my drink again. "Whatever this is, though, I feel like I might be able to face Mom and Caius." I started to turn away but stopped midstride. "This isn't addictive, is it?"

Simone expelled a heavy gust of air, pressing her hand against her chest. "No, of course not. *Aracondo* would never forgive me for that."

"No." I shook my head and picked up my cup again. "He probably wouldn't."

A sheepish smile crossed her face. "You'll let me know if you need it again, won't you?"

"Yeah." The weight of everything that lay ahead of me pressed down on my shoulders, making me sigh dramatically. "I imagine there will be a lot of late nights ahead of me."

## Chapter 13



"*S*chmendrick." The door snicked shut behind me, and I said a silent prayer that he was okay. "I have to go to Ravenwood. Are you coming with me?"

He trotted to the top of the staircase and blinked slowly at me, his tail weaving through the air behind him. "Ah, Ravenwood, home of a thousand different traumas and, of course, bitter sorcerers. Will you grab my emotional support treats for me, Molly?"

"If you still need rest after yesterday, I can go on my own." With my arms folded over my chest, I rocked back on my heels, hoping I didn't look too antsy, hoping I wasn't projecting how badly I wanted him with me.

Like a kitten and not a timeless cat, he trotted down the steps and rubbed his head against my leg. "I'm feline fine." With a flick of his tail and a smug smirk, he strolled to the kitchen, stopping to look back at me. "You didn't expect an overgrown salamander to keep dragon me down, did you?"

Normally, hearing one of his bad puns would have made me roll my eyes, but right then, I couldn't even make myself groan. Warm relief that pooled inside me, and I smiled.

Dressed in black slacks and my teal silk shirt, I reached for the door handle. The runes sparked against my skin, and blue light cascaded down from the frame, spiderwebbing across the wooden door. It traced the Ravenwood crest, erupting from the bird's talons in a fiery glow.

A new engraving covered the door. A massive dragon rested its head on its front feet. Its body curled around a pool of water. Its tail touched its claws, forming a perfect circle. I stood on a ledge overlooking the massive beast, an ant in comparison.

My shoulders dropped, but I fought the urge to scurry away. Instead, I walked into the great hall with my head held high. Even though no other guardians or council members had shown up yet, I knew somebody somewhere was watching. They always were.

Taking my place in front of the dais, I stepped out of my heels and waited for the Arcane Council to arrive. Schmendrick settled in the shadow beneath the stage and, with a wink at me, curled into a ball of floof that would have been invisible if I weren't looking.

Staring up at the banners behind the dais, I wondered if our ancestors would be proud of us, the Ravenwood line. Did my mother's concern for appearances come from them, or did they care more about right and wrong? Would they have stood by and watched as Caius abused his own stepdaughter? Would they have replaced the council members for standing by and watching it happen?

As sorcerers, it seemed to me that our contribution to the world should be in finding ways to help others. We had the means. Didn't that make it our responsibility?

But Mom and the council only seemed to care about sorcerers and being the enforcers of magical beings. Of positioning themselves above others.

Standing beneath the domed ceiling, I realized I never should have left. I should have fought for the Ravenwood Cabal to use our strength, our power, and our magic to make the world a better place, not only for sorcerers. For everyone.

And once Kur was sent to rest again, I would find a way to make that happen.

There were so many illnesses that magic could cure. So many wrongs that magic could right. We could feed the world if we worked with humans. We couldn't create food, but we could increase the yields of the crops. We could purify water and make it accessible to everyone.

We had that power, but we were afraid to show ourselves to the world. Afraid to let people know what we could do.

And so we hid from humans, blended in with them, made them believe that sorcerers, werewolves, vampires, fae, and dragons were all fantastical creatures. We let them believe that magic was merely sleight of hand.

Walking over to one of the stone columns, I traced the raven-headed gryphon that was etched into it. My family's protectors. What would they think of what we'd become?

"Oi, Molly." Storm's voice echoed through the great hall, snapping me out of my internal deliberations. "Yer early."

With a grin, I turned to him. The man was quickly becoming one of my favorite guardians. He was steady, honorable, someone I could count on. "I thought maybe if I showed up super early and dressed nicely, the council might ignore me."

"Fat chance o' that happenin'." His laughter boomed through the columns, bounced off the ceiling, and was contagious.

I strode toward him. "What brought you here, Storm? Why this cabal?"

"Believe it or not." His grin was lopsided, and he rubbed the back of his neck. "Lorelei."

Trying to figure out what I wanted to say, I stared at him for a second, but the only thing that escaped my mouth was, "Huh."

"Yeah." He shrugged one shoulder before tucking his hands in his pockets. "We were together for a coupla years." His gaze flicked to the ground before he looked back up with a faint smile touching his lips. "But I like it here. There's always somethin' keepin' me busy, ya know? And I've learnt heaps."

Lorelei had done her best to make my life miserable. I knew she was different around other people, so I shot Storm my most sincere smile. "Well, I'm glad you're here. It's nice to see a friendly face at these meetings."

Caelan joined us at that moment. "If you want a friendly face, start playing by the rules." His hazel eyes were surrounded by dark circles that drained the vibrancy from them.

"It's lovely to see you, too, Cae." Smiling at him, I stepped back into my heels. Just because I couldn't give him what he wanted, that didn't stop my heart from going out to him. His brown hair looked like it hadn't been combed (or washed for that matter) in days. It hung limply to his shoulders, the curls that I'd always loved pulled straight by grime. His dress shirt was buttoned crookedly, and he wobbled when he tried to stand still.

Pulling my gaze from him, I watched Nahvienne stride into the room. Her blue hair rippled behind her like a wave—fluid, effortless, and impossible to look away from. Her smile brought with it the peace found when gazing at a mountain reflection on a calm lake. "Hey, Molly. Are we training tonight?"

"I brought my gear." Her soothing nature relaxed my muscles and put my mind at ease. "But I won't know until I get my orders." Emphasizing my point, I nodded toward the dais.

She walked over and squeezed my hand. "Do what you have to." The compassion in her blue eyes was genuine, something I wasn't used to seeing in the cabal.

A lump formed in my throat. I tried to swallow it down, but it lodged there. Since there was no way I'd be able to talk around it, I nodded my head, hoping she could see my sincerity as plainly as I saw hers.

The rest of the Ancestral Guardians filed in. Lorelei arrived after the Arcane Council, minus my mother, was seated. Caius smiled at her. "Good evening, Lorelei."

Schooling my features into a serene mask, I did my best to hide my annoyance, but my hands curled into fists. The smirk that crawled over Caius' lips let me know my reaction hadn't gone unnoticed.

Focusing on Schmendrick, I ignored Mom walking across the stage, taking her place on the dais, and Siobhan calling the meeting to order. No matter what I did or didn't do, Caius would never accept me, and why did I care anyway? Why did I keep coming here? Keep looking for approval? When would I learn?

A stinging slap dragged my attention to the present.

"What the hell?" Rubbing my arm, I snapped my head toward Caelan.

He shot me a look that said, *You're screwed.* "Your mother—" he waved at her, teetering dangerously, somehow managing to right himself before toppling over "—has been calling your name." He rubbed his mouth with the back of his hand. "Stop dreaming about wolves and pay attention."

Heat crept up my neck and onto my face when I glanced at the council. Mom stared down at me with her arms folded over her chest and her toes tapping impatiently. "Yes?" The word left my mouth coated in guilt and embarrassment.

"Oh, goody." Caius smacked his hands together and leaned toward me. "She's returned to the world of the living."

Mom still hadn't said anything, but her eyes locked on mine, unblinking, icy. She didn't speak, only looked at me like she was trying to decide if I was worth the breath.

The frosty weight of her glare made me shiver. "Sorry."

"Do you have more important things going on than returning a dragon to sleep, or do you think you can tell us what you learned from your father?" The chilly tone in her words bit into my flesh, burning like frostbite.

"He was no help." The urge to fidget was hard to ignore, but I fought it, refusing to rub the back of my neck or rock back on my heels. "He said the old gods don't have the power to put Kur back to sleep."

She tilted her head just enough to look down her nose at me. A quiet exhale left her nostrils—measured, scornful. "So we are doomed."

## Chapter 14



The words slid from Mom's tongue, and though she didn't raise her voice, the judgment in her posture said enough. "That is what you would have us believe. Is it not?"

"Not at all." My chin lifted confidently, and I straightened my shoulders. "I believe there is always hope. Always. And I will do all that I can to find a way to put Kur back to sleep."

A flicker of satisfaction ghosted across Mom's lips—so brief I almost missed it. She dipped her head in a slow, deliberate nod, the kind that wasn't agreement so much as quiet confirmation.

As if she'd been waiting for me to say exactly that.

As if I'd just proven her point.

The chill in her gaze didn't thaw, but it settled—less like a blizzard now, more like black ice, waiting to lure someone to their death. She stepped back, returning to her throne.

Siobhan strode to the center of the dais. "As many of you already know, earlier this afternoon, we welcomed another sorcerer to the Ancestral Guardians." For a breath, her mask slipped, revealing hope she dared not voice, glimmering in her eyes. "Nox is a blessing, sent to us when our need is dire. His magic is the strongest we've seen in a long time. He will be working with you—" she waved her hands, encompassing all of the guardians "—to return the dragon to sleep."

She lifted her arms above her and tipped her head back. "Once again, we thank you, Ravenwood Citadel, for imparting your wisdom and bestowing your strength upon us. May our mission to return Kur to his eternal post be blessed with success. The Arcane Council is now adjourned."

I waited for the other guardians to turn around to leave. Once they did, I followed.

"Molly." Mom's voice stilled my steps. "See me in my office."

I glanced over my shoulder, but she wasn't looking at me. "Here, or in the manor?"

"We are here, aren't we?" She tilted her head fractionally, eyes narrowing just enough to make the dryness in her voice sting.

"Yes, Mother." As I turned, I pinched the bridge of my nose. I loved my mom. (I swear I did.) But loving her was easier from a distance.

Nahvienne squeezed between Caelan and me. "It's safe to say you won't be training today." Her smile faltered for a heart-beat. "Maybe tomorrow."

"Yeah, maybe." Rubbing the back of my neck, I glanced down the hallway. "I'll probably have to write, *I will not space out in council meetings,* 5 or 6,000 times or clean her floor with a toothbrush or something stupid." Joking seemed like a better option than dwelling, but realistically, Mom would come up with something worse to punish me with. Hopefully, none of the alternatives involved Caius.

Caelan snickered, not because he thought what I'd said was funny, but because he wanted to see me fail. "Ever think of, oh I dunno… maybe actually payin' attention?" He swayed slightly, blinking slowly like the room tilted a bit too much. "You could quit—quit playin' the victim for a second." A hiccup of a laugh slipped out, sharp and breathless. "The villain ain't a victim." He staggered down the hallway, bouncing into the wall every few steps.

His words were a blade, piercing my heart before twisting, so the bleeding and pain would never stop. My hand pressed against my chest, and I watched him stumble away, whispering the lie I needed to believe—that it wasn't Caelan talking. It was the alcohol.

Nahvienne's cobalt curls bounced as she strode toward me, her jaw clenched. "You okay?"

Still rubbing the ache his words left behind, I lifted one shoulder.

Her gaze followed him, hard and narrowed. "He's not even mad at you. He's mad at fate or the universe or whatever, and he's too drunk to know the difference."

Storm cocked his head and crossed his arms over his chest. "He needs to sleep it off before he drowns in his own bitterness." His tone was light, but the tight line of his mouth said he was not impressed. "I'll make sure he doesn't knock himself out on a doorframe." He followed Caelan, his boots thudding in a slow, steady rhythm.

"You know, if you need to talk, I'm here." Nahvienne's voice was quiet, as if she were afraid she would scare the words away. Her body angled toward me, just slightly. Her eyes searched mine, and in them, I saw a flicker of loneliness that matched my own.

Grabbing her hand, I squeezed her fingers. "I, uh, well, I've never really had a friend, but I'd like to." My gaze darted from her toward Mom's office. If I kept Mom waiting much longer, she would send out a search party after me, or worse, Caius.

"You need to go." Nahvienne squeezed my hand back before letting go. "I'll be in the arena. Stop by when you're done, even if you can't train with me."

My stomach tightened at the thought of facing Mom. "I'll do my best." My lips lifted in what I hoped could pass as a smile, but it felt like a poor imitation.

My heels clacked against the stone floor, echoing through the corridor, making it sound like someone followed behind me. Standing outside Mom's door, I sucked in a deep breath and held it for five seconds before releasing it. Then I did it a few more times. Right before I knocked on the door, Schmendrick rubbed against my legs. "Hey, Buddy." Stalling a little longer, I reached down and petted his head.

"If I go in there with you, your mom will have a cat-niption fit." He tipped his head to the side to get scratches all over.

"Yeah." I straightened up and tugged my sleeves down, hoping I looked good enough to avoid that lecture. "I'll be okay."

"Then I shall see you at home." He disappeared as if he'd never been there.

The Ravenwood Crest was carved into the center of Mom's door. I knocked right below the bird's beak. Unlike the front door, magic didn't create a new image for me to ponder. "The door is open, Mahlia."

"Mahlia," I whispered under my breath, frustrated that after all this time, she couldn't call me Molly.

Pushing on Mom's door, it opened without a sound. Expecting to find her alone behind her desk, I straightened my shoulders and took a step.

The next one faltered, bringing me to a halt.

A man stood near the window, shrouded in shadows. Tall—at least a head taller than Jayden—with dark hair that brushed the collar of his black jacket. He was unnaturally still, as if he had always been part of the room, some silent, unsettling fixture.

My breath hitched. Every instinct screaming at me to flee.

Not because he moved or even looked at me—he hadn't. For too long, I stood frozen like prey spotting a predator.

Then he turned, slow and deliberate. His gaze caught mine, and my skin prickled. His eyes were dark, so dark I couldn't tell where the irises began and the pupils ended.

"You're late." Mom's voice released me from the fear that had held me frozen. "Molly, meet Nox. I'm sure the two of you will be perfect together." She lifted her hand to her mouth as if to cover her faux pas and chuckled. "Oh, dear me, I mean *work* perfectly together."

## Chapter 15

*"Time spent with cats is never wasted." -Sigmund Freud*

$\mathcal{N}$ox slipped across the room like a shadow. I'm not sure I saw his feet move as he made his way toward me. He stopped too close, and his scent wafted over me. It was foreign, something I'd never smelled before, but it set my magic on edge and curled my toes in my heels.

He held his pale hand out, and I lifted my trembling one to meet it. Instead of shaking it, he drew it toward his mouth and kissed the back of it. His lips held the heat of a thousand suns, but frost crept up my spine. "It is a pleasure to meet the daughter of the archon. I am certain we will find Kur and return him to his post."

When he dropped my hand, a chill settled over me. "I didn't expect to meet you so soon."

Mom sat behind her desk with a smug look covering her face, and I couldn't help but wonder why she was pushing me toward this man. Everything about him warned me away. From the way he stood eerily still to the predatory look in his eyes.

He was dangerous.

Of course, Mom liked him.

He wasn't a wolf.

*But he's not your mate.*

The whisper slid into my thoughts like an unexpected guest. I slammed the door on it, refusing to invite it in, to delve deeper into my feelings, while standing in the viper's den.

"Why weren't you in the council meeting?" I took a slight step back, hoping he wouldn't notice, but he tracked the movement.

Mom strode toward us, her ebony skirt swirling around her legs like fog. "Nox was getting settled in. He'll be staying at Ravenwood Manor until he finds a place to call his own." She settled one hand on my arm and one on Nox's. "Isn't that lovely, dear?" She sucked in a breath as if an epiphany had suddenly struck her. "Wouldn't it be nice if you came home? Then the two of you could get to know each other better."

"Does Caius still live with you?" I shook her hand off me.

She pressed her fingers to her stomach. "Why, of course, he does, Molly? Why wouldn't he?"

"I figured he did, but I'm sure I made it very clear—crystal even—that I wouldn't live under the same roof as that man." My jaw tightened as I folded my arms over my chest—a barrier between us. Small and insignificant, but a barrier, nonetheless. My eyes narrowed, locked onto Mom's. One foot slid half a step back, my weight shifting, ready to turn and walk away. The moment hung heavy in the air. My shoulders tightened, like a bowstring pulled taut.

Seraphina's smile faltered. Her outstretched hand hovered a second too long in the space where I'd been. She snapped it back, fingers curling into a loose fist. Her spine stiffened, chin lifting as her steely gaze settled on me. She took a deliberate step forward, her skirt whispering against the floor, radiating that unshakable, queenly poise she wore like a second skin. Her hands folded in front of her, the gesture deceptively calm, like the peace before a storm. "Molly, stop goofing around. It's time for you to come home. Step up. Learn to become the next archon."

"Mom, I love you, but that isn't my home, and this isn't the place to discuss it." I shot Nox a smile that I hoped conveyed my sincere apology. "I can't live there. Not with him."

"Oh, psh." Mom waved her hand through the air like I was an annoying gnat that she could swat away. "Everything Caius did was to help you get stronger. He never really hurt you, and he wouldn't. He loves you as if you were his own."

My mouth fell open, hanging there as if the hinge to shut it had broken. As I stared at her, rage and disbelief warred inside of me, battling to be my dominant emotion. She couldn't truly believe that, could she?

No matter how hard I searched my memories, I couldn't find her anywhere in them—not during his punishments, and certainly not during the worst of them. When I'd cowered in my room, waiting for my tail to grow back, I'd hidden under the bed with only Schmendrick beside me. In those moments, he was the only one who ever cared, the only one to comfort me.

"Being archon is no walk in the park." Her features transformed, turning hard, unsympathetic. Not like she was talking to her daughter, who had been abused, but more like a stranger she had no time or patience for. "There are constant threats. He only wanted what was best for you, for you to be ready, to be strong."

My breath caught in my throat, forcing my shoulders to go rigid, bracing myself against an invisible blow. For a moment, my gaze dropped to the floor, but when it lifted again, my eyes blazed with fury and betrayal. My voice came out low and sharp, trembling not with fear—but with restrained rage. "You can believe that if you want, but I know better. That man is evil incarnate. And he enjoyed every second that he tortured me." Needing to get away from her and from the memories held in this place, I spun on my heel, fully intending to leave.

She grabbed hold of my arm, her grip strong. "I did not dismiss you yet." Her fingernails dug into the soft flesh of my wrist. "You and Nox need to come up with a plan. Kur must be neutralized before the Primordial Waters overflow and destroy everything that your ancestors built."

"Really, Mom?" I stepped closer to ease her hold. My jaw clenched, and I had to force it open before I cracked a tooth. Miraculously, my voice came out even. "That's what concerns you? What our ancestors built. What about everyone else? Everything else? You realize there's more to this world than the Ravenwood line, don't you?"

Nox lifted Mom's hand from my arm, holding it as tenderly as a newborn babe. "Seraphina, it is late, and I traveled far to get here. Perhaps Molly and I could meet tomorrow to discuss our plans."

"Oh, Nox." Mom's voice dropped into a flirtatious lilt, and a mask slipped over her features, transforming her once again. "That is a wonderful idea. It will give Molly and me time to hash everything out."

While her hand was still in his, I slipped closer to the door. "Actually, I am supposed to be training with Nahvienne right now." I plastered on my phoniest smile. "Council's orders."

## Chapter 16



Jogging through the hallway, I burst out the front door. Mom would not let my escape slide so easily, but I needed to get away from her, needed to breathe.

The fresh air (as unnatural as it was) filled my lungs and calmed my racing heart. Outside the cabal, colorful leaves were falling from the trees. The nights were brisk, but at Ravenwood Estates, Mom kept it spring or summer year-round. The sky was always blue. Rain only ever fell overnight. It never snowed.

For so many of the sorcerers, it was paradise—the perfect weather day in and day out—but for ones like me, ones who loved rainy, cloudy, gloomy days, it was monotonous.

Looking up, I gazed at the sky above me. Light pollution hid the vast majority of stars, but the ones that shone through helped calm me further.

By the time I reached the arena, my head felt clearer. The clang of swords reminded me I didn't have mine with me, and I wasn't dressed for training. Sure, on TV, women battled in heels and fitted dresses, but I struggled to walk across the floor in them. I was more like one of those cats that flops onto the ground and refuses to move until the offensive clothing is removed.

Stepping into a shadow next to an archway, I stepped out beside my car. A glance through the driver's side window made me realize that leaving seemed like a great idea, but then I remembered Nahvienne's expression. With a sigh, I grabbed my duffel and swords off the back seat and shadow walked into the arena.

Nahvienne sparred with Thorn Wilder. My first day as a guardian, I'd met him, but we had only nodded at each other since then. His long, dark hair was pulled back in a low ponytail that bobbed as he blocked Nahvienne's advances. Sweat dotted his forehead as he fought to hold his position.

But like water does to earth, Nahvienne pushed him back, slowly gaining ground. Her strikes fell quicker, harder, until Thorn lifted his hands. "Okay, I give." He laughed. "Next time, hand-to-hand combat; I need a win every so often."

"Oh, you think you can best me in that, do you?" A playful grin tugged at her lips, and she smacked his arm. "We'll see."

They strode toward the benches, and I stepped into the light. When Nahvienne's eyes met mine, her smile lit up her whole face. "You came." She gave me a once-over. "Are you staying?"

I lifted my duffel bag. "Yeah, I just need a minute to get changed."

"Great! We'll see what you've got." Still buzzing with adrenaline, Nahvienne bounced lightly on the balls of her feet. She gave Thorn a mock salute, then turned back to me, hands settling on her hips in challenge. There was a spark in her eyes, mischief and excitement tangled together.

Rubbing the back of my neck, I lifted one shoulder in a half-shrug. "I won't be near the challenge Thorn was, but I'll do my best."

Our swords clashed together. Nahvienne fought me using her left hand, instead of her right, and even then, she was better, faster, stronger, but my skills were increasing. My arms ached, but I fought through the pain, focusing on blocking each strike. Soon, there was nothing in the world except Nahvienne, our swords, and me.

The rhythm of the dance was all I knew. Strike. Block. Step. Step. Strike. Block.

Nahvienne lunged, and if she had less control, her blade would've taken my hand off. "Enough for now." She backed up and walked to the benches along the side of our training space.

Ember and Lane had joined Thorn there while we'd been sparring, looking way too entertained for bystanders.

"Not bad, Molly." Thorn held his fist out, and I bumped mine against it.

"You lasted longer than I expected." Ember raked her fingers through the black hair that hung over her shoulder, then swept it over the shaved side of her head. "I heard you didn't even know what the pommel was for."

Heat rushed up my neck and onto my cheeks.

"Don't listen to her." Lane's voice was deeper than the Mariana Trench. He leaned forward, planting his elbows on his knees. Tattoos covered every visible patch of skin on his arms. "You've got natural talent, but you need to hone it."

Picking up a towel, I wiped the sweat off my face. "Thanks, but I've got a long way to go."

"Maybe, but we all start somewhere." Thorn turned his attention to Nahvienne, and his expression softened. "Nahvienne's a great teacher. You'll be a pro in no time."

She walked over and pecked him on the cheek. "Such a flatterer." Snatching a water bottle out of the cooler, she downed most of it in one big gulp before focusing on me again. "So… what punishment did Seraphina have lined up for you?"

I rolled my eyes. "Apparently, she wants to hook me and Nox up."

"Hook you up." Nahvienne's head jerked back, her curls bouncing as her eyes narrowed. "Really? What the hell!"

Ember's mouth fell open. "Wait—like romantically? That's…" She flopped her hair back over to the side it belonged on. "Wow. Even my mom doesn't meddle that bad."

"Yeah, well, he's powerful." I tried (unsuccessfully, I might add) to keep the bitterness out of my voice. "And nothing appeals to Mom more than power."

Thorn tipped his head to the side, confusion twisting his eyebrows. "She knows you're with Jayden, right?"

"She doesn't approve. He's a wolf, and the Ravenwood line has not been sullied by lesser breeds before." Plopping down on the bench, I leaned against the wall. "Thanks, but no thanks. I mean, have you met him?"

When all of them shook their heads, I continued, "There's something off about him. I don't know what, but he kinda creeps me out."

"Maybe he's just got that brooding *I-eat-my-enemies-for-breakfast* vibe." Ember smirked. "Some girls are into that."

Lane snorted, the sound so strange coming from him. "And some have better survival instincts than you, Em."

"I wasn't talking about me." She smacked the back of his bald head.

"Sure, you weren't." He nodded.

"Maybe he just doesn't make good first impressions." Thorn scratched the back of his neck, his brows pulling together. Then he shrugged, offering a crooked grin. "Not everyone does. Anxiety or shyness, or just you know, being you. Some people aren't good at it."

My chin dipped toward my chest. "Yeah, could be. I guess I'll find out tomorrow. I have to meet with him to come up with a plan to return Kur and put him to sleep. Between working, training, and the guardians, it's hard to fit in a life."

Nahvienne toyed with the end of her cobalt curl, her brow creasing. "Have you considered quitting your mundane job?"

"The thought's crossed my mind, but I don't want to give up the life that I fought for to let the one I fled from take over everything." Pushing to my feet, I smoothed my palms down my thighs. "I've got training with Jayden first thing in the morning, so I should get going. You two, have a good night."

"Get some rest, rookie." Ember hopped off the bench and grabbed her sword. "You'll need it if you're sparring with a wolf."

As I strode away, I forced myself not to look back. It was hard to reconcile Lane with the memories I had of him. He'd tormented me, but I needed to remember that sometimes people changed. Sometimes, they grew up.

Once I was beneath the archways of the arena, where the other guardians could no longer see me, I scanned the area, making sure no one was watching when I shadow walked to my car.

Just as I stepped into the darkness, I saw them—two eyes catching the faint light, unblinking, fixed on me. My stomach clenched.

Nox tipped his head, a faint smirk twisted his lips, before he slipped into a shadow of his own, disappearing as if he'd never been there.

# Chapter 17



*N*ox stalked me through my dreams. He watched me from the shadows as still as a big cat hunting its prey.

When I woke up, I felt like I hadn't slept at all. Unease settled over me, making me startle at every noise as I stomped into the bathroom.

"You're jumpier than a cat in a rocking chair factory. If you drank coffee, I'd tell you that you'd had too much already." Schmendrick leapt up onto the bathroom counter, dipping his paw in the stream of water running in the sink. "What's going on?"

"I don't know." I pulled the brush through my hair in harsh, punishing strokes. "I don't want to meet with Nox. I have a feeling Mom is going to keep pushing to get me to live there and keep shoving Nox and me together." Slamming the brush down on the counter, I flipped my hands into the air. "Jayden isn't going to like this at all."

"A little competition will do him some good." His green gaze flicked from the water to my face. "Maybe he'll finally figure out that chasing you is a lot more interesting than chasing his own tail."

Leaning my hip against the cabinet, I scratched Schmendrick's back, making him arch higher. "Yeah, but when will I even have time to spend with him?"

"Isn't that where you're going this morning?" The words were spoken between purrs.

"For training, but I'm talking about real time spent together." When I pulled my hand away, he reached for it, letting me know he wasn't done. "Getting to know him. Trying to figure out if he's the one."

"My dearest Molly—" he flopped onto his side, then rolled until his belly was facing up "—I believe you already know the answer to that question."

*But he's not your mate.*

The words from the previous day came back to me, daring me to examine what they meant, why they'd snuck up on me, but I shoved them back again.

"Do I?" Crossing my arms, I tapped my fingers on my sleeve, too anxious to stay still. While chewing on my lip, I studied the brown tiled floor. "I mean, how many people end up with the one after their first try? And what about Caelan?"

"What about him?" Schmendrick stretched in that way only cats can, flicking his tail as if brushing off my words. "It seems like you made up your mind about him when you left Ravenwood the first time. If you'd wanted eternity with that boy, you wouldn't have left him behind." He jumped off the counter, not making a sound, and swaggered to the doorway, looking over his shoulder at me. "So why is he even part of your equation now?"

"He's hurting." The weight of Caelan's pain pressed down on me as if it were my own, maybe because I was the cause of it or maybe because he'd been my only friend for so many years. "And I feel like I need to put him back together."

"You're not his purr-sonal savior." He rubbed against the doorframe before leading me into the hallway. "If he doesn't want help, you can't purr-suade him to get it."

I followed him downstairs, where he immediately jumped onto the couch. "Are you coming with me? I'm sure you and Jayden can hurl some puns at each other."

"And miss my morning nap?" He cracked one eye open enough to let me see the disdain in it, as if I couldn't hear it in his voice. "I think not."

Jayden stood by the archway leading into Castle Unicorn's main grounds. As soon as I parked my car, he strode toward me with the confident, familiar gait that made my heart skip a beat. The chilly November air nipped at my cheeks and nose, but the second he pulled me into his arms, his warmth chased the cold away.

Without a word, he dipped his head, and his mouth crashed down on mine. His lips were warm, urgent, demanding. My breath caught as his hands slid up to cup my face, fingers tangling in my hair.

My mouth opened instinctively, wrapping my arms around his waist, feeling the heat of him press against me.

When he pulled away, his forehead rested against mine, his breath coming in heavy bursts that misted slightly in the cold morning air. "Missed you yesterday." His voice was low and rough. He brushed my hair back, tucking it behind my ear, as if he needed to keep me close, to hold onto this moment for a little longer.

My body melded against his, savoring the heat that radiated off him. "Sorry about that. I'd've definitely rather been with you." Stepping back enough to look into his eyes, I gave him a small, frustrated shake of my head and sighed. "Between Mom and Caelan and Nox, it was a shit show."

Jayden's hands slipped to my lower back, his fingers flexing. His voice came out low, edged with a protective growl. "Who's Nox?"

"Jealous much?" My brow arched, and I pressed my palms against his chest, pushing away from him, leaving the smallest breath of air between our bodies. I clutched his shirt and gave it a playful tug. I wanted to be annoyed with him, to accuse him of not trusting me, but for some reason, I found his reaction endearing. "Nox is someone I *have* to work with, not someone I *want* to be with."

He lifted his finger, drawing it from my temple to my chin. Tiny shivers danced along the path. "How closely will you be working together?"

"Not as closely as Mom would like, but too close for my comfort." Closing the space between us, I leaned into his touch.

He dropped his head until his mouth was right next to my ear. His breath turned my insides to goo. "Be sure to tell him you're mine."

*Mine.* The word coiled through my body, settling in my stomach, and reanimating the butterflies that only took flight for him.

I could've stayed in his arms all day and into the night, but I flattened my hands on his chest and pushed him back. "Training."

"I thought we were."

My eyebrows lifted, silently asking, *How?*

"I was training your lips to only desire mine." He bent down, trailing kisses along the path his finger had blazed just moments before. "Did it work?"

Sliding my hands from his chest to his waist, I pulled myself closer. "We might need to keep working on it." I smiled against his lips, savoring the feel of his breath against mine. "Practice makes perfect, you know."

I fought the urge to step closer, to snuggle into him and wrap my arms around him. But we were supposed to be training, so I hooked my foot behind his. Then I pushed him back at the same time that I jerked my leg toward me, knocking him off balance. As he fell, he grabbed hold of me, pulling me with him.

He landed flat on his back, with me crushing him. His hands slid beneath my shirt, resting on my sides. "If this was what you wanted, you could've asked me." His grin was mischievous.

I stared down into his amber eyes. Humor lingered in their depths. "What did Malachai mean about our mate bond?"

His face blanched, and his grip on my sides slackened. "It's not… not in place until we, uh… actually mate."

"Oh." The heat that had pooled in my belly rushed to my face. "Oh. Then what?"

He brushed his thumb along my cheek. "Then you can walk away, but I can't." His eyes closed, and when they reopened, they were filled with a raw honesty that made my heart clench. He wasn't hiding the impact this would have on him. He knew the significance of his words and that he couldn't take them back.

His vulnerability weighed on my soul like an anchor pulling me beneath the waves. I held his gaze until I thought I'd be able to talk without my voice shaking. "I guess we'd better not rush into things."

His thumbs brushed my sides, and shivers trailed his touch. "I guess I'd better win your heart first."

I pressed my hands against his chest and tried to push myself up.

Clutching my waist, he rolled over, pinning me against the ground beneath him. His body draped over mine like a weighted blanket, but I wasn't there for comfort; I was here for training.

Shifting as much as I could, I arched my back, trying to shove him off balance. I twisted sharply and rolled to the side. Instead of breaking free, I found myself pressed up against him, our legs tangled, his arm sliding down my leg like it belonged there.

His lips lifted, lazy and wicked, amused. "Not sure if you're trying to win or just get closer." His voice was husky, and my heart tripped over itself in response.

*"Artists like cats; soldiers like dogs." -Desmond Morris*

"Maybe… I want both." My words slipped out softer than I intended. I leaned in, brushing my lips over his. The cold ground beneath my body was a harsh contradiction to the heat rushing through me. I pulled my head back, still feeling his breath caressing my face. "I think I need to find a new trainer."

"Don't you dare." His eyes glowed with his wolf, and the growl that rumbled through him was more animal than human. He kissed my forehead and sprang to his feet, stretching his hand down to me.

His fingers were rough and warm against mine, and they lingered a fraction of a second longer than necessary. Even with the chill in the air, my skin felt overheated, too aware of every inch of him.

"All right, no more horsing around. Serious training." His grin was a weapon, double-edged and sharp.

If I wasn't careful, it would pierce my heart like Cupid's arrow, and I was already so close to falling. "May I use your restroom before we continue?" My voice was too even, too controlled. It took everything I had to keep the fire burning within me restrained, and I knew that he knew it. With his wolf senses, there was no way my act was fooling him, but I was grateful that he played along, grateful he didn't push me too hard.

"Sure." He kept his fingers twined through mine as he led me inside.

Closing the bathroom door, I slumped against it, giving myself a moment to breathe. Once my heart rate slowed, I walked to the sink, turned on the faucet, and splashed cold water on my face.

Training.

With Jayden.

With his body pressed against mine.

I filled my hands with more water and held them against my face.

I could do this.

I *would* do this.

And I would wait to move on until I knew for a fact whether Jayden was or wasn't what I wanted in life. I couldn't hurt him like that. I couldn't bind him to me, then leave him behind if he wasn't the one.

I turned off the faucet, dried my hands, and walked to the door. Jayden waited in the hallway for me, leaning against the opposite wall. He appeared relaxed until I noticed the tightness in his shoulders and the small tic in his jaw when he clenched his mouth and released it before clenching it again.

"Ready?" Holding my hand out, I hoped he would take it.

His fingers twined through mine. "We have a gym in the basement if you'd rather be out of the cold."

"No." I shook my head and pulled my bottom lip into my mouth. I was going to need the cool air to keep me from igniting under his gaze.

Three hours later, my muscles were sore, and I was wound tighter than a serpent coiled about its prey.

And I was on my way to Ravenwood to meet with Mom and Nox.

## *Chapter 19*



*T*hings were not looking up. While gripping the steering wheel, I rolled my shoulders, trying to loosen the tension in them, but it was no use. The image of Nox standing in the shadows haunted me, his dark eyes gleaming as I disappeared.

All my life, I'd been told that I was the only half-demon, half-sorceress, but after seeing him last night, I couldn't help but wonder if he was like me. If maybe I wasn't as unique as I'd been led to believe.

If he were a hybrid, that could explain his otherworldliness. There was something feral about him. Even though he'd spoken only a few words and had made my getaway possible, he seemed untamed somehow. Maybe it was just his eyes. They were unsettling. Maybe Thorn was right. Maybe Nox wasn't the type of person who gave a good first impression.

My thoughts occupied me for the whole drive, making it go by too quickly. I pulled in front of the citadel and turned the engine off. Sitting in my car, I took several deep breaths before finding the courage to get out.

The unnatural warmth of Ravenwood Estates pressed down on me. The magic hung heavy in the air, and the hoodie I'd thrown on when I finished training became stifling. Pulling it off, I tossed it into my car, leaving me in a t-shirt and jeans that Mom would hate.

As I walked up the path, the manicured lawn of Ravenwood Manor caught my attention. Knowing I would be late and not caring, I strode across the grass to the wrought-iron fence surrounding my old home. "Vak, are you out here?"

A lizard scurried across the yard, making his way to me. When he was right across the fence from me, he lifted onto two legs. He was dressed identically to the last time I'd seen him. His maroon scales stood in stark contrast to the green grass. He pulled his hat off and bowed so deeply that his snout nearly touched the ground. "How can I be of service, Miss Mah—Molly?"

"If it's not too much trouble and won't cause you any harm, I wonder if you could locate something for me." Unable to hold still or keep my focus on the kobold, I tucked my hands into my back pockets and lifted onto my toes.

He straightened up, looking me in the eyes. His were a blend of brown and gold. The highlights danced in them, constantly changing the exact hue. "I am forever indebted to you. Your wish is my command." His voice was lower-pitched than the first time I'd met him, leading me to wonder how afraid he'd been of Caius and what would have happened to him if I hadn't removed the dandelions from the yard.

*Actions have consequences.* The thought rang through my mind, a reminder. Something I needed to remember always.

I chewed on my lip. I didn't deserve his gratitude. "All I did was clean up the mess I made. I shouldn't have put you in that position to begin with."

"If it's all the same," he bowed with a flourish, "we humbly disagree. If we only thanked perfect people, no one would ever receive our gratitude." When he straightened up, he clutched his hat in his hands. "You helped us, and that's all that matters."

"My mother had a dagger in her office." A shiver rippled through me when I thought of the blade. "It was not a nice weapon, made from a sacrificed virgin and a corrupted unicorn."

He tipped his head to the side and scratched behind his horn. "I know the blade you speak of." His voice lowered, and the air seemed to grow colder. "*MaunDagnir*. It is cursed."

"I must find it."

Vak's tail stilled, and the spines along his back lifted ever so slightly. "Miss Molly—" he blinked deliberately, then exhaled through his nose, a low, smoky sound "—you should not use it. It twists and corrupts. It will destroy you."

"I don't want to use it." Remembering Schmendrick's dislike for Vak last time we were here, I didn't know how much I should divulge, but my instincts told me Vak was trustworthy and reliable. "I want to prevent it from being used on me."

Still clutching his hat in one taloned hand, Vak reached for the sword sheathed on his back as though he thought a threat was nearby. "I will do all that I can."

"Then I will be indebted to you."

Knowing how much it would irritate Caius, I strolled across the yard and onto the stoop. The raven carved into the massive wooden door stared at me, daring me to reach for the handle. Wiping my hands on my jeans, I lifted them toward the knob. My fingers trembled, but I inched them forward. The runes burned against my skin, and blue lightning struck the top of the door, trailing down the wood, branching out as it made its way past the shield.

Jayden formed first. His features were a blend of man and wolf. Then the light drew an image of me, standing next to him in my demon form. Across from us stood Nox. My eyes darted between the two of them. Even half-turned, Jayden appeared less feral than the sorcerer.

"What are you showing me?" I pushed the door open, watching as the image faded away, wondering why my ancestors had ever thought this magic would be helpful.

Stepping onto the tiled floor, I walked down the hallway. When my footsteps didn't echo through the citadel, I glanced at my feet. Sneakers. Once again, I'd entered a den of vipers weakened.

# Chapter 20



Caelan staggered down the hall toward me, his steps uneven, his shoulder brushing the wall for balance. "Seraphina's not—" he paused, brow furrowing as if chasing the thought "—not here. Her office is... in the manor." He wiped the back of his hand over his mouth, then let it hang at his side like it was suddenly too heavy. "You'd know that"—his voice was quiet, his words slurred—"if you gave a damn about being part of the cabal."

My hands tightened into white-knuckled fists. My fingernails bit into my skin, grounding me. "Thank you, Caelan." Before I could say something I would regret, I spun on my heel and retraced my steps to the door.

"When are you gonna stop pretending you're not one of us, Molly?" A bitter laugh caught in his throat.

Against my better judgment, I looked over my shoulder at him.

"You keep actin' like you're not." He leaned a hand against the wall as he looked at me, his glassy eyes rimmed in red. "You *are*. Always were. Whether you like it or not."

I froze.

The words sank in like cold rain seeping through my clothes—slow, heavy, inescapable.

I wanted to laugh. I wanted to scream. Instead, I stood there, staring at the pristine tile in front of his feet.

"You say that now." I looked up, meeting his gaze. "But don't you remember the way they treated me? The way they whispered like I couldn't hear them. The way they acted like I was a curse, a plague that would doom them all." My voice shook—not with weakness, but with the weight of everything I'd swallowed down over the years.

Squeezing my fists, my nails dug even deeper into my palms. "You don't get to say I'm one of you just because you're drunk and feeling lonely."

"Molly—" He reached toward me, wobbling like a ship in rough seas.

I didn't wait to hear what he had to say. Didn't care. Spinning around, I strode toward the door with my head held high.

The door shut behind me with a finality that said this chapter of my life was over. Whatever Caelan and I could've been, whatever we were was finished. Whether we could move past this or not would remain to be seen.

The sun practically blinded me when I stepped outside. Squinting my eyes against it, I stormed over to the manor. Caelan's words echoed through my mind with each step I took.

And I realized that Schmendrick was right. (I mean, of course, he was. He always was.) Caelan was not my problem. He needed to figure this out on his own. He needed to decide if he wanted to quit drinking or to drown himself in alcohol. There was nothing I could do for him. The choices were all his.

I couldn't give him what he wanted, and I couldn't fix him.

Opening the gate, I stepped onto the path and steeled myself for what I would find on the other side of the door.

I was late.

I was dressed inappropriately in Mom's eyes.

And I was sure she could come up with at least a hundred other things I'd done wrong.

The steps loomed in front of me—oppressive, foreboding—but I climbed them anyway and walked through the front door like I still lived there. The dimly lit house was stifling. Burgundy curtains smothered the windows, choking out the light. The carpet matched the drapes. The dark wood trim sucked up what little light the weak bulbs offered, leaving only half-formed shadows behind.

Mom's laughter tinkled down the stairway, and I followed the sound to her office. She was perched on the edge of her desk, her posture relaxed and inviting. Her head was tossed back, genuine joy lighting up her face. Her dress had slipped open, baring her legs, which stretched toward Nox—close enough to brush his knee.

He sat stiffly in his chair, spine ramrod-straight, like he'd never once considered slouching. His head snapped toward me, and Mom's gaze followed.

"Oh, Mahlia, dear." She rose gracefully, and the silver fabric of her skirt shimmered, scattering tiny prisms across the room as it settled back into place. With a casual elegance, she let her hand linger on Nox's shoulder. "Nox knows so much about the Mesopotamian gods. The two of you will have Kur back to sleep in no time."

Her fingers trailed down his arm as she sashayed toward me. She leaned in as if she were about to kiss my cheek, but she pulled back. Her nose wrinkled. "What have you been doing? You smell like sweat and dog."

"Training." The sudden urge to draw her in for a hug nearly overwhelmed me, but I fought the impulse, knowing what it could cost me. "Like the council ordered." Plopping down in the leather armchair next to Nox, I shot him what I hoped would pass for a smile while trying to repress a shudder. "I think you're putting the cart before the horse, Mom. First, we have to find Kur. Until then, it doesn't matter what we know."

"My studies have long centered on Kur and the Mesopotamian pantheon." Nox cleared his throat and adjusted the cuffs of his shirt as if to refasten a button that wasn't undone. "I am well-versed in their histories, mythologies, and associated rites. Therefore, I am certain that locating Kur will not be an issue." His dark eyes locked onto mine, and it was like staring into an unending chasm—vast, cold, and hollow. There was no light in them, no flicker of life. Only the weight of something ancient and unknowable.

For a moment, I forgot how to breathe. Frozen, as if caught in the gaze of a predator—one who hadn't decided if I was a threat or prey.

Finally, I forced myself to blink, the moment breaking. With a shake of my head, I reminded myself I didn't know him and shouldn't judge him based on a couple of superficial meetings held in Ravenwood Estates. Everything here was more menacing. My emotions and my instincts were on edge, especially in Ravenwood Manor, where so many of my ghosts lived.

Unable to turn my back on him, I looked at Mom, keeping Nox in my peripheral vision. My hands rubbed my bare arms, trying to remove the chill that had settled over me. But the unease didn't vanish. It clung to me like the remnants of last night's dream.

"Good." The word slipped out, weak and worn. Swallowing hard, I relaxed the tension in my shoulders and slumped in my chair, the complete opposite of Nox's rigid posture. "Where do we begin?"

Mom positioned herself behind her walnut desk, flipping her long, blonde hair over her shoulder. "I am so glad you two are working together. I just know you're going to get on fabulously."

Somehow, I resisted the urge to roll my eyes. It wasn't Nox's fault that he was stuck with me or that my mother was acting like she was Cupid's emissary. So, instead, I stood and clapped my hands together. "All righty then. Let's go find us a dragon."

## Chapter 21



Nox followed me out of Mom's office and down the stairs, his steps silent. Having him behind me made the hair on the back of my neck stand at attention. My hand shook as I trailed it along the banister. When we reached the landing, I turned to him, holding my breath and willing my heartbeat to calm.

"Since you know where we're going, you should probably lead."

Without a word, he grabbed my hand and pulled me into the shadows next to the staircase. Darkness surrounded me for a breath before everything changed.

Nox pulled away from me as we stepped into a world where the sky was a bruised violet that lightened to gray as it neared the horizon. Jagged stones jutted from the cracked, scarred ground like broken teeth. Black peaks rose in the distance—ominous, looming. Chunks of rock floated on a gentle breeze, defying gravity.

My hand lifted—seemingly of its own volition—to touch one, but I yanked it back before my fingers could make contact.

Folding my arms tightly across my chest, I tucked my fists into my sides. "Wh-where are we?"

"The Primordial Waters." Nox's voice was low and solemn, like someone standing at a gravesite. "Where the world began. And where it will, one day, end."

He didn't look at me—just continued to stare into the distance.

I followed his gaze.

The Primordial Waters churned in slow motion, stretching so far it became impossible to tell where they ended and the world began. The surface rippled and shifted—from inky black, to the silver of starlight, to a purple so deep it matched the color of my hair. Mist floated above it in slow, billowing wisps, as if the air itself was remembering how to breathe.

The wind carried with it the smell of petrichor and something older. Something long forgotten by the world.

My hands fell to my sides, and I stepped forward, drawn as if in a trance. With each step, a song hummed through the air—soft at first, then steadily clearer. Straining to hear each note, I tipped my head, listening. The melody captivated me. Haunting, wordless, ancient. It felt entirely new and impossibly old all at once, slipping through my mind like a half-remembered dream. Echoes of the past. Promises for the future.

The waves lapped at the ground, and I stopped before the Waters could touch me. Glancing down, I expected to see my reflection in the dark surface.

Instead, I watched stars being born. Land rising from the sea. Mountains spewing fire.

And a shadow—coiled around the basin. Massive. Ancient. Watching.

Kur.

My breath caught.

Awe washed over me, thick and suffocating.

The Waters inched forward, rising to greet us. I wanted to back away, but my body seemed to be held in place by the miracles I bore witness to. How many had stood where I was? How many before me had beheld the universe being forged?

I didn't belong here. I'd done nothing to deserve this honor. I was small. Insignificant. A thorn in the paw of eternity.

The Waters crept over the toes of my shoes, and I stumbled back a step, colliding with a floating rock. It slammed into my shoulder—sharp, sudden—tearing me from my trance.

Ever so slowly, I reached up and tapped my fingers against the stone, pushing it away, watching as it drifted along its new path. "H-how?" The word caught in my dry, scratchy throat. How long had I been standing there, observing? "How did you know about this place?"

Nox strode to the edge of the Waters, not looking into it but over it. Ribbons of lightning laced through ominous clouds. No thunder boomed, but the melody in the air crescendoed. "I have spent my life researching Kur and the Mesopotamian gods."

"Your life." A chuckle snuck out before I could stop it. "You're what, twenty-five? So… you've spent a couple years researching?"

He didn't smile or roll his eyes. "I am a bit older than I look."

"That's really not an answer, you know?" Then silence lingered while I waited for him to say something else, but he just stared over the Waters, his expression unreadable—like he couldn't decide if it soothed or tormented him. Reaching out, ever so slowly, I rested my fingers on his forearm. "Why did you bring me here?"

Nox finally turned to face me, and his expression shifted as he looked down at my hand. "I wanted you to see them. Before they remember how to wake up."

"They?" Dread coiled in my stomach, and my gaze darted around, scanning the shadows, searching for some monster. But Kur was already awake, already gone from this place.

Nox's mouth twitched—somewhere between a smile and a grimace—as he nodded toward the Waters' edge. "The Waters." He patted my hand before gently prying my fingers loose. "They're rousing. Their slumber is nearing its end."

He turned and walked away from the Waters' edge, skirting the jagged rocks that made up the archaic landscape. His footsteps were soundless and left no tracks in the dirt. "Besides, there may be a clue here, something to show where Kur went."

The dry, cracked ground crunched beneath my feet as I followed Nox. With each step I took away from the Waters, the melody grew quieter, fading out of existence. Straining my ears, I listened until it was nothing more than a memory, and then I hummed the tune, not wanting to lose it. Unwilling to forget the power those notes held over creation.

The ground changed as we climbed higher. Scorched basalt and glassy obsidian rose in molten waves that were frozen in mid-scream. The bleached corpses of trees littered the slope we climbed.

"What are we looking for?" Tapping my fingers against a floating rock, I sent it hurtling away from me. It struck one of the pale trunks with a hollow, resonant *crack*. A piece broke off, twisting and tumbling through the air before landing with a sharp thud.

It didn't sound like a dried chunk of wood, hitting stone.

Detouring from Nox's path, I strode toward the downed tree, inspecting it. The splintered edge looked nothing like wood and everything like bone.

"It can't be," I whispered as I straightened up. My heart thudded as my gaze swept over the area, seeing everything with new eyes.

This wasn't the remains of an ancient forest.

It was a graveyard.

# Chapter 22

*"Cats do not have to be shown how to have a good time, for they are unfailing ingenious in that respect." -James Mason*

Massive, ancient bones surrounded me.

My eyes darted across the ground, straining against the dim light of the never-ending dusk. Femurs lay half-buried in hardened lava. Ribs arced from the earth like broken bridges. A shattered skull yawned open in a silent scream.

I stumbled back a step, heart hammering in my chest, goosebumps rising all over my body. My fingers curled instinctively, summoning a flicker of magic to my palms like a second heartbeat. The air felt thinner suddenly—charged, watching.

"What the hell, Nox?" My voice choked out tighter than I meant it to be. Wide-eyed, breath shallow, I turned to him. "Why are we walking through this? Why are *they* here?"

Nox stepped beside me, his eerie black eyes sweeping over the scattered remains without flinching. "This is what happens when the Primordial Waters wake. It doesn't matter what you are—god, monster, mortal. They unmake everything."

"How can we stop it?" Hoping to stifle my shivers, I folded my arms over my chest. "Without Kur. Is there a way?"

"Kur stood guard—against his will—for thousands of years." Nox's voice was calm, but he didn't look at me. His eyes remained on the bones scattered across the slope, unblinking. His fingers flexed once at his sides, then stilled. "Would you subject another to that torture, to that isolation?"

I turned and stared at the Waters below us. The mirror-like surface had been replaced by fierce ripples as the Waters surged outward, rising higher with every breath I took.

"No." I bowed my head. "Though… I would do it… If I could."

A long silence followed. When I finally looked at him, Nox was watching me—really watching me—with a strange stillness. His usual edge, the sharpness I'd come to expect, was dulled. Not gone, but tempered.

He inclined his head slightly, as if in recognition. Not mocking. Not cold.

Respectful.

The simple acknowledgment threw me off balance.

For the first time, I saw something in him that wasn't a shadow or threat. Something softer. Something… human.

"We should keep moving." He turned away.

I followed more willingly now, not because I had to, but because I wanted to. "How is it that an expert on Kur shows up exactly when we need him?"

His shoulders rose as he laughed. The sound was a glimmer of light in this darkness. "In all honesty, your mother pulled the strings. She's very persistent and doesn't know how to take no for an answer."

"You're right about that." The snort that followed my words wasn't very ladylike. (Mom would be so disappointed in me.) "*No* has never been an answer she's cared to hear. Although it's a word she uses frequently herself."

He slowed his pace until he walked beside me, his steps matching mine. "It seems she believes we would be a good match." He didn't look at me as he said it, but his hands slid into his coat pockets—a gesture that felt almost… uncertain. "I don't believe she's overly fond of your wolf."

"I know for a fact she isn't." Bending down, I picked up a loose rock. The top was as smooth as glass, but the bottom was rough and pitted against my skin. Before I tucked it in my pocket, I turned it over in my hand, studying it. Two sides that reminded me of Nox. A souvenir of this strange expedition. "But I have to admit, I don't exactly like the man she chose to spend her life with."

He glanced sideways at me then, something flickering behind his eyes—amusement, maybe. Or understanding.

We walked in silence. Comfortable for a change. When we were about to crest the peak, I broke it. "I feel sorry for Kur." A sudden chill worked its way beneath my skin, and I wished I were wearing one of my hoodies. The familiar comfort—the warmth, the weight, a place to tuck my hands, to hide their fidgeting—would have eased me in this strange place.

"Why?" Even with him standing right next to me, his quiet voice barely carried to my ears. "He is a beast, is he not?"

"He might be." I breathed the words, just a whisper on the wind, bracing for Nox's disagreement. "But think how lonely it would be… holding the Primordial Waters back. Day in, day out… for eternity."

A shadow flickered over his expression, there and gone before I could make sense of it. "We all have our cross to bear. Some are just a little heavier than others."

"Yeah." Whether that was true or not, I wasn't sure. Some people skated through life like nothing touched them—but maybe that was what they wanted the world to see. Maybe everyone was hiding something under the surface, buried where only they could feel it. "Still—" I swallowed hard, curling my fingers in the hem of my shirt "—to have no reprieve. No one to help carry that weight. At least I've got Schmendrick to help me through the worst of it."

Nox didn't answer right away. He stood still for a moment, his gaze cast out over the jagged landscape below. The wind tousled his dark hair, and he didn't seem like a shadow come to life anymore—but something vulnerable and maybe a little broken, too.

"You're lucky." A wistful smile tugged at his lips. "To have someone."

There was something in the way he said it that made my chest ache. As I studied his profile, I realized he looked younger somehow—the hard lines of his face softened by dusk, making him appear more real.

"You don't?" I lifted my hand, wanting to comfort him, but unsure how he'd react.

He didn't meet my eyes. "Not anymore."

A silence stretched between us—no longer uncomfortable, but heavy with shared understanding.

"I'm sorry." The words weren't enough. They never were, but they filled the space when there was nothing else to say, no way to encompass all the feelings.

He gave the smallest shake of his head, as if to dismiss it, but his voice was quieter than before. "Don't be. Some burdens aren't meant to be shared."

We crested the ridge in silence, but this time, it was Nox who broke it. "Who is Schmendrick?"

"He's my cat, who's not really a cat." Flipping my hands up, I shrugged. "One of the fae calls him *Aracondo*, but nobody will tell me what that means, and I haven't had a chance to figure it out."

"*Aracondo*." The word rolled off his tongue with a familiarity that I envied. "If he will not tell you what it means, I would be remiss to spoil it for you. I am certain you will find out in time."

Exhaling through my nose, I shook my head. I should've expected as much, but I wanted answers. "I hate being kept in the dark."

"But you are not afraid of it." Nox's words came slower than normal, drawing his brows together, not in confusion, but in thought. He looked at me—really looked at me as if seeing my soul—and for a fleeting moment, his expression softened, as if the truth of it surprised him. "So many others are. So many fear the darkness inside and out."

The wind changed, carrying something strange with it—heat, like breath exhaled from deep beneath the earth, and a scent I couldn't place.

I stopped walking.

Just beyond us, the land dropped into a basin. A massive gouge in the earth, like a wound that had never healed. Stone lay shattered and burned. Concentric rings etched the blackened earth, spiraling inward toward a raised platform of volcanic rock.

And at its center stood a throne—or maybe an altar—melted, fused to the ground by some great heat. Cracks spiderwebbed across its surface. The obsidian shimmered faintly, throbbing like a heartbeat.

Carved into the stone behind it was a single symbol.

One I didn't recognize, but my magic seemed to.

It recoiled instinctively, humming in warning, but I inched closer, squinting to make out the etching.

A crescent moon with a half-lidded eye hung over a spiral. Three wavy lines radiated downward.

"Nox." My finger lifted, stopping before touching it, but tracing it in the air. "What is that?"

He didn't answer right away. "Kur's mark." His shoulders slumped like a man defeated. "A reminder of what once was. Or maybe a promise of what could return."

"This is where he was held, isn't it?" A chill passed over my skin, and I rubbed my hands over my arms, trying to warm them.

Nox's eyes didn't leave the altar. "Perhaps. Or one of many places."

My magic pulsed again—a warning perhaps, but of what, I was uncertain. "Why would he leave his mark?" My voice was little more than a breath.

"To be found." He shrugged. "Or maybe to be remembered."

Glancing down, I shivered. "This place isn't safe, and I don't see any clues as to where Kur disappeared to."

"No." He turned away, his expression unreadable. "We should move on. There are some doors that are better left unopened."

We walked back to the top of the hill, away from Kur's destruction. Overlooking the Primordial Waters, we stood in silence, two silhouettes on the edge of something ancient and awesome. Something powerful and terrible. Something that could end us all.

## Chapter 23



"Where have you been?" Schmendrick lifted his head off the back of the couch (apparently not having moved an inch all day) and squinted at me like I'd disrupted his ten-hour nap on purpose. His eyes narrowed as he took in the sight of me. Then he opened his mouth, drawing in the scent through his vomeronasal organ like a connoisseur judging a spoiled bottle of wine.

"You smell like something ancient mixed with…" He trailed off, tilting his head to the side. After a long, hard stare, his green eyes widened, whites showing around his irises.

"…Dragon."

He slowly sat up, appearing relaxed, but the steady flick of his tail gave him away. "Tell me you didn't adopt another pet. The wolf is bad enough."

My mouth opened, prepared to answer him, but he cut me off with a low, uncharacteristic growl.

"What have you been doing?" He rose onto his haunches, stretching his neck as high as it would go, trying to catch another whiff.

Tapping my foot against the beige carpet, waiting to see if he'd let me get a word out this time, I stared at him. "I thought you always knew where I was."

Schmendrick blinked slowly, then turned his head and gave one shoulder an absent-minded lick. A classic deflection move. "I usually do. But when you vanish off the face of the Earth for *hours* and come back smelling like myths of gods and monsters, I start to wonder if I should have you microchipped."

He glanced at me again, tail thumping once against the couch. "So... Where. Were. You?"

"Nox took me to the Primordial Waters to see if we could figure out where Kur went." I expected Schmendrick to throw in his two cents, but for once, he didn't.

Staring beyond him, I let my vision drift out of focus while I remembered. I didn't want to let it go. The feeling. The song.

The melody was already slipping away, but I wanted to hold onto the notes, to hear that tune every day. "It was..." How could I describe what I'd seen? What so many others didn't even know existed?

"...Awe-inspiring. Ancient. *Alive.*" Focusing on Schmendrick, I fought the desire to step into the nearest shadow and return, to stare into the Waters' depths and watch galaxies being formed. "Everything was still. Like the world had been holding its breath for thousands upon thousands of years."

Trying to wrap my mind around what I'd seen and figure out a way to put it into words, I shook my head. "It wasn't just water. It felt alive. Like it knew I was there. Like it remembered me."

Schmendrick walked to the edge of the couch and stretched his paw out, settling it on my arm. "I know, Molly." His voice was soft, almost reverent. "I've seen it."

While I petted him (scratching everywhere he demanded), I told him about all that I'd seen, all we'd found, and how my opinion of Nox had changed.

Once I finished, Schmendrick jumped off the couch and trotted toward the kitchen. "You've been gone all day, and I was *this* close to starving to death."

"Oh, Buddy. That only works if you can show me how close you mean." Shaking my head and smiling over his dramatics, I followed him. When he jumped up onto his chair, I went to the cabinet, unlocked it, and pulled the treats out. I dumped a hefty serving onto Schmendrick's silver platter and made him wait while I put the container away.

"Next time, you're planning on hanging out with Nox, why don't I tag along?" He watched every move I made, practically drooling while he waited for me to set his plate in front of him.

Stopping halfway to the table, I tipped my head toward my shoulder, wondering what Schmendrick's sudden interest in Nox was about. "I'm sure it's going to become an everyday ritual. Mom wants Kur found, and she thinks Nox and I are the ones to do it."

"Not to mention that she's hoping that if you spend enough time with him, you'll forget the dog." He set his foot on the table and shifted his weight as if he were about to run across the surface to get to the treats.

Knowing he would be embarrassed if he lost control, I set the platter in front of him. "Not to mention." I pulled a glass from the strainer and filled it with ice before adding water. Then I sat across from him. "You could've come along today."

"I had important things to do." He snatched up a morsel with his claws and held it in front of him. "They're called catnaps for a reason."

## Chapter 24

*"The way to get on with a cat is to treat it as an equal—or even better, as the superior it knows itself to be." –Elizabeth Peters*

My alarm had gone off several minutes ago, but I wasn't ready to open my eyes or get out of bed, so I lay there, trying to focus on the song I'd heard. Every time I thought I'd grasped one of the notes, it drifted away. The harder I focused, the more I lost of it.

Flopping onto my back, I petted Schmendrick, hoping his soothing purrs would help revive the memory. When they didn't, I tossed the covers back and shuffled over to my dresser.

"What is it, Molly?" Schmendrick didn't bother opening his eyes.

Wiping the sleep out of my eyes, I walked into the bathroom and set my clothes on the counter. "I can't remember the melody. It slipped from my grasp."

"None can." He yawned, showing a mouth filled with sharp teeth. "It was not meant for this realm."

Slipping the hair tie off the bottom of my braid, I pulled my fingers through the plait I'd slept in. The strands were still wet from my shower. "So, it's going to haunt me forever?"

"I would love to answer yes to that, but since you know how to shadow walk, I'm sure you'll risk life and limb to return to hear it again." He stood, walked in a few circles, and curled up on my bed again. Once he was situated, he peeked up at me, his green eyes solemn. "Don't go alone. Whether you take me or Jayden or even Nox. Just don't go alone."

"I can take care of myself, you know?" I put toothpaste on my toothbrush, and right before sticking it in my mouth, I turned toward him. "See, I'm doing it now."

His ear flicked. "The Primordial Waters are fickle. Yesterday, they sang to you. Tomorrow, they might swallow you whole. Don't go alone."

"Fine. I won't." I spat my toothpaste into the sink and rinsed my mouth. "Are you coming with me to Castle Unicorn?"

He cracked one eye open, the green vivid against his black fur. "Do you need a chaperone?"

"Once again, I can take care of myself." Tugging my pajama shirt off, I dropped it on the counter and pulled on a sports bra. When my toes caught on my leggings, I stumbled a bit. "I might not be great at it, and I don't always like to, but I am capable." As I walked back into my bedroom, I tugged on a hoodie. "But, I need to see Nox when I'm done training."

"Don't leave Jayden until I am with you." He flipped his tail over his eyes, signaling the end of our conversation. "Leave my treats on the table. I'll be down for them in a bit."

The drive to Castle Unicorn was torturous. Even with the radio playing, my mind kept searching for the melody that had slipped through its grasp like smoke. It was there—perched on the edge of memory, like a dream that drifts away as soon as you wake up, waiting for me to find it.

Even though it was mid-November and the air had a bite to it, I gave in, rolling my windows down and cranking the music. But still, the tune tickled my thoughts, teasing me before dancing off again.

Coming to a stop in front of the gate at the bottom of the driveway, I pushed the button for the intercom. "Can I help you?" The voice that answered was unfamiliar.

"Yeah, uh, Molly here to see Jayden."

The gate slid open. "I'll let him know you're here. Drive safely."

The drive wound through the dormant trees. Their leaves littered the ground. The once vibrant colors were muted browns. A couple of wolves ran through the forest. I expected them to chase my car, but they disappeared, hidden by the mottled sunlight that streamed through the branches.

Jayden wasn't waiting for me by the gate like he normally did. A small, empty feeling tugged at my chest. Glancing around, I grabbed my swords off the back seat and strolled along the pathway into the backyard. Koi clung to the bottom of the moat, the water too cold for them to be active.

Garrett strode toward me from underneath the covered patio, his footsteps measured and sure. He towered over me, making me feel like a child caught doing something she shouldn't. "Molly." His chin dipped in a deep, acknowledging gesture—less formal, more weighted with intent. "Jayden is dealing with an issue right now." His blue eyes flashed gold for a heartbeat when his wolf stirred, tension flickering just beneath the surface. He reined it in with practiced ease, his voice smoothing. "Why don't you come sit with me for a moment?"

It sounded like an invitation, but the weight in his tone said otherwise. He was the alpha. His invitations didn't beg—they expected.

My chest seemed to hollow out a little more with every step toward the table Garrett seemed to prefer, my steps cautious but obedient. Setting my weapons on a bench beside it, I tried not to feel like I was being assessed.

Garrett pulled out a chair for me, the scrape of wood gentle but deliberate. As I sat, he moved to the seat across from me, his posture calm yet undeniably commanding—shoulders squared, hands resting on the table, thumbs loosely hooked together like he was ready to listen but still very much in control. "How is your training going?"

Warmth crept up my neck, blooming into a flush that burned my cheeks. My mind betrayed me with images—Jayden's hands wrapped around mine as we sparred, his breath on my neck, the heat of our bodies locked in motion. "Good." The word emerged, rough, half-swallowed. I dropped my gaze to my swords, pretending they needed studying. Training with Nahvienne was far less… charged. "I believe I'm improving."

Garrett didn't respond immediately. He watched me with a stillness that reminded me of a predator right before it lunged—not threatening, but undeniably alert. "Would it be easier with someone other than Jayden?" His voice was mild, but his eyes were sharp and assessing.

I looked into them, holding his gaze until I remembered he was the alpha. "No." I trailed my fingers along the grain pattern in the table. "We've come to an agreement. I, uh—" I cleared my throat, trying to bury my discomfort deep inside of me. "I don't want to hurt him, but I'm not a wolf. To me, the bond seems forced, and I want to get to know him before we—" (Yeah, it didn't stay buried long at all.) "Well, you know."

"That's admirable of you, Molly." He folded his arms over the table. His biceps were easily the size of my thighs. "Not all potential mates care about the devastation they leave behind when they enter a relationship with a wolf."

The sliding door opened, and Ariella stepped out, carrying a platter stacked with breakfast options. A young boy followed behind her with a pitcher of orange juice, one of water, and one of coffee.

"Help yourself." Garrett settled back in his seat and nodded at the delicious-smelling food.

After glancing at the spread, I focused on Garrett again. "I can't eat if I'm going to train anytime soon."

"Eat." His eyes flashed again. "Jayden won't be in a position to train you when he returns. His wolf will be riled."

Sticking my fork into a pancake, I pulled one off the stack and covered it in strawberries and blueberries before pouring syrup over it. Then I snatched a couple strips of bacon, biting into one immediately. It was cooked to perfection and practically melted in my mouth.

When I poured myself a glass of OJ and one of water, Garrett chuckled. "Melissa said you didn't drink coffee, but you work at her favorite coffee shop."

"I can't stand the smell of it, but Viv offered me a job when I needed it." I took a sip of juice. "I can never thank her enough for that."

Garrett's amusement faded into something quieter. He leaned forward slightly, resting one forearm on the table, the other hand curling loosely near his mouth as if holding something back. His gaze held mine—not challenging, just steady, thoughtful. Then he nodded once, slow and sure, the motion carrying a quiet kind of weight. Respect.

"And, this brings me to the next topic I'd like to discuss with you." He piled bacon, eggs, hash browns, and pancakes onto multiple plates. "Have you considered becoming the next archon?"

My hand froze halfway to my mouth. A thick drop of syrup slid off my pancake and hit the table with a soft splatter. "I-I haven't really thought about it. So much has happened since we had that talk." I set my fork down and leaned back, suddenly not sure I could take another bite even if I wanted to.

## Chapter 25

*"A cat understands how to be pleasant in the morning. He doesn't talk." -Tamora Pierce*

Garrett shoveled enough food into his mouth to feed a small army, then watched me carefully as he chewed. Whatever he'd seen on my face must have made him decide to drop the subject. "I hear you're hunting for a dragon."

"Trying to." I pushed my food around my plate with the fork. Garrett's eyebrow lifted as if in challenge, so I stabbed a strawberry and popped it into my mouth. The sweet taste exploded across my tongue and resurrected my appetite. "It'll be easier once we know which realm he's on."

"If you need help, don't hesitate to ask." He wiped the egg yolk off his plate with a piece of toast before eating half of it in one bite. "The world belongs to more than sorcerers, and it's up to all of us to protect it." His eyes flashed to the rich amber of his wolf, and he nodded toward the tree line. "Jayden."

I turned just as a wolf burst through the trees, light brown fur rippling as he bounded across the lawn with effortless grace.

My breath caught.

Jayden didn't run—he *soared*.

Sunlight caught in his fur, turning it gold. His muscles rippled beneath it as he ran. He was beautiful—wild, untouchable, free.

In human form, he carried so much weight, like the world expected too much of him. Sure, there were times when he let his guard down, let himself relax, but never like this. Running with the wind, he belonged.

I couldn't tear my gaze away.

He was breathtaking like this—radiant, carefree, and utterly himself.

A strange ache settled beneath my ribs. I told myself it was nothing, just awe or leftover adrenaline, but watching him stirred something deeper. A longing I didn't understand. A pull. Something.

Something I couldn't name.

The way my heart raced as he drew nearer didn't make sense. Yeah, he was a wolf (and a massive one at that), but I'd seen the other wolves run through the timber. I'd watched them nip at the car I'd been driving, but I'd never felt like this. Never felt... drawn.

But the other ones had only been nameless wolves. Unknown to me in their furry bodies. This one, though, this wasn't just any wolf. It was Jayden, and I would've recognized him even if Garrett hadn't told me who it was.

Watching him like this made me feel something I didn't understand. Something I couldn't place. Something between wonder and want. The urge to join him enveloped me. The desire to run alongside him so strong, it left my heart fluttering and my thoughts scattered.

He was so different like this. And yet still Jayden. Still the man who made me feel safe and challenged and sometimes left me exasperated beyond words.

He turned his head slightly, as if he knew I was watching. As if he felt me there.

Unsettled by the ache in my chest when I couldn't see him anymore, I turned away.

My gaze was drawn back. Pulled by some unseen force.

Jayden ran with the wind at his heels, and I realized how fortunate I was to witness this moment, to witness him, wild and free.

As Jayden neared us, Garrett stood and pulled the sliding glass door open. Jayden's eyes locked onto Garrett's for a fraction of a moment. Then his gaze flicked to me before he ran inside.

Garrett crossed his arms over his chest and leaned against the wall, waiting.

A minute later, Jayden stepped outside, wearing nothing but gray sweatpants that hung low on his hips, breath fogging slightly in the cool morning air.

Scratches laced his arms—thin red lines that looked like claw marks. A streak of dried blood trailed from his shoulder to his ribs—from the look of it, not his own. His fists were clenched tightly at his sides, his chest heaving with the remnants of a run that was more chase than exercise.

Seeing him battered made my heart clench. I wanted to go to him, but everything about his stance warned me away. And I began to doubt my earlier thoughts.

Did I want to be a part of this? Was it the life I longed for?

My fork slipped from my fingers, dropping onto my plate. The thought of taking another bite made me queasy, so I pushed the food away from me.

Garrett didn't move. He only watched me, calm as ever.

Jayden's gaze scanned the lawn, then the patio, finding me and lingering. Just long enough for me to know he hadn't forgotten I was there. Then he turned to Garrett.

"Martin and Devon." His voice was low, clipped with anger. "They crossed the western boundary. Far enough in to send a message, nothing more. Left their scent everywhere."

The names triggered something in my memory. "Romeo's." The word slipped out, and even though it had only been a shade above a whisper, Garrett and Jayden turned toward me.

After our date at Romeo's, the two wolves confronted Jayden in the parking lot. Devon, all cocky swagger and smirking confidence, had thrown the first verbal blow—taunting Jayden, saying I needed a *real* man. At the time, I hadn't known Jayden believed I was his mate. I hadn't realized how deeply those words would cut.

I had ended it—but for them, it clearly wasn't over.

Garrett's brows drew together. "What did they want?"

"To taunt us… me." Jayden flexed his hands like he still needed to bleed the fight out of them. With each pump of his fists, his wounds oozed more blood.

Garrett watched, giving Jayden the time he needed, not pushing him.

"They knew I'd be the one to respond. They led me on a run, then circled back to the edge and waited. No real at-tack—smirking, posturing, being dicks. They transformed long enough for Devon to tell me that loner wolves don't need leash-es, and Martin asked if—" his gaze flicked to me, and he winced "—the *witch* still had me under a spell."

My stomach flipped. Garrett didn't look at me, but I felt the shift in the air between them.

"I wanted to rip their throats out." A muscle ticked in Jayden's jaw, then again. "I nearly did, but they escaped through the barbed wire fence, off pack territory." He stared into Garrett's eyes for longer than I'd have thought possible. "I didn't follow."

Garrett was silent for a beat. Then he gave a single, approv-ing nod. "You did right."

"I still want to go back and rip their throats out." Jayden kept his voice low, but the fierceness in it was louder than if he'd shouted. He exhaled a heavy breath, but it did nothing to relax him. "They'll be back. They want to test our boundaries. Maybe more."

He glanced at me again—brief, unreadable.

Something hollow opened up inside me. The ache I'd felt while watching him run twisted into something darker. The blood streaking across his chest held my gaze captive. His words looped through my mind, assaulting me again and again—*I wanted to rip their throats out*. Each repetition sliced into me like a blade.

His wildness and freedom had called to me. I had longed to join him, to be a part of that world, to feel that abandon.

Standing in front of me, he looked more like a storm. Thunderous, raging, brutal. Burning with the need to fight.

*Dangerous*. But still him.

My chest tightened.

Too tight.

My breath hitched.

The edges of my vision darkened.

The chilly November morning became scorching.

Their voices disappeared behind my heartbeat and the blood pounding through my veins.

My fingers dug into the chair's arms as I tried to anchor myself.

Sunlight glinted off Jayden's skin, blinding me. Squinting, I tried to breathe.

But I couldn't.

Jayden turned toward me as if called by my panic. His amber eyes, still more wolf than man, met mine, and I silently begged him to look away, to not see me unraveling and weak.

My gaze dropped to the ground, avoiding the sympathy and worry that resided in his eyes.

"Molly?" Garrett's voice was gentle, careful. He stepped closer to me, but I refused to look.

My mouth floundered. My answer settled on my tongue, but the words wouldn't form.

Tears pricked at my eyes, heating them, but I held them back. My hands trembled, and my breaths came too fast, too shallow. Doing me no good.

I needed to run. To hide. To get away.

But I couldn't move.

Warm fingers wrapped around mine.

Jayden.

His touch soothed me, and I slowly began to breathe again.

The world quieted, but my thoughts still screamed.

# Chapter 26



*L*etting go of my hand, Jayden crouched next to me, balancing on his toes. His feralness had been replaced by a calm, soothing presence. The Jayden I'd grown accustomed to.

"You okay?" His voice was steady, even. Nothing like the man who'd declared he wanted to rip the other wolves' throats out.

Nodding, I kept my eyes averted; I couldn't look at him, couldn't let him see the lie. "Yeah."

On the edge of my vision, I saw his chin drop toward his chest.

"I'm fine, Jayden." The sliding door hissed open, then snicked shut. Garrett was gone, giving us a moment. One I wasn't sure I was ready for.

Jayden exhaled through his nose, slow, controlled. "I didn't say you weren't."

"I don't know what happened." My fingers clenched on the arms of the chair, then let go. The motion repeated again and again as I tried to relax, tried to keep from falling apart entirely.

His fingers brushed mine, a light touch, soft as a butterfly landing on my skin. "You don't have to explain."

"It's… a lot." I tipped my head so I could see him a little better without looking directly at him. "This life."

Jayden nodded slowly, like he was afraid of spooking me. "It is." He stared straight ahead. His jaw was tight, but everything else appeared loose, relaxed, like someone approaching a wild animal, afraid one wrong move would spook it, make it dart away, never to return.

"I don't know if I can do this." The words crept out on a breath.

His gaze flicked toward me, but the mask he wore was unreadable. "You don't have to decide right now."

The Gordian knot twisted in my stomach, pulling tighter and tighter, impossible to untie. "It feels like I do."

"You don't." He squeezed my fingers, then stood, backing away from me. "Take all the time you need."

Those words had to break him. He wanted this—us—so badly that I could feel it, but he didn't try to get me to commit. He didn't give me a speech, didn't try to sway me. Just gave me a steady shoulder I could lean on if… when I needed to.

"Thank you for… for not making this a thing." I glanced at him and then away.

He settled his hand on my shoulder for a fraction of a second. "We all break sometimes."

Something about the way he said *we* filled the hollow chasm in my chest. Was that why he'd retreated after telling me about the dragons? Was this how he'd felt?

Jayden padded toward the door, barely making a sound as his bare feet crossed the patio. But when the door closed behind him, it echoed—louder this time. Final.

And just like that, I was alone again.

The uneaten breakfast food sat on the table, and the smell made my stomach roil and churn—the grease of the bacon and eggs and the sickeningly sweet smell of the pancakes and syrup.

I leaned back in my chair and tried to count to ten, but my thoughts spiraled before I reached five.

"You have a dragon to catch, Molly." Schmendrick's voice was lazy and exactly what I needed to hear. "Feuding canines shouldn't be your focus right now."

He leapt onto my lap, a warm, familiar weight, and I began petting him without thinking. The motion, his purring—both anchored me. For a moment, the silence didn't feel so heavy. For a moment, I didn't feel lost and alone.

Instead of taking up his customary position on the passenger seat, Schmendrick curled up on my lap for the drive to Ravenwood. I didn't tell him that I needed him, that I would fall apart without him, but somehow he knew.

I parked in front of the manor. The raven-headed gargoyles stared down at me from their lofty perches on top of the roof. The house itself was dark and foreboding. The deep gray stone and shadowed porch were nearly as black as the memories buried inside them.

Pushing open the wrought iron gate, I stepped onto one of the ebony stones. Movement in the bushes caught my eye and halted my steps.

Schmendrick hissed and arched his back. His tail doubled in size, and his claws swiped through the air in front of him.

"Miss Molly." Vak ignored Schmendrick, snatched his hat from his head, and bowed so low I thought he might kiss the pristine yard.

Schmendrick positioned himself between Vak and me, dropping his head and front legs to the ground and wiggling his butt, preparing to pounce.

Vak's eyes flicked from Schmendrick to me. "We have located that which you seek."

"You have? Where?" I asked at the same time that Schmendrick jerked upright and turned his focus on me. "What have you done, Molly?"

Bending down, I tried to scratch Schmendrick's head, but he pulled away. "I asked them to help me find the dagger."

"You made a bargain with them?" Schmendrick's tail lashed through the air behind him, his ears twitching with agitation. "They are fae. Do you know nothing of this world you live in?" He paced a tight, angry circle on the lawn in front of me. "Next, you'll be offering your name, your blood, and your firstborn in exchange for a warm sunbeam and an empty box to nap in."

A cold weight settled in my stomach. I hadn't thought it through—not really. I mean, I knew that Schmendrick didn't trust him, but I should've asked him why. I should've demanded answers from him. (But would he have answered me?)

Leaning against the closed gate, I pinched my eyes shut. The words had seemed harmless, but under Schmendrick's fierce stare, they felt like loaded weapons I'd casually handed over. My mouth went dry. Regret bloomed sharp and fast, curling into fear. What had I done? What had I given away without realizing it?

Schmendrick went still, the way only cats can—tense with unspoken judgment. His tail twitched once, sharply, like a blade slicing the air. "Brilliant. Let's auction off your soul next." His head whipped toward me, his ears lying flat against his head, as if a horrifying thought had struck him. "At least tell me you didn't thank him."

I stared into the distance, my gaze settling on the Guardians of Ravenwood Citadel without really seeing them. "I don't believe I thanked him, but I might've told Vak that I'd be indebted to him if he found it."

## Chapter 27

*"I have studied many philosophers and many cats. The wisdom of cats is infinitely superior." -Hippolyte Taine*

Schmendrick froze mid-pace, his pupils narrowing into slits. "You *what*?" His voice was low and dangerous. "You didn't just invite trouble—you marched straight into it with a giant bow tied around yourself."

"I didn't think—"

"No." His fur bristled along his spine. "You didn't. That's the problem." He paced along the stone pathway, claws tapping rhythmically with each step. "Debts with the fae are binding. You might as well have carved a contract into your bones or signed in blood. And Vak?" He paused, staring hard at me. "Vak doesn't do favors. He collects them."

A chill ran down my spine. "What do I do now?"

Schmendrick gave me a long, weary look—the kind that said he'd already started composing my eulogy.

"What's the price?" I turned toward Vak, my voice quieter than I meant it to be.

Vak tilted his head. "Ah, now she asks. You offered a debt freely, Miss Molly. I simply honored your request."

"She didn't understand what she was offering." Schmendrick stopped between us. "She left this world behind to live with humans."

Vak turned slowly toward Schmendrick, his voice edged with steel. "Come now, cat. Surely you, of all creatures, understand the weight of a fae debt."

A chill skittered across my skin.

Schmendrick's ears flicked back, his eyes slitting. "Debts are a petty game for lesser fae. I don't play by your rules."

I froze.

*Lesser fae?* What did that make Schmendrick then?

My breath caught as the weight of his words settled like a stone in my gut. I'd known he was more than a cat, even a fae cat, but it seemed he was even more than I'd guessed. More than he'd ever let on.

Vak chuckled low. "Of course. My mistake." His eyes glittered as they slid back to me. "Still, one never quite knows which rules apply… until they're broken. Be that as it may, ignorance is not a defense."

Schmendrick remained still, his tail twitching once.

Vak tilted his head, the movement unnervingly fluid, like a predator considering a new angle of attack. "I wonder, though—do your rules come from age or rank?"

Schmendrick bared his teeth in a slow, deliberate yawn. His eyes never left Vak's, and his claws unsheathed lazily into the grass. "You're assuming I follow rules at all."

My skin prickled. The air between them felt charged—like an electrical storm gathering strength.

Vak's smile didn't reach his eyes. He clasped his hands behind his back, but one foot shifted, angling his body subtly sideways—less like submission, more like readiness. "They are written for all of us. Are they not?"

Schmendrick rose, slow and graceful, his back arching in a sinuous stretch that made the muscles beneath his fur ripple like shadows. His tail flicked once, then twice—sharp and agitated. "Careful, kobold." His voice dropped, low and ancient, deeper and darker than I'd ever heard it. "You're starting to sound like someone who wants to find out."

Vak went still.

Utterly still.

Even his breath seemed to stop, as though he knew the slightest misstep could unleash something he wouldn't be able to put back.

I didn't move. Couldn't. My heart thudded in my chest, loud enough I was sure they could hear it. The space between them buzzed with the kind of tension you feel before a fight breaks out—or a spell detonates. I didn't understand the rules they were playing by, but it was clear neither of them was bluffing.

And Schmendrick…

He'd spoken like something old. Something dangerous. Something that didn't follow rules because he'd written the rules.

Or, he was the reason rules existed in the first place.

My pulse thudding, I took a step back. The space between them was suddenly too still, like the air before a lightning strike. As I looked from one to the other, my skin began crawling with the sensation that I was witnessing something far older—and far more dangerous—than I understood.

Vak held up both hands in mock surrender. "Perish the thought. I'd never presume." But his smile lingered a heartbeat too long.

My eyes darted to Schmendrick. His gaze was unreadable now, far away, as though watching something I couldn't see. My heart kicked harder.

What was he?

"What do you want from me?" Wrapping my arms around myself, my fingers dug into my sides.

"Nothing—yet. I'm not sure I can collect." Vak raised one of the ridges above his eye, like a human lifting a single brow, the corner of his mouth twitching. "If I remember right, I indebted myself to you first. *Forever indebted*, if memory serves me."

Schmendrick narrowed his eyes. "Which means she can't owe you anything. Not unless you're rescinding your oath." His tail lashed like a willow switch. "There are rules against that. The consequences are devastating."

"No need to get dramatic, cat. This... is merely a complication of terms. I'm sure we'll figure something out." Vak turned toward him slowly, still smiling. "At any rate, debts are best ripened with time." His gaze shifted back to me, sharper now. "A debt offered, even in ignorance, has weight. But perhaps we're simply… even now."

Schmendrick rubbed against my leg. The contact startled me, pulling my gaze from Vak. He sat heavily on top of my feet, anchoring me. "The dagger." He licked his paw, slow and deliberate, then paused. "Where is it?"

"Caius has it." Vak watched Schmendrick warily, as if this version of the cat was more frightening than moments before. "He keeps it on him. Always."

The name hit me like a punch in the gut. I clutched my stomach, trying to hold myself together, to hold my fear in. "You're sure?" (Of course, he was sure.)

Everything fell into place. Of course, it was Caius. How could I have suspected Mom or Malachai?

Caius had never hidden his hatred for me. The way he'd treated me… the things he'd done to me growing up. His casual cruelty.

He wouldn't flinch at taking my life. Especially if it meant more power for him.

But Mom… she would never believe me. Never take my side. Not without proof.

Vak nodded, and his voice dropped to something softer, something filled with pity or remorse. "Quite. Though I'd be careful if I were you. Caius doesn't share well."

Schmendrick's claws flexed into the top of my shoes.

*Dammit.* I was in Ravenwood wearing sneakers. *Again.* I'd been prepared for training with Jayden that hadn't happened, and I hadn't changed.

"Of course, he has it." Schmendrick's tail curled around my ankles. "*Of course.* Why not hand it to the most paranoid, power-hungry bastard on the continent?" Every hair on his back stood on end.

Vak turned toward the bushes, already beginning to disappear into the shadows. "You asked for truth. I delivered. The debt remains… complicated." He looked over his shoulder, something unreadable in his gaze. "Do be careful with what you seek, Molly. That dagger should never have been found."

## Chapter 28



"Come, Molly." Schmendrick bumped my shin with his head. "Let's meet with Nox and find a dragon." He blinked at me slowly, then trotted toward the porch. His long tail stuck up, curling at the tip, making it look like a question mark. "Once we've accomplished that, we can deal with fae bargains and cursed blades."

My feet felt like lead boots had been strapped to them as I followed him inside. Every time we crested one hill, another larger one loomed in front of us, and I didn't know if I had the strength to keep climbing.

The house was dark. I trudged up the stairs, each step a chore. Even once I found Kur, I had no idea how to get him back to the Primordial Waters—much less convince him to guard them again.

Or even if it was right to expect him to.

I'd meant what I'd said to Nox: I would take Kur's place if I could. He'd already done his time. Already spent thousands of years in solitude, holding the Waters at bay.

And what had he done to deserve that punishment? What could anyone do to deserve five thousand years of solitary confinement?

With each thought, my steps grew heavier until I finally reached the top. I slogged my way to Mom's office to find her alone, behind her desk.

Her gaze raked over me from my feet up to my face. Her lips pinched together when she noticed my shoes, and her expression grew tighter as she trailed her way to the messy bun that pulled my purple hair back.

"Hello, Mom." I didn't have the energy to fight with her, so I tried my best to be polite. "Where's Nox this morning?"

Schmendrick jumped onto the chair in front of her desk and began kneading the seat (with his claws out), drawing Mom's attention away from me.

"Schmendrick." She smacked her hands together. The noise shattered the silence that held the manor captive, but he didn't even glance at her. "Molly, get your cat off my chair."

He jumped down and shot me a smug look. *She's not focused on you anymore.*

*Thanks, Buddy.*

Mom tugged at her blouse sleeves, pulling the imaginary wrinkles out of them. Then she smoothed her hair back. "Nox returned to his cabal to gather some of his research." She flicked her fingers dismissively. "Most of the other guardians are training in the arena. Take your cat and join them. Then see Caelan. You need to learn what it means to be part of the cabal."

My steps were lighter on the way down the stairs. I felt like I had a moment to breathe for a change.

"Oh, and Molly." Mom stood at the top of the stairs; one hand curled around the banister. Her posture was stiff, commanding—like a queen about to pass judgment.

My stomach plummeted. Nothing good ever came after those words. Turning toward her, I swallowed. "Yes." I tried to match her tone, but it came out too thin.

*"Will to will, mind to mind.*

*Sever the bonds that hearts confine.*

*Attach anew those I desire.*

*By blood and breath and mother's ire,*

*Her magic to his now re-aligned.*

*And be their hearts forever entwined."*

Magic forged her words into a blade—elegant, deadly—that pierced my heart. The influx of power and pain dropped me to my knees.

She didn't need to speak the spell aloud. Sorcerers rarely did.

But she wanted me to hear it, to know she was in control.

She wanted me to understand exactly what she was taking.

She didn't want Jayden and me to drift apart over time. She wanted us to end, knowing she'd been the reason.

She wanted me to know that she was stronger than fate, more powerful than destiny.

*"Soul to soul, ties unbind.*

*Make the clock rewind.*

*Let past desires be now unmade.*

*The tether loosed, the promise will fade.*

*What once was held, now be released.*

*And in its place, let new love increase."*

She stared down at me, her hand lifted and her fingers weaving her words into steel—hard, unbreakable.

My magic surged to the surface—instinctive and raw—like a tidal wave, crashing into hers. It wrapped around her spell, straining to deflect it, fighting for the right to choose my path. Not willing to have my destiny forged by her words.

Gasping, I doubled over. Pain cracked through my ribs like lightning. Schmendrick rubbed against me, anchoring me, keeping me from drowning beneath her power. His strength flowed into me, and finally, I dragged in a shaky breath.

The dark, oppressive room whirled around me as I pushed to my feet. I gripped the banister, attempting to put an end to the dizziness, and glared at Mom (no, I wouldn't call her that anymore)—Seraphina. No mom would do what she'd done. She dropped her hand, and the smile she donned was wicked, twisting her beauty into something malicious, treacherous.

"No daughter of mine will run with wolves." Seraphina's voice was cold and harsh. "Only a strong sorcerer—one like Nox—will win your heart and your hand. The Ravenwood line will continue growing stronger. I will not allow it to be diluted by a mongrel."

I wanted to respond with something witty, something that would show her she hadn't won, but I couldn't think over the battle raging inside of me.

"Run along now, dear." She waved in a shooing motion before retreating to her office.

The dark hallway held me captive for several seconds. When I felt like I could move without toppling over, I staggered toward the door. Clutching my chest, I wondered if Seraphina's spell had taken hold or if my power had overcome it.

My heart clenched, remembering how I'd left Jayden less than an hour before, wondering if that would be our last encounter and what would become of him if Seraphina had her way.

When I opened the door, Caius stood on the other side, reaching for the knob.

My breath hitched in my throat, startled by his sudden appearance. My eyes darted to his side, scanning for *MaunDagnir*—wondering if it was strapped there.

He clicked his tongue against the roof of his mouth, shaking his head in mock disappointment. But the gleam in his eyes betrayed him.

Not concern.

No. I recognized it for what it was. I'd seen it too many times to count.

Too many times to forget.

Malice.

Excitement to catch me at a disadvantage.

Alone.

Where nobody but Schmendrick would witness his cruelty.

I wanted to run.

But I needed to stand up to him.

"How many times—" he stepped toward me, and I fought my instincts, refusing to back away "—Dear Mahlia, must you be reminded to dress appropriately when visiting Ravenwood Estates?"

Blood thrummed through my veins, pounding in my ears, and my heart raced faster with each passing millisecond. "And what exactly is appropriate attire for hunting a dragon?" I tried to inch past him, but he shifted, blocking the doorway and any hope of escape.

He reached for my shoulder, sparks dancing across his fingertips. "For starters, not sneakers."

I caught his wrist before he made contact and shoved it back.

His eyes narrowed, and menace tightened his lips.

But I didn't flinch. I refused to give him the satisfaction of seeing me cower.

Then I stepped closer. Close enough that the malice in his eyes flickered, shifting toward fear. "I know what you're up to." My voice was low but sharp enough to draw blood. "And I will stop you."

# Chapter 29



*I* strode out the door and to the gate with my head held high, hoping Caius couldn't tell how anxious I was about turning my back on him. Hoping he didn't take the opportunity to plunge *MaunDagnir* between my shoulder blades.

My only solace was that Schmendrick was with me. He would warn me of any danger or protect me if he needed to.

He trotted along beside me, looking to all the world like a normal cat and not whatever he truly was. "I can smell your brain burning, Molly. What's on your mind?"

With that one question, my dam broke. "What *are* you? What's going to happen with me and Vak? Did Mom's spell work?" The words tumbled out in a rush, tripping over one another in their hurry, like holiday shoppers on Black Friday before the internet was a thing. "How am I going to find Kur? How can I convince him to go back and guard the Primordial Waters? And will I ever hear their song again?"

I didn't even pause to breathe. "And *what are you*? Why do you stay with me? Why *me*, of all the people in the world? Why me? And Jayden—" His name snagged in my throat. I pictured both sides of him that I'd seen earlier in the day—his wolf breaking free from the trees, wild and free, and him standing on the patio, blood smeared across his chest like war paint.

The second version scared me.

The violence that rolled off him.

I didn't think he would ever turn it on me, but he *could*.

And unlike Seraphina, I refused to invite cruelty into my home and call it love.

Schmendrick stretched his front legs as far as they would go, his claws scraping against the sidewalk as he dragged them back. "I am your friend—your companion. The same as I've always been." He padded alongside me. "I came to you because your magic called to me. I stayed with you because…" He glanced up at me, the green of his eyes swallowed by dark pupils. "Because I love you, Molly."

A lump formed in my throat, and my heart swelled and ached all at once. Tears pooled in my eyes at his unexpected admission. In all the time he'd been with me, he'd never said those words, not out loud. I'd always wondered if I would come home one day to find he had moved on.

After all, he wasn't mine.

"I've loved watching you grow into the woman who stands before me now." He blinked at me—slow and unhurried—the way cats do when they trust you completely. "I can't wait to see who you will become."

Something in my chest cracked open, letting light spill through the fissures, washing away the shadows I carried. He'd seen all of my flaws, all the bad parts of me. All of my fear and uncertainty, and somehow, he was still proud of me. I crouched next to him. Pressing my forehead to his, warmth and peace flowed through me, easing my fears. I scratched his chin, then trailed my fingers along his spine, sinking them into his thick, silky fur. "I love you, too, Buddy." The soft words caught. "I don't know who I'd be without you, and I don't want to find out."

For a moment, the world stilled.

No dragons. No faerie bargains. No mothers with cruel spells.

Just me and my cat. And that was enough.

He leaned into my touch, a purr rumbling through his body, warm and steady against my palm. "When was the last time Seraphina's magic worked on you?"

I blinked as the weight of the world crashed onto my shoulders again. The peace I'd clung to the moment before fractured, and all of my questions slammed into me again, pounding against my brain, begging for answers. Pressing my hands against my skull, I focused on what he'd said, repeating the words to myself, trying to drown out my thoughts. "Remember when she used it on me to make me finish my supper? Canned spinach." The memory made me shiver with disgust. "Yuck."

"Even I wouldn't eat that garbage." A bug zipped past me, catching Schmendrick's attention. He sprang into the air, spinning as gracefully as a ballerina. He swatted the fly mid-flight. It dropped to the ground with a buzz, and Schmendrick landed neatly beside it. "Next time you see Nox, you'll know if the spell worked or not." He started walking again, tail flicking lazily behind him, as if the incident with the fly had never happened, and I followed.

Silence stretched between us while I turned that over in my head, looking at it from every angle, trying to make sense of it. "Why not when I see Jayden?"

"Whether Seraphina's magic worked or not, you have a history with the wolf. He was your first date, the first man you felt comfortable enough to fall asleep next to, your first *real* kiss." He looked at me pointedly. "That peck between you and Caelan under Seraphina's desk really doesn't count."

Schmendrick was right about a lot of things, and more often than not, but my kiss with Caelan counted as my first. I may have been young and innocent when it happened, but it was real, and it had meant something to both of us.

"Jayden felt his mate was threatened." His voice snapped me back into the present. "What would you do to protect those you love?" He flung the words at me. They were weighted and broke through the shield I'd built around my heart.

It took me a second to realize Schmendrick had moved on to one of my other questions.

Jayden. The question I couldn't make myself ask.

I pictured Jayden on the patio again, but this time, I saw him differently. The fury radiating off him. The blood smeared across his chest. The way he'd said, *I wanted to rip their throats out.* It wasn't coming from a place of violence. It had been coming from fear. From a desire to protect.

I'd been like those cubs to him. All he wanted was to keep me safe, and if something happened to me, he would carry those scars forever, too.

"And can you imagine any circumstances where you'd turn that rage on a loved one?" Schmendrick watched my face even though he knew what my answer would be.

I shook my head. "No, I can't."

"As far as the Primordial Waters are concerned" —his voice softened, making me wonder if he knew something about them that I didn't—"either they'll recede or they won't. Sometimes things happen, and there's nothing that could've prevented them."

A tiny crack formed in the weight I carried. With each shaky breath, it expanded, racing across the surface but also reaching deeper.

My burden shifted, sloughed off in a slow, groaning slide, like a glacier calving into the sea. Slow. Thunderous. Impossible to stop. It didn't take everything with it, but enough.

Enough that I could finally straighten, draw in a full breath, and let relief rush in like sunlight through storm clouds.

Ever since being dragged back into this world, I'd taken the burdens and responsibilities as if they were mine, and mine alone. But they weren't. None of them.

It wasn't up to me to fix every problem. I just needed to play my part. To help where I could and to step back when I couldn't.

My steps were lighter as we continued walking to the arena. When we reached it, I stared down at him. There was one more thing I needed to know. One more thing I had to have answered before he clammed up again. Trying to find the courage to ask him, I chewed on my lip.

"Spit it out, Molly." He sat and looked up at me. His ears flicked—his only sign of anxiety.

Drawing in a deep breath, I tried to ease into it gently, but my mouth didn't get the memo. The words tumbled out. "Did you wake Kur?" I pressed my fingers to my lips, waiting for his answer.

"Not intentionally." He turned his face from me. He didn't blush. (He was a cat after all.) His ears twitched back, and his tail flicked guiltily.

I stumbled over my next thoughts. "Why? How?"

"I've been searching for *MaunDagnir's* antithesis." He wrapped his tail around his paws and glanced at me. "Legends claim it was with Kur when Ereshkigal bound him to the Primordial Waters, but I felt no trace of *GwathNahtar*."

I stared at him—the black cat who had come to me so long ago—and wondered (not for the first time) how I could know so little about him. "What else do you do while I'm at work?"

"Whatever needs done." He trotted into the arena before I could ask anything else.

## Chapter 30



$\mathcal{N}$ahvienne stood across from me. Waves of cobalt hair cascaded down her back, rippling with each lunge toward me. Our swords crashed together. Every move released some of my doubts, my stress, my frustration. Exercise grounded me, focusing my mind and my body on something besides *what-ifs*.

"You're getting better every day." She grinned as she lunged toward me again.

Parrying her strike, I pivoted to the side. "I should be better. I should've started training as soon as I was old enough to hold a sword."

"Could've. Would've. Should've." Her blade struck mine, and she twisted, nearly wrenching the sword from my grip. "You can't change the past. All you can do is move forward."

Backing up a step, I waited for her to make her move. A gentle spring-like breeze blew through the arena, blowing my hair off my neck, and for once, I was grateful that the weather in the cabal was controlled.

Nahvienne's blade swept toward my legs, and I jumped, my feet scraping the air above the blow. "Good." She nodded.

My arms ached from holding the sword. I'd been relying less on my magic and more on my muscles.

She struck again, faster this time. Steel collided in a blur of motion, but my footing slipped on the grass.

Nahvienne caught my wrist mid-fall, yanked me upright, and twirled us both away from the momentum. "Losing your balance in a real fight could be the end of you." She kept hold of my arm, not letting go of my gaze. "Trust your instincts. Always be aware of your surroundings. You have to count on more than your blade in a battle. You have to count on yourself." She let go of my arm and squeezed my shoulder. "You've got this, Molly."

Swallowing the knot of emotion her words stirred, I nodded. For so long, I'd been told I wasn't good enough—not only from one person, but from all directions. It was going to take a while for me to find my self-worth. "Working on it."

"I know." Stepping back, she raised her sword again. "Now show me how much."

We circled. Her weight shifted, her hips projecting her next move. I struck first—an upward slash that she blocked effortlessly, but it forced her off-center. I followed it with a quick spin and jab toward her side.

She dodged, avoiding the sting of my blade by a hair's breadth. "Better." She was panting slightly, almost as tired as I was for a change. "Again."

We circled. I didn't wait for her to strike. I feinted right, then slashed left, catching her off-guard. Our blades locked, and I pushed forward, my muscles trembling with effort.

Her eyes sparkled. "That's it. You're reading me better."

She broke the lock and stepped back, testing me with a quick jab. I parried, then turned the motion into a graceful spin, catching her blade with mine and deflecting it.

We paused, breathless. For once, Nahvienne didn't immediately lunge back in.

"You're not just reacting anymore." She lowered the tip of her sword toward the ground. "You're *thinking*. Seeing a step ahead. Choosing your moments."

I nodded, heart pounding. "I still have a long way to go."

"We all do." The soothing tone of her voice made me think of a gentle stream. Its water flowing steadily. "But you keep showing up, keep trying. That matters more than anything else."

Her words settled in my chest, making me feel lighter.

She raised her sword again. "One more?"

My muscles begged for a break, just a few moments, but my competitive side won out. I grinned and shifted my stance. "Yeah. En garde." Ignoring the ache in my legs, I lunged forward.

We danced, blades clanging together, each clash vibrating up my arm.

Finally, Nahvienne stepped back, lowering her sword. "That's enough for today."

I let my blade drop with a grateful exhale, sweat clinging to my brow.

She nodded. "You're getting there."

And for once, I believed her.

## Chapter 31

*"Like all pure creatures, cats are practical." –William S. Burroughs*

Caelan sat behind his desk. Dark circles ringed his blood-shot eyes, and his shirt looked like it had been lying in a crumpled heap before he slipped it on. It was so out of character for the normally pressed and polished person I'd known.

With a heavy heart, I knocked on his door and stepped into his office without waiting for an invitation. Schmendrick trotted in at my side. He leapt onto the chair across from Caelan's desk and eyed him critically. "You look like something even I wouldn't drag in."

"It's great to see you, too, Schmendrick." His words stuck together like his tongue had forgotten how to form them.

Schmendrick's ears rotated. "Of course it is." He lifted his paw and licked it, still watching Caelan.

"Seraphina sent me here to '...*learn how to be part of the cabal.*'" I picked Schmendrick up, then sat where he'd been, placing him on my lap.

Caelan snorted and leaned back in his chair. "She should've done that years ago."

My fingers tightened in Schmendrick's fur. Caelan was hurting and looking for a fight. That much was obvious, but I refused to let him goad me.

Instead of looking at him, I let my gaze wander over his bookshelf, searching for his special edition copy of *Alice's Adventures in Wonderland*. But like the Caelan I'd known, it was gone.

He spun his chair so that he was facing the window instead of me. "When are you going to stop pretending, Molly?" His tongue had sharpened. His words cut through the tension in the room, slicing into me.

My head snapped back. "What are you talking about?"

"You know we're meant to be together." He reached for the glass of scotch that sat next to the nearly empty bottle on his desk.

I stared at him while he slammed back his drink. What could I say to that? Once, I might have agreed. I'd believed it for a long time. But after he'd shown up at Harvest Moon looking at me like I was the enemy, like he hated me… I'd stopped believing. I'd given up on the idea of us and moved on.

He refilled his glass with the last of the scotch. "He's using you, Molly."

"For what?" I rolled my eyes, but he didn't answer, just lifted the scotch to his lips. "Don't you think you've had enough to drink?"

He held my gaze while he tipped the glass back and emptied it. Then he wiped his mouth with the back of his hand. "How much I drink is none of your damn business." He staggered over to the corner where he kept his alcohol and grabbed another bottle of scotch. "Power, Molly. He wants power."

"Really? Power?" Unable to remain sitting while a storm raged inside of me, I pushed myself to my feet. "That's the best you've got?"

He set his glass down. It wobbled on the edge of the stand before falling to the ground and shattering. He didn't flinch. Just stared at the broken shards for a second, then picked up the bottle and drank straight from it. "If the fae attack again, the wolves'll need us." His words slurred.

"Bullshit!" I slammed my palm down on his desk like a lightning strike, my voice rumbling with the force of thunder. "You know that was all lies. You know we betrayed them."

"He's not even a sorcerer!"

"Neither am I." I tilted my head. Transformed. My horns spiraled from my skull. My fangs glinted. And I stared at him through soulless black eyes. "Or had you forgotten?"

"Molly…" He slumped into his chair, broken. Tears glistened in his eyes. "I've loved you since we were five. I can't live without you." He reached for the bottle, hand trembling. "See what I've become."

"Cae." My voice softened, the storm momentarily diminished, but I didn't reach out to comfort him. I couldn't solve his problems for him, and I couldn't coddle him, couldn't let him think there was a chance for us. "If you loved me—*truly* loved me—you wouldn't have treated me the way you did."

His chin dropped to his chest. "I do love you, Molly, but I was hurt." He lifted his gaze to me, his hazel eyes pleading with me. "I wanted to hurt you."

"That's not love." Clutching Schmendrick to my chest, I stood. "That's abuse, and I deserve better."

## Chapter 32



Caelan's head was bowed over his desk. Tears carved trails down his cheeks. The bottle of scotch rested in his lap like a weight he didn't know how to put down. My fractured heart broke a little more, but I walked out the door anyway. There was nothing I could do for him. Nothing I could say to help him.

Schmendrick squirmed until I set him on the ground. As I straightened up, I resisted the urge to look back. I hoped Caelan would figure things out. That he would move on. And that we could eventually be friendly again (or maybe even friends). But I couldn't be responsible for him anymore.

Hurrying through the hallway to the door, neither Schmendrick nor I spoke until we stepped outside.

As soon as the door closed, I stopped, hoping some of the tension would drain from me. The magic in the air clung to me like a wet t-shirt, and I doubted I would get any relief while I was there.

Schmendrick brushed his head against my leg. "Besides training with Nahvienne, today was a *cata*strophe."

A humorless chuckle escaped me. "It sure was."

He wove between my legs, and every time he touched me, some of the weight slid off—slowly, like shadows retreating before the dawn.

My house had always comforted me. Whether it was because I'd believed the other sorcerers didn't know it existed or because of its quiet solitude, I wasn't sure. But that wasn't the case when I returned from Ravenwood.

The interior was dim. The only light spilled in from the hallway. Feeling as trapped as the tigers at the Henry Doorly Zoo, I paced from one end of the living room to the other.

On my umpteenth pass behind the couch that Schmendrick slept on, he cracked one eye open. "Call him, Molly."

His unexpected voice made me jump. In a futile attempt to calm my racing heart, I pressed my hand to my chest, then tipped my head toward my shoulder. "What?"

"Call him." He stretched to his full length, then curled into a ball, covering his eyes with a paw.

I'd been thinking about Vak. About the faerie bargain I may or may not have made with him.

But as Schmendrick's words sank in, my thoughts shifted to Jayden and the way I'd left him.

How could I call him after that? How could I explain? How could I expect him to understand?

"Molly." The command in Schmendrick's voice left me with no choice but to pick up the phone and dial Jayden's number.

It rang once. "Molly." His relief washed through the line, unexpected and disarming.

It took me a few seconds to find my voice, to figure out what to say. So many thoughts raced through my mind, but I settled on the simplest, most direct thing. Some of the toughest words to say. "I'm sorry, Jayden." They came out on a breath, smothered in guilt and regret.

"Hey, now." The Jayden I'd come to know over the past several weeks resurfaced—steady, warm, unshaken. "There's nothing to apologize for."

His words were an arrow that pierced my heart. "There's—" I swallowed hard and pinched my eyes shut, thinking of everything that had happened since I'd seen him. "There's so much you don't know."

A long breath filled the silence. It stretched on, and my stomach tightened with every beat of my heart. When he spoke again, his voice was softer—careful, like he didn't want to spook me. "Have you eaten?"

The change of subject threw me. It took several breaths before I registered what he said. "No, I haven't."

"I'll order a pizza from Casey's and bring it over. What do you want on it?"

"I don't care as long as pepperoni is one of the toppings." My fingers twisted the hem of my shirt, wrapping around it until I had to let go and start over.

"If you want, I can call you back as soon as I place the order."

I shook my head (like an imbecile). "No. I need a shower." I paused, the fabric still clenched in my hand. "We'll talk when you get here."

On my way upstairs, I patted Schmendrick's head. "Thanks, Buddy."

"Always, Molly."

## Chapter 33

*"Cats have it all—admiration, an endless sleep, and company only when they want it." -Rod McKuen*

$\mathcal{W}$hen I heard the knock, I was drying my hair. Water dripped from the tips, soaking the strands until the purple appeared almost black, but that didn't matter. What did matter was Jayden standing on my stoop. The towel hit the counter and sloughed off onto the floor. As I bounded down the stairs, I heated my fingers with magic and dragged them through the tangles.

Schmendrick glanced up from his perch on the back of the couch and flicked his tail. "Better get that before he starts barking."

Shaking my head, I tried to suppress my grin. Then I padded barefoot across the carpet, my heart doing that ridiculous fluttering thing it always did around Jayden. As I reached for the doorknob, I sucked in a deep breath, trying to steady myself.

Jayden stood on my stoop, a pizza box in one hand, a can of tuna in the other. The porch light softened him somehow, brushing gold across the sharp lines of his face and catching in the waves of his hair. For a moment before he stepped inside, he looked less like a beast and more like a boy.

"For the lady. Pepperoni, beef, and sausage. I hope that's okay." He looked a little uncertain as he set the pizza on the stand.

Backing up a step, I motioned for him to enter. "Sounds delicious. Thanks for this."

"And for His Royal Purrness." He set the tuna on top of the box before unlacing his boots.

Warmth bloomed in my chest, growing into a full-fledged smile. "A man after my cat's heart." I chuckled. "I like it."

Schmendrick let out a pleased chirp, jumped off the back of the couch, and trotted forward to rub against Jayden's legs.

Jayden petted Schmendrick, then pulled me in for a hug. "You look better than you sounded on the phone."

His woodsy scent wafted over me, surrounding me in a comforting cocoon and hardening my resolve to be the one to choose my path.

"That's a low bar." Snorting, I wrapped my arms around his waist and leaned my head against his chiseled chest, listening to the steady rhythm of his heart.

He didn't laugh, just rubbed his hands in slow circles along my back. "You don't have to explain anything until you're ready. I'm here. That's all."

My throat tightened, and I twisted his shirt in my fingers like it might keep me from unraveling. "I'm sorry."

His hands stilled, his fingers splaying across my back.

"I believe someone mentioned tuna." Schmendrick jumped onto the stand and pawed at the can.

I pulled back, but Jayden held onto me. "No, I'm sorry." He leaned back enough to look into my eyes. "For scaring you. But, Molly, I would *never* hurt you."

The intensity in his gaze—so open and vulnerable—struck me. I met it without flinching. "I know."

Schmendrick reached for me, a not-so-subtle reminder that he was waiting. "If no one else is going to acknowledge the emergency here, I will. Starving cat." He tapped his paw on the can. "Open this immediately."

"Patience is a virtue, kitty." Jayden's mouth twitched into a smile as he glanced from Schmendrick to me, a quiet warmth in his eyes that made my heart stutter.

Schmendrick jumped down and trotted toward the kitchen. "It may very well be, but it isn't one of mine."

Jayden followed him, carrying dinner. He set the pizza on the table, then opened the can. Without needing to be told, he grabbed Schmendrick's silver platter out of the strainer and dumped the tuna onto it. "There you go, Your Majesty."

While he tended to my cat, I put plates and napkins on the table. "I have water, milk, or Dr. Pepper."

"I'll have whatever you're having."

After adding ice to two glasses, I pulled a couple cans of pop out of the fridge.

Jayden and I sat at the table. He waited while I grabbed a slice of pizza, then did the same.

We ate in silence. The kind of silence that didn't need to be filled.

Not yet, anyway.

Jayden wiped his mouth with a napkin, then dropped it onto his plate. He waited quietly until I had almost finished my pizza. Then, keeping his voice low, he broke the silence. "What did you do today?"

The crust in my hand was suddenly the most interesting thing in the room. "I went to Ravenwood. It was…"

"You don't have to talk about it. But if you want to—" he set his hand on top of my empty one "—I'm here."

I didn't want to, but I thought of Nox—tried to imagine him sitting here with me, comforting me. No matter how hard I tried, I couldn't picture it. "I know. You're too good to me."

"Sorry." He huffed a soft laugh. "I'll try to be a jerk next time."

"It might make things easier." He didn't know what I was talking about, but he didn't press.

He leaned back in his chair and arched a brow. "I brought a can of tuna for your immortal, talking cat. That's gotta count for something."

"Of course, it does." Schmendrick looked up from his platter. "You'll make a fine servant."

"Right." Jayden kept his expression neutral. "I live to serve."

Schmendrick licked his plate. "Good. When I'm done, you can clean my dish."

Laughter burst from me—a deep, unexpected sound that carried through the house and made me believe, if only for a moment, that everything might turn out okay.

Jayden's eyes met mine, and a tender smile lifted his lips, spurring my butterflies into flight. "His Royal Hiney can insult me a million times if it means I get to hear you laugh like that."

My cheeks flushed, but I didn't look away. "Thanks for coming over."

"Thanks for calling." Something shifted in his gaze—unguarded, sincere—and the vulnerability in it sent warmth flooding through my body.

## Chapter 34



*T*he bell jingled as I stepped into Harvest Moon. Viv poked her head out of her office. "Oh, hey, Molly." She smiled, and I wondered (not for the first time) why I couldn't have a warm, caring person like her for a mother.

"Hey, Viv." Stuffing my phone into my back pocket, I nodded at the table closest to me. Centerpieces made of small pumpkins, gourds, and fall leaves gave the shop a festive, cozy feeling. "Looks good."

She shrugged as if it wasn't a big deal, but a small, pleased smile tugged at her lips. "Yeah, it's almost too late, though. Thanksgiving's only a week and a half away. Then I'll have to decorate for Christmas." She started to walk back into her office but paused, stopping in the doorway, looking uncertain.

"There's room for you and your young man at our table if you'd like to join us for Thanksgiving dinner."

"Thank you." My heart plummeted into my stomach, and I turned my back to her so she couldn't see my face. Who knew what would happen in the next ten days? Would Jayden be a part of my life? Would I even care? "We haven't talked about it yet, but I'll ask him if he has plans."

Viv shifted her weight, fingers curling around the doorframe. "I would've asked sooner, but with that whole situation with your mom, I thought you might go there?" Her voice rose at the end, turning the statement into a question.

"No." The word slipped out on a chuckle. "Mom doesn't cook, and Caius would be there." (And he might carve me instead of the turkey.)

She patted me on the shoulder, startling me. Her steps had been so quiet that I hadn't heard her move from the doorway. "Well, you're always welcome to celebrate with us."

A lump lodged in my throat, preventing me from responding. Reaching up, I grabbed her hand, squeezing her fingers in silent thanks.

The door swung open, bringing in a rush of cold air. Simone stepped inside and flipped the sign to open. "As cold as it is this morning, I imagine it'll be busy." She pulled on her apron and headset, combing through her hair with her fingers until not a single platinum strand was out of place. "How's your *cat*?"

"Well-fed, even more well-rested, and snarkier than ever."

Simone poured herself a cup of coffee and held the mug between both hands, warming them. "No doubt planning world domination."

"No doubt." The image of Schmendrick perched on his throne, issuing orders to his servants, made me laugh out loud.

Viv slipped out from behind the counter and started back toward her office. "Isn't that the way with cats?" She smiled fondly. "Dogs are content being servants, but cats want served."

Simone sauntered over to me after the morning rush died down. "How's your wolf been?" She waggled her eyebrows.

With every cup of coffee I'd made, every customer I'd helped, and every receipt I'd handed out, I'd been trying to forget the way Jayden had looked when I'd told him about Seraphina's spell. He'd tried to hide his fear, tried to convince me he didn't believe it would work, but the devastation was evident in his expression, in his stance, in his voice. And most of all, in those forlorn-looking amber eyes of his.

"I'm not so sure he's mine."

She tossed her head back and laughed. "Of course, he is. A near-sighted cyclops could see the puppy love pouring off him."

"Yeah, well, Seraphina doesn't like him." While I wiped down the counter, I explained what had happened at Ravenwood.

"So he follows you into the Abyss to save your mother, only for her to cast a spell on you to get rid of him?" Her aqua eyes flashed with fury, and for a moment, I glimpsed her power simmering beneath the surface. "What a bitch. What an absolute bitch! She has no right to take that decision from you."

The bell above the door jingled, and a pleasant smile replaced the fury on Simone's face—a mask more convincing than my shapeshifting ability. "Welcome to Harvest Moon. Can I help you?"

I was grateful that she asked because the hurt and indignation that had bubbled up inside of me weren't as quick to disperse. Excusing myself, I hid in the restroom until the maelstrom inside of me had diminished.

Nicole arrived at 3:30 to relieve me. Even though I was beyond peopled out for the day, I did my best to smile at the bubbly high schooler. "Have a good one." Yanking my jacket off its hook, I pulled it on and trudged to the door.

The click-clack of heels followed behind me. Simone caught up to me as soon as I stepped outside. "Hey." She grabbed my shoulder, stopping me from escaping to my house.

Fighting my desire to flee, I turned cautiously.

She held something out to me—a necklace made of pink and gray stones. The pendant was rose quartz with a hole in its center.

Tipping my head to the side, I lifted my eyebrow and tapped my foot impatiently. "I don't need to see the fae. I can see you just fine."

"Just put it on, will you?" She rolled her eyes.

Not sure what to expect, I slipped my hands under my hair and fastened it around my neck. *Never trust the fae.* Seraphina's voice rang through my head, but how could I trust anything she said or did?

Simone grabbed the pendant. She stuffed a pouch into the hole and chanted something I didn't understand. A flash of light flared between us, then she let go.

Lifting the necklace, I studied the pendant. Gold and silver veins streaked through the stone, glowing faintly in the afternoon light.

Simone waited for me to complete my examination. "Next time you see Nox, I want you to hold this while you chant this spell."

*"Fate be mine to change or bind.*
*No spell may touch my soul or mind.*

*My heart is my own to lose.*
*Love is mine to choose.*

*No other will take away my fate.*
*I will be the one to decide my mate.*

*With will unbroken, I reclaim my fire.*
*Forever my own, free of false desire."*

"Actually—" she backed up a step and gazed at the amulet "—why don't you do it next time you see Jayden, too? It can't hurt."

My mouth hung open, my eyes darting from the amulet to Simone. "When—? How—?" My jumbled thoughts refused to form into coherent sentences.

"You deserve the right to choose." Her voice hardened, and something flickered across her expression. Something that made me believe she knew what it was like to have your choices taken from you. "Everyone does."

Looking down at the pendant again, I wrapped my fingers around it. Then I met her gaze, and my words came out softer than I expected. "I don't know how or when you found the time to do this…"

My voice thickened with emotion. "But I'm truly grateful." Before I could second-guess myself, I stepped forward and pulled her into a quick hug, unsure how she'd respond.

Her hands hung at her sides for a moment before she returned the embrace. Then she stepped back and smirked. "I'm just that amazing."

## Chapter 35



For the entire drive to Ravenwood Estates, I'd fingered the necklace while reciting the spell. Maybe Nox was a great guy, and maybe I'd choose him on my own in the end, but if this would help ensure the choice was mine, I wouldn't ruin the chance by forgetting the words.

As I turned into the subdivision, the gray, overcast skies of the real world transformed into a deep cerulean blue, dotted with puffy white clouds. Tension tightened my grip on the steering wheel, and I blinked my eyes against the sudden brightness as I turned onto Ravenwood Drive.

Nox stepped through the manor gate and strolled toward the citadel. His black slacks were perfectly pressed with crisp creases, and his charcoal shirt shimmered faintly. With his pale skin and dark hair, he reminded me of the vampires I'd read about in novels, but in reality, their hair came in all hues, and the older ones could walk beneath the sun.

Pulling up to the curb, I shifted into park. Before I even shut the engine off, I clutched the pendant and recited Simone's spell.

*"Fate be mine to change or bind."*

Nox slowed, then turned. His black eyes bored into mine as if he knew I was casting a spell on him… on us.

*"No spell may touch my soul or mind.*

*My heart is my own to lose.*

*Love is mine to choose."*

The pendant warmed in my grasp.

*"No other will take away my fate.*

*I will be the one to decide my mate."*

Nox strode toward me, his strides lengthening. Power writhed behind his eyes, and his hand lifted.

*"With will unbroken, I reclaim my fire.*

*Forever my own, free of false desire."*

A surge of power enveloped me, blanketing me in a pink glow before it sank into my skin. The magic felt like the first drops of rain on a spring day—cool, refreshing.

Nox's head tilted, and his hand dropped to his side. As he watched me, the power drained from him.

My boots scraped against the ground when I stepped out of the car. Hopefully, either my will or Simone's pendant (or maybe even both) had worked.

"What was that?" Nox's voice was a low rumble that reminded me of Jayden's and Garrett's when their wolves were close to the surface. "I felt your power rise and thought danger was near."

Grabbing my sword and stiletto off the back seat, I strapped them on while I tried to figure out how to answer him. "Seraphina cast a spell on me yesterday." My teeth latched onto my bottom lip, pulling it into my mouth. How could I tell him what she'd done? What would he think? "She, uh…"

"She does like to be in control, doesn't she?" He held his hand out, and I stared down at it.

*Do I dare take it?* If I touched him, would Mo— (she didn't deserve to be called that anymore) Seraphina's spell take hold? Schmendrick said it would activate next time I saw Nox, but did he mean a glance would do it, or did he mean the next time I was around Nox for an extended amount of time?

"What is it, Molly?" The concern that flashed through his dark gray eyes surprised me.

Tentatively, I reached out, hoping, praying that my choice wouldn't be made for me. When our fingers touched, nothing happened. No zing. No butterflies flapping their wings. Nothing.

"She doesn't like the choices I'm making. The life I've chosen." This was too personal to share with a man I'd only recently met, and yet, I couldn't stop the words from coming out. "And as you know, she doesn't approve of Jayden."

"Why is that, though?" There were no shadows that we could step into, so Nox pulled them toward us. The darkness beneath my car spread out, stretching and lengthening, defying the sun's light. We stepped into it. "Wolves are honorable."

The world shifted, and we stepped into the land surrounding the Primordial Waters. Kur's symbol stared at me from behind the shimmering obsidian.

Dropping Nox's hand, I shivered. "I don't know which sorcerers raised you, but in the Ravenwood Cabal, wolves are hated, lesser beings." Out of reverence for this shrine, I kept my voice low.

"But not you?"

My magic thrummed inside of me. Powerful. Ready. "No. I'm not better than anyone. Maybe better at things, but on the whole, we're all equals." Avoiding Nox's eyes, I folded my arms across my chest and shifted my weight. "And I try hard not to hate. I still have some work to do on that front, though."

"Don't we all?" He chuckled, but the sound lacked warmth and humor.

The cracked stone we'd seen last time we were there pulsed, drawing my attention. "So what is that?"

His body tensed, and for a moment, I didn't think he would respond. "Kur was told it was a throne." His gaze was fixed on the fractured obsidian. "That he would be worshiped and ascend as a god."

When he didn't continue after several long seconds, I broke the silence. "But it wasn't?"

"No, it was an altar." His jaw clenched, and his voice dropped. "And when he sat upon it, he couldn't rise. Betrayed, his blood spilled, mixing with the Primordial Waters. Ereshkigal bound him—not with iron or shackles, but with words. Words that stole his choices. Words that forced him to forever guard these shores."

We stood still for a moment, staring at the broken altar, and silence crept over me like a killing frost. The song that had once transfixed me—the lullaby of water and magic—was gone.

"Why are we here?" My voice was a shade above a whisper.

"Kur will return to the Primordial Waters." Nox spoke with so much conviction, like he knew Kur. Like it was more than a theory. Like it was truth. "We'll find him here if we keep returning."

"Why would he come back?"

"When Ereshkigal bound him—" he crouched, running his fingers across the cracked stone "—she not only imprisoned him, but she also gave him a home. A place where he feels he belongs… even if he doesn't want to."

He rose slowly, as if the weight of his words pressed down on him. When he turned toward me again, there was a deep sadness inside his black eyes. "He was trapped there for five thousand years. It's all he knows."

## Chapter 36



We turned from the altar and walked to a ledge over-looking the Waters. I wrapped my arms around myself, hoping to hold everything in—my thoughts, my doubts, my fears. But even still, heaviness settled in my chest, thick and stifling. Every step was a struggle as if weights had been strapped to my feet. I peered over the cliff.

The Waters had risen.

Where smooth stones had once lined the shore, only jagged rocks and the bones of long-forgotten gods jutted above the surface. The Waters lapped at them with quiet persistence, gentle but unrelenting, shimmering with unnatural color—inky darkness veined with silver and violet, like starlight trapped in liquid shadow. The air was thick with moisture and memory, each breath damp and heavy, tinged with magic and something old.

"It's higher." My voice scarcely rose above the hush, but Nox heard it. "Significantly."

Silence blanketed the realm, thick and unnatural.

It was uncomfortable, but I didn't know how to break it.

Nox glanced around as if he felt the same. "So, where is this cat I keep hearing so much about?"

As far as I could remember, I'd only mentioned Schmendrick to Nox one time, but perhaps Nox felt the oppressiveness and wanted the silence broken as much as I did. "He had other things to do today." Even though I was finally learning some of Schmendrick's secrets, I doubted I'd ever know them all.

"One of these days, I'll meet the famous Schmendrick." He held his hand out. "The dragon is not here. We might as well move on."

We stepped into a shadow and stepped out into the desert. After the humidity of the Primordial Waters, I shivered in the cool, dry air.

The sky stretched wide and endless. A black tapestry splattered with twinkling shards of silver. The Milky Way spilled across the heavens like a river of light edged in pinks and purples. Its shimmering currents wove between countless pinpricks of starlight. A cool breeze stirred, carrying the faint scent of sand and stone.

Turning slowly, I took in the vast emptiness that surrounded me, but all I could see were silhouettes of ancient ruins and distant hills.

"Where are we?"

"Uruk." Nox's voice held a quiet reverence that was laced with wistfulness. "One of the larger cities of Sumer."

I blinked at him. Once. Twice. "Sumer? You mean Iraq?"

"This is the land Kur knew." His gaze swept the horizon, sharp despite the darkness. "He will be drawn to this place."

I tucked my hands into my pockets, then pulled them out, and folded my arms across my chest, shrinking into myself. "Even if he were here, we'd never see him. I can hardly see *you* standing next to me."

The moonless sky left the landscape in near-total darkness. The wind whispered through cracks in the ancient stone, dry and restless.

"Is there no other way to bind the Waters?" My foot twisted, my toe digging into the desert sand. "Does a guardian need to be involved?"

Nox didn't look at me. His voice was steady and sure. "Would it be so bad if they were free?"

"They'd destroy everything."

He shifted. "Again, I ask… would that be so bad? The world would be remade. Maybe it would be better."

"Maybe it would." My words hung in the dark like smoke on a still night. "It might be better for Earth, but it wouldn't be better for *us*. For any life that exists now."

The sky stretched endlessly above, a canvas so wide that I was only an infinitesimal drop of paint on its fabric. Without the moon, the stars crowded the heavens—bigger, brighter, and more numerous than I'd imagined. A single shooting star tore across the sky, a slash of silver fire that vanished as quickly as it came.

"I'd like to stop them if we can." Even though I could feel him next to me, hear him breathing, out here, I could almost convince myself that I was the only person on the planet. "The world could definitely be better, but there's a lot of good, too. And if we try… maybe we can use that to fix what's broken."

A silence more deafening than the one at the Primordial Waters filled the air. After several heartbeats, Nox finally broke it. "As long as greed and hatred reside in the hearts of men, that will be a hard battle to win." He turned slightly, the movement stirring up dust and sand. "However, if that is what you wish, I will search my tomes."

## *Chapter 37*



$\mathcal{W}$e stepped out of a shadow into Seraphina's office.

She sat behind her desk, her fingers steepled in front of her, and Caius perched on the edge like a smug gargoyle. "He says Ereshkigal won't help us stop the Primordial Waters. It seems it cost her too much last time." Her lips pressed into a thin line, voice laced with disgust. "A soft-hearted goddess. No wonder she's been forgotten."

Caius chuckled. "But not you, my darling. When you asc—"

Nox cleared his throat.

Mom's (dammit! Why was it so hard to quit calling her that?) head snapped up. Her blue eyes narrowed, then widened slightly as she registered us.

"Well, if it isn't the happy couple—" she paused and covered her mouth with her fingers like she hadn't meant to say that "—of explorers. Any luck locating Kur?"

Swallowing the spike of anger rising in my throat, I rubbed the pendant Simone had given me. Had it worked? Would Seraphina's spell have been immediate, or would it creep in slowly like rust devouring a car? Was it already affecting Nox? Had he offered to help because he wanted to… or because something had shifted in him, drawing him toward me?

"Molly." Mom's voice cracked like a whip. "Quit fidgeting with that gods-awful necklace, and answer me."

My jaw clenched. The way she sat upon her chair like a queen on the throne made me sick. And Caius, lounging at her side like her king consort, only made it worse.

"No." Nox stepped forward as if he were shielding my body with his. "However, Molly suggested an alternate route that we plan to investigate."

I blinked. We. Since when was there a we? And why was he defending me?

Seraphina's expression turned saccharine sweet. "No need to try to protect Molly from us. We'd never hurt her." She stood and sashayed to Caius' side, her aqua dress floating around her legs. She trailed her fingers across his back before resting them lightly on his shoulder. "However, your chivalry is honorable. It's so nice to see a young man so concerned for our daughter's well-being. Isn't it, Caius?"

"Much better than some dim-witted, slavering beast." He tilted his head, eyes gleaming with cruel amusement. A shark circling its prey, waiting for the right moment to strike.

My fingers brushed the hilt of the stiletto belted at my hip, and I bit the inside of my cheek. Hard. Holding back the words that would have given me away. Refusing to let them know that I hadn't fallen for Nox—not yet anyway—even if he was falling for me.

Instead, knowing what they would think, I slid my hand into Nox's, lacing my fingers through his, and dragged him toward the door. "Come on. We have research to do if we're going to save the world."

Seraphina giggled like a schoolgirl, and Caius winked at Nox. "Research." He chuckled. "Right… Don't do anything I wouldn't do."

Nox pulled me against him. He was all lean, sculpted muscle beneath his clothes, and I was shocked by the way mine melded with his. Without realizing what I was doing, I nestled closer. My body reacted before my brain could catch up.

I stiffened, but before I could pull away, we were swallowed by a shadow.

An erratic heartbeat later, we stood next to my car.

His head dipped until his lips brushed my ear. To an outsider, it probably looked intimate. To me… it *felt* like more than that.

My breath hitched.

This was Nox.

Mysterious. Dark. Dangerous. Nox.

But suddenly, there was more to him, and things were more complicated than I'd expected.

"Why didn't you tell me?" His words caressed my ear, sending warmth rushing through my body.

"I planned to." Curling my toes in my boots, I clutched his forearms. "But then we were at Kur's altar, and Seraphina's spell slipped my mind until we were standing in front of her."

"Don't keep me in the dark again." His breath against my skin sent a shiver racing down my neck. Danger and disappointment braided together in his voice, making it low and rough.

I swallowed. "I won't."

"Good." He stepped back, giving me room to breathe. "Until tomorrow."

He disappeared into the shadows, leaving me alone beneath the stars.

And for a moment, I stood there—my heart thrumming, my head spinning, unsure if it was fear, guilt, or something far more dangerous.

My fingers latched onto the hilt of my sword, grounding myself with something solid, something real.

As soon as I pulled out of Ravenwood, I pushed the button on my steering wheel. "Call Jayden."

"Hey." Jayden's voice was guarded, tight in a way that made my chest ache. He knew I'd met with Nox after work. And in that one word, I could hear his fear. Not the loud kind. The quiet, gnawing kind that slowly wears you down.

Had it haunted him all day?

"Can I stop by?" My voice cracked a little. After the loneliness I'd felt looking over the Primordial Waters and the confusion of being near Nox, I needed to see a friendly face.

And not just any. *Jayden's.*

"Good or bad?"

I paused—too long.

"I don't know." The words were a hushed truth, one I didn't want to speak at all. One that I hated with everything in me.

Guilt gnawed at my gut, and I twisted my hands on the steering wheel. "Simone gave me a spell to counteract Seraphina's, but I don't know…"

I hesitated.

There was no sound on the other end of the line. Not even his breathing.

"I don't know how long it should take for me to fall."

Jayden didn't answer right away. The silence felt weighted. Condemning. Like he knew what I'd been thinking when Nox's body pressed against mine. When his breath caressed my ear.

"I'll be waiting." His words grounded me.

But guilt pressed down, heavier than before.

Jayden was pacing when I pulled up. Long, tense strides back and forth over the sidewalk. His shoulders nearly touched his ears.

My heart twisted. *I'd done that to him.* And if I fell for Nox, it would destroy Jayden.

Not merely a broken heart. Not something he could get over.

He stepped behind a tree, and for a moment, I could breathe.

Castle Unicorn rose up in front of me. Not hard and cold like Ravenwood Manor, but warm and alive in the soft glow of the landscape lighting.

It looked safe. Welcoming.

Parking next to the wrought iron gate, I steeled myself before climbing out.

Jayden stopped pacing. He shoved his hands into his pockets and watched me—didn't move, didn't speak.

The weight of everything he wasn't saying hung in the air between us, rooting him to that spot, preventing him from rushing to greet me.

"Simone said to cast the spell on you, too."

At the sight of him, butterflies had sprung to life in my belly. Their wings still fluttered—nervous, frantic, uncertain.

But I didn't know if it was because I wanted him to kiss me… or because I was scared it was already too late.

He held his hands out at his sides, open palms facing me. "Whatever you need to do." His voice was steady, even if his eyes weren't. "Whatever makes you mine."

## Chapter 38



$\mathcal{M}$y heart raced, but the trust I found in Jayden's amber eyes soothed my rising anxieties. Stepping closer to him, I grasped the pendant and willed this to work.

Magic flared, power flowing through my hands into the amulet.

*"Fate be mine to change or bind."*

The wind gusted, carrying Jayden's scent to me—cedar, fresh air, and leather.

*"No spell may touch my soul or mind."*

Light spilled through my fingers, tiny god rays, brightening Jayden's face, wrapping him in a warm glow.

*"My heart is my own to lose.*

*Love is mine to choose."*

With those words, my desire for this to work rose. I imagined Simone standing in front of me. The harsh angles of her face as she said, *You deserve the right to choose.*

*"No other will take away my fate."*

I pictured Seraphina when she'd cast the spell on me—smug, callous, and uncaring.

*"I will be the one to decide my mate."*

Images of Jayden and Nox flashed through my mind. Both of them as lonely as me. Both of them deserving of love. But only one could be mine.

*"With will unbroken, I reclaim my fire.*

*Forever my own, free of false desire."*

A brilliant flash of light burst from between my fingers, casting shadows and sparks through the night. A multitude of tiny embers that drifted through the night sky like fireflies.

"Is it done?" Jayden's voice was little more than a whisper.

My shoulders lifted at the same time my eyes dropped. "The spell is. But…" My voice faltered, caught on the lump in my throat. "I don't know. It'll take time."

He stepped closer and lifted his hand toward my face, stopping just shy of touching me. The uncertainty in his eyes tightened my chest.

I closed the distance, leaning into his palm, savoring the feel of his warm fingers brushing my cheek.

"No matter what happens—" his voice caught "—I will cherish every moment we spent together."

The embers floated higher. Their sparks flickered, vanishing one by one into the dark. I watched them go, a lump rising in my throat.

"Only time will tell." Lowering my gaze, I met Jayden's. His eyes searched mine, looking for answers I couldn't give him.

"Stay here with me tonight." His voice was soft, vulnerable. "Just let me hold you while you sleep. In case…" He swallowed hard, and his eyes glistened. "In case I never get the chance again."

My throat tightened, trapping the words I wanted to say. I nodded, not wanting to be alone either.

Dawn would rise full of uncertainty. But I knew we had a better chance if we faced it together.

My fingers fumbled across the nightstand, groping for the offending device. A low groan froze my hand.

Lamp light blinked on, and I winced at the brightness—until my eyes adjusted, and I remembered where I was.

Jayden propped himself up on one elbow beside me, shirtless and sleep-ruffled. His dark blond hair stuck out in all directions, his eyes were half-lidded, but when he looked at me, his face lit up.

My heart caught in my throat. His smile, the warmth in his eyes, the scar catching the light—I pressed every part of him into my memory.

I hadn't expected to feel so safe.

I hadn't expected to want this so badly.

I'd been happy alone.

I hadn't needed anybody but Schmendrick.

I couldn't let Seraphina's spell take my choice from me.

Moments like these were too special, too few.

I needed more of them.

And it terrified me that I might not get the opportunity to find out where this relationship could go.

"Good morning, beautiful." He brushed a kiss over my cheek as he handed me my phone.

"Good morning." Schmendrick's head rose from the end of the bed like a judgmental sphinx. "But I prefer *handsome, all-knowing,* or *my most beloved liege* over beautiful."

He stretched his front legs as far forward as he could while lifting his butt higher and higher. Then he tramped up my legs before fluffing my belly. "Imagine my surprise when you didn't come home to give me my treats." He sat and curled his tail around himself. "Then I find you here, reeking of dragon and dog and something older than time."

"Nox and I went to the Primordial Waters yesterday." I rubbed Schmendrick's ear, loving the velvety feeling. "We didn't find Kur."

Schmendrick leaned into my hand. A deep purr rumbled through him. "He will be found when he's ready."

## Chapter 39

*"In its flawless grace and superior self-sufficiency, I have seen a symbol of the perfect beauty and bland impersonality of the universe itself, objectively considered, and in its air of silent mystery there resides for me all the wonder and fascination of the unknown." -H.P. Lovecraft*

I handed Mary her vanilla breve and attempted a smile. She patted my hand, her skin soft from years of giving massages. "Whatever's bothering you, I hope you get it worked out."

"I appreciate it." Since finding out Simone was fae, I'd been working on removing *thank you* from my vocabulary.

"If you can't, a massage might help." She laughed as she walked toward the door. When the bell tinkled behind her, I let out a hefty sigh and walked over to Simone.

She was wiping down the countertop near the drive-thru window. Her blonde hair was haloed by the light streaming in. If I hadn't known about her secret identity, I would have guessed that she was an angel or a high elf.

"How will I know if the spell worked?" My fingers twisted my hoodie strings together, rolling them up, then releasing them. When Simone noticed my fidgeting, I tucked my hands into my pockets, then pulled them out again, and crossed my arms over my chest, clutching my sweatshirt while I waited for her to answer.

Her perfectly sculpted brows pinched together. "You won't be attracted to Nox." There was a dry quality to her voice that couldn't be mistaken for anything other than *what a stupid question.*

"But—" Letting go of my shirt, I picked up a stir stick, twisting it forward and back, while I tried to arrange my thoughts. "Will I know immediately, or do the spells take time to work?"

She didn't answer right away. Instead, she folded her cleaning cloth and placed it beside the register before turning to me. Her touch was light when she patted my arm, but her voice was firmer. "From what you've told me about Seraphina, I believe she would want it to happen instantaneously, severing any ties you have to Jayden in a blink."

"Th—" So much for the practicing I'd been doing. "That's good to hear. I hope you're right."

"Your mother is like a snake that sheds its skin." She met my eyes. Her aqua ones shimmered, not with pity or sadness, but with truth. "Nothing has changed—not like when a caterpillar transforms into a butterfly. She may shimmer a little brighter for a few days, but she is the same power-hungry sorceress she always was."

My hackles rose, and I opened my mouth to defend Seraphina. But the words wouldn't come.

Why would they?

Simone was right.

The bell above the door tinkled, and I trudged back to the front counter. A phony smile lifted my lips. "Welcome to Harvest Moon. How can I help you?"

While I served the last coffee of my day, a pumpkin crème cold brew, I thought about what Simone had said. By the time I walked the two blocks home, dread no longer writhed in my gut when I thought about seeing Nox. For the time being, my choices seemed to be mine and mine alone.

"Shall we see if we can catch a dragon?" Schmendrick sat at the table, his silver platter licked clean in front of him. He'd scarfed down his treats while I'd changed out of my work clothes and into my battle gear: comfortable leggings, a worn tee, and a baggy hoodie. All black. Better for hiding in shadows.

He jumped down and trotted to the darkest corner of the kitchen. "No need to drive, Molly." His voice was low and coaxing. "It's time to embrace your magic."

He was right, and we both knew it. But after hiding for so long, the instinct to stay small, normal, was so hard to shake.

Still, I focused on the ashy smudge stuck between the wall and the floor. Shadows stirred in response, lengthening and creeping across the gray-flecked tiles, slinking closer to me as the darkness deepened.

Bending down, I scooped up Schmendrick, cradling him with one arm and absently petting him with my other hand. Then I stepped into the shadow.

And stepped out into Seraphina's office.

Schmendrick sneezed.

"Bless you." My voice cracked through the silence like a gunshot on a still morning.

He squirmed in my arms, so I set him on Seraphina's desk. If she'd have been in the room, she would've thrown a conniption—but what she didn't know wouldn't hurt her.

Schmendrick sniffed the air, his tail flicking once. Twice.

"Why does it smell like dragon in here?" His nose twitched, and he sneezed again.

His words froze me.

The only thing I smelled was Ravenwood Manor: musty books, lemon-scented cleaner, and a trace of Seraphina's perfume—faint, floral, and ghostlike, as if she'd just slipped away.

Schmendrick doubled in size—not because his fur stood on end, but because the magical being beneath the feline guise shifted, breaking through. With another look around the room, he hissed, and a low, menacing growl rumbled through his body. "Danger and deception are at play here."

The hair on the back of my neck lifted.

With my gaze sweeping the room, I turned slowly. Shadows clung to the corners—heavy and dense. My stomach clenched as I searched for the source of my unease.

Nothing moved.

Nobody was there.

But the feeling of being watched lingered.

I swallowed my fear and licked my lips. "Let's get out of here, Schmen."

He nudged his head against my leg, pushing me into the shadows. "Go to Malachai. Demand he take you to Ereshkigal. Find out all they know about Kur and why Seraphina would harbor him."

"What about you?" My breath caught in my throat. I didn't want to be alone. I wanted to stay together—with him.

He rubbed his head against my thigh. "I must follow my own path." His body slowly shrank to its normal size. "I cannot enter the Abyss without an invitation, and alas, one has not been given for thousands of years."

A stair creaked. Schmendrick's gaze snapped to the door, then back to me. "Go now, Molly. Be safe."

As I stepped into the shadow, Schmendrick disappeared, and something cold and heavy settled in my chest.

## Chapter 40



The shadow spat me out into Taras Mor, and I staggered and stumbled like someone whose heart had been ripped from its cage. My steps dragged, and my arms hung limp at my sides. Malachai's guards didn't awaken, didn't try to stop me. Their stony faces stared at me from the archways they stood beneath, eyes blank and bodies unmoving.

Black stone surrounded me. The floors, the walls, the statues. All of it, but somehow this castle in the heart of the Abyss didn't feel as dark or dangerous as Ravenwood Manor had.

My steps echoed through the vast space as I strode toward Malachai's throne, hoping I would find him there. Wondering why the statues hadn't sprung to life—why they didn't stop me.

The massive chair sat upon the obsidian dais.

Empty.

Runes flickered like the charred husks of trees left behind after a forest fire. Black to red when kissed by the air.

Searching the room, I turned, wondering where to find the lord of the Abyss.

"Molly." Malachai's deep, booming voice rumbled through the hall, echoing back and forth.

One hand flew to my chest, the other to my sword.

He stepped out of the shadows. His dark hair pulled into a low ponytail, concern etching his handsome face.

Relief at seeing him threatened to overwhelm me. The loneliness I'd felt when Schmendrick vanished evaporated at the sight of him.

"What brings you here?"

My shoulders sagged, my breath catching on a sob I barely swallowed. I counted to ten and then back to zero. It wasn't the time to break down. "Seraphina's office smells like dragon. Schmendrick sent me to find out everything about Kur. Why she would aid him."

"She will do anything and everything for power." He slung his arm over my shoulders and pulled me against his side.

My body stiffened, caught between wanting to retreat and wanting comfort. Then I let my head fall against him.

His warmth seeped into me—comforting—but it stirred a deep sadness for all the lost years, all the times his hugs might have mended what was broken. My hands twitched at my sides, like they wanted to reach for him but didn't quite know how.

"You know that." His soft voice hitched, and I realized I wasn't the only one who'd missed out on having a father/daughter relationship.

My arm lifted slowly as if unsure what to do, where to settle, finally wrapping around his waist, my fingers squeezing his side. "I need to know what Ereshkigal knows."

He hesitated, his gaze going distant for a moment, then he rubbed his jaw. "I don't know if she'll tell you anything. The world has all but forgotten her, and that sort of betrayal cuts deep." He stepped away, pulling his warmth with him, and a shiver ran through me.

Wrapping my arms around myself, I tried to hold onto some of the comfort I'd felt.

Staring into the distance, Malachai lifted his hand. "Ereshkigal. Lady of Irkalla. Queen of the Dead. Keeper of the Seven Gates. Come forth."

Following Malachai's gaze, I saw nothing except the black, gleaming walls of Taras Mor.

Then there was a shimmer in the air, like a heat wave rising above the pavement on a hot summer's day. It flickered, growing taller and wider.

Until…

Ereshkigal arrived with a thunderous boom, making the ground tremble. I stumbled back a step, flailing my arms to catch my balance. Shadows writhed around her like living creatures. She stood at least eight feet tall, towering over me—towering over Malachai—cloaked in darkness and despair. Her skin was the color of storm clouds rolling across the plains.

Ebony wings flared out behind her. Their vast, jagged edges blotted out what little light there was in Taras Mor.

She carried a scythe with a serrated blade that reminded me of a raven's talon. And atop her head sat a heavy onyx crown with seven points tipped with blood-red stones.

Her eyes were bottomless pools of darkness, and when they settled on me, I felt as if I'd been laid bare in front of her. As if she could see every thought, every deed, every misstep I'd ever made.

She didn't look away.

And I couldn't.

She strode toward me and snapped her wings closed. A gust of air rushed from them, slamming into me with the force of a derecho, shoving me back another step. It pulled the breath from my lungs and flooded me with the scent of a graveyard at midnight—iron gates, freshly disturbed soil, and the raw ache of grief.

Beneath her gaze, my lungs seized. I couldn't move. Couldn't tear my gaze away.

"Erie." Malachai's voice snapped like a whip. "Don't kill her. Please." The last word carried a desperate edge. He leaned forward, one hand held palm out between us.

Time seemed to still as the goddess pulled her focus from me and turned it on Malachai.

I blinked, holding my eyes closed longer than necessary while I sucked in a lungful of air that tasted like hot summer nights and forgotten dreams.

Breathing it in, I slowly opened my eyes, cringing like a child expecting to be scolded—expecting a goddess's wrath.

Ereshkigal's countenance softened, and she transformed. Ebony hair flowed down her back, catching the light like a river on a moonlit night. Her skin was the warm brown of sunbaked clay, and her eyes shifted. Amber, deep and luminous, filled with the memory of every soul she'd guided to the afterlife.

Malachai studied my face for a moment before conjuring three black recliners situated around a coffee table brimming with food and drink. "Sit."

"Why did you call me forth, Mal?" The goddess settled across from me without noticing me. "The gates cannot go unguarded."

He waved his hand at me. "My daughter, Mahlia, needs to know all you know about Kur. Lest the Primordial Waters overflow, destroying all life."

"No." The word was barely a breath—filled with so much sadness and dismay—but her head snapped up. "I cannot admit that many souls at once, and who will remember them?"

Malachai dipped a corn chip into queso, rolling it from side to side until a glob of cheesy goodness dropped back into the bowl. "Nobody, Erie. But if Kur isn't returned, that's exactly what will happen."

She leaned back in her chair and sighed. Heavy. Resigned. And suddenly, she looked like every sleep-deprived customer who had ever set foot into Harvest Moon. "Kur wants the same thing everyone wants."

"What's that?" My head tipped toward my shoulder, and I tried to figure out what everyone wanted. What did I want?

She lifted her hands palms up, and a soft smile tipped the corners of her lips. "A connection to another living being."

Leaning forward with my elbows braced on my knees, hope flickered in my chest. "Where will he go looking for it?"

"Anywhere." She lifted a shoulder in a tired shrug. And for the first time, I realized her wings, scythe, and crown had disappeared when she transformed into her human-looking guise. "He'll probably start with places he once knew. And he will be called back to the Primordial Waters frequently."

"How?" My voice cracked on the word. Straightening, I pushed up to my feet and began pacing in front of the recliners. The scent of melted cheese and salsa turned my stomach. "How can he be in all these places and not be seen? How did he get into Ravenwood Manor? Isn't he a massive dragon?"

Ereshkigal's hand traced a circle on the armrest of her chair. "He is. He is also magic. He can shadow walk. He can fly. He may appear as a dragon or in any other form that he desires to take. As large or as small as he chooses."

"Then how will I know him when I see him?" I flung my arms into the air, then let them drop.

"I doubt you can." Her gaze roved over me, and I got the impression that she found me lacking. "In the past, you may have been able to sense his power. He wasn't well-versed in hiding it." Ereshkigal's eyes narrowed, lashes casting long shadows on her cheeks. "But now… now I cannot say. He's had thousands of years to perfect that skill."

"Great." Sarcasm dripped from the word, and I slumped, bowing over the back of the recliner. "Just great."

"Schmendrick should be able to sense him." Malachai looked like he'd sacrificed a huge part of himself to admit that. His jaw clenched, and he nodded as if settling an argument with himself. "Don't go anywhere without him." He stared up at the ceiling high above us. "Including here." He raised his voice as if Schmendrick was listening to us. "Yeah, you furry nuisance, you're invited so long as you cause no trouble."

Schmendrick appeared like a shadow in the dying light. His tail flicked with smug satisfaction. He rubbed against my leg, then stopped in front of the goddess, dipping his head in a surprisingly humble bow. "Ereshkigal."

Ereshkigal's brows lifted in surprise, and her gaze sharpened with recognition. "What are they calling you now, Tha'—"

"Schmendrick." He gazed up at me, his green eyes soft, loving. "It's the name Molly gave me when she was five. And it's the *only* name that will be used in her presence."

Ereshkigal dipped her head. "As you wish."

My gaze narrowed on the black cat. Everyone except for me seemed to know who or what he really was. The way Malachai dipped his gaze, the way Ereshkigal didn't argue—I was the only one left standing in the dark.

As frustrating as it was, I knew he had his reasons. That he'd tell me if he could.

My fingers sank into Schmendrick's fur, rubbing his head. Then I met Ereshkigal's gaze. "Nox also believed Kur would return to places he knew. We've gone to the Primordial Waters a couple times now and to Sumer once, but today Nox is nowhere to be found."

## Chapter 41



*E*reshkigal stared past me. "I concern myself with the dead, not the living. I do not know who this Nox you speak of is."

Glancing over my shoulder, I strained to see what she saw, but whatever her eyes were fixed on—Irkalla, maybe— remained beyond my sight.

Her gaze found me again, dark and unreadable. "You may be able to lure Kur with a spell, but unless you are prepared to bind him, I would caution you: let him be."

Biting my lip, I drew it into my mouth as I weighed the wisdom of my next question. "Is there nothing you can do?"

"This battle no longer belongs to me. My role ended when the world forgot me." She seemed at once to diminish and to grow more severe. "Kur was not just some beast that I chose to guard the Waters." Her eyes, sparkling with unshed tears, met mine. "He was my everything. But he was the only one with the strength to stop them from overwhelming the world."

A heavy silence settled over Taras Mor, and I sank into the recliner again. Schmendrick jumped onto my lap, curling into a purring ball of fluff.

"My part in all of this is done." She stared off into the distance once more. "And I must return to my duties."

She stood, and with a nod at Malachai, she walked back the way she'd come—disappearing like smoke in the night.

"I know you don't like being reminded of it." Malachai wiped a hand down his face and cleared his throat. "But you are half-demon."

My chest tightened, but the sharp sting the reminder usually brought didn't settle over me. The more I learned about my parents, the more I wondered which half of me I should worry about.

"I am."

"You hold within you the power of manipulation." His eyes met mine, then darted away.

The thought of forcing someone to do what I wanted settled in my stomach like a dropped anchor. "I can't do that."

"Can't?" Malachai's voice was barely above a whisper. "Not even to save the world?"

"I-I don't want to force him to go back." I couldn't hold his gaze. Maybe I was wrong. Maybe I was being selfish.

But I couldn't force Kur to guard the Primordial Waters. I couldn't take his choices—

Not when I'd fought so hard to keep my own.

Almost subconsciously, I began petting Schmendrick. His soft, silky fur comforted me, grounding me like nothing else could. "I would take his place if I could."

Malachai's jaw clenched. "You'd take his place?" His voice was hard, disbelieving. "You'd give up your life for someone you don't know?"

He stood and paced, his hands clenching into fists at his sides. "You think you're being noble?"

I flinched.

Schmendrick cracked an eye open. The green the only color amongst the darkness of Taras Mor.

Malachai stepped closer, lowering his voice. "If you take his place, you'll die." He grabbed the arms of my recliner, leaning in until his face was inches from mine. "Maybe not immediately. But you will, Mahlia. And I *can't* let that happen to you."

Schmendrick sat up. His ears flattened on his head, and a low growl rumbled through him.

Malachai backed off. "I know you don't believe me, Molly." He lifted his hand, and a lowball glass materialized in his grasp, filled with amber liquid. He tipped back in one swallow. "But I love you. Since the first day I saw you—no, before that. Since the idea of you, I've loved you, and I've always wanted what is best for you."

Liquor poured into his glass from an unseen bottle. "Taking Kur's place isn't best for you. It isn't best for him or even for the world."

"Maybe not." Plucking Schmendrick off my lap, I stood with him tucked against my side. "But I can't manipulate him.

I'll think of something else." My steps were slow but sure as I made my way to Malachai, then rested my hand on his arm. "I have to go get yelled at by Seraphina for not being dressed properly. I don't want to get yelled at for being late, too."

Not wanting to face the images in the door, I shadow walked into Ravenwood Citadel's great hall. The Arcane Council was already seated on the dais, and the Ancestral Guardians stood in front of them.

"So much for not being late." Setting Schmendrick on the ground, I strode to my position with my head held high.

Seraphina stopped talking mid-sentence, her eyes locking onto mine, not letting go until I took my place.

"I am sorry for my late arrival and my attire." To keep from fidgeting, I folded my hands behind my back. "I have been in the Abyss, discussing Kur with Malachai and Ereshkigal."

Seraphina's eyes widened in horror. "You stood before a goddess dressed in *rags*?"

"No, we sat in recliners."

Storm snorted and tried—badly—to cover it up with a cough.

"The goddess didn't seem to care about my clothes." Meeting Seraphina's icy gaze, I held it without flinching. "She seemed more concerned about the possibility of the world ending."

Thaddeus stood and gave Seraphina a respectful nod. "Perhaps we, too, should focus more on that and less on how our guardians dress." Folding his hands behind his back, he walked in front of the seated council members, meeting each of their gazes as he passed by them.

The only sound in the room was the click of his hard-soled shoes against the marble dais.

Siobhan smiled at him, warm and friendly. Encouraging him without saying a word.

Seraphina and Caius had mastered their looks of indifference long ago. (Most likely as toddlers, judging their parents' every action.) And they wore them as Thaddeus passed them by.

"Their duties are significantly different from ours. They are sent into dangerous situations where comfort and functionality are what should matter more than appearance." Thaddeus's pace was steady, each word polished.

Nadia nodded. Her dark curls, loose instead of bound tight as usual, bounced with the motion—softening her normally sharp features. Approval was written plain across her warm, brown face.

Stroking his beard, Alden's gray eyes flicked to me, and he shook his head, clearly not agreeing with anything Thaddeus said, but then disagreeing came naturally to him.

Leonora, Darian, and Isadora looked down their noses at me. Their lips curled in the same disgust I had seen on their faces growing up. I half expected them to tell me to go outside and play, to get out of their sight.

Thaddeus turned at the end of the dais and walked past all of them, not stopping at his empty chair. The banners on the wall waved in a breeze I couldn't feel, as if the great hall breathed with us. "Each of the guardians should be shown respect, whether dressed in *rags* or formal wear."

Eveline's eyes were closed, and if not for the gentle tapping of her foot, I would've thought she had nodded off. I didn't know her well enough to know if she agreed with Thaddeus or if she was composing a ballad in her head.

Lucian drummed his manicured fingers on the arm of his chair. From what I'd seen in the past, I knew he agreed with Thaddeus, that he wanted to add his two cents, and that he wouldn't interrupt Thaddeus.

As Thaddeus neared Eryndis, she leaned forward, a lazy smile tugging at her lips. One finger traced the carved arm of her chair in a motion that was anything but absentminded. When his eyes flicked to hers, his stride hitched—the barest stumble in his otherwise flawless composure.

Her smile deepened, triumphant, as though she'd planned it all along. "Well said, Thaddeus." Her voice was low, husky, and meant only for him.

Wondering if there was something going on between the two of them, I tipped my head to the side.

Orion stared into the darkness beneath the archways, not seeming to notice Eryndis flirting, not looking up when Thaddeus approached, not glancing at the guardians or giving a hint about his thoughts. The man would make a fine gargoyle—never blinking, never speaking a word, probably convinced that he was mysterious instead of creepy.

When Thaddeus passed Orion, he pivoted and started back. "We shouldn't expect them to run home and change before every meeting." Reaching his chair, he sat—a king upon his throne. A leader like the cabal needed. Not out for power. Not driven by greed. But good, honest, and filled with integrity.

Alden's fingers stilled in his beard as he glowered down at me. "Especially not that one." He pointed a crooked finger at me. "She can't get here on time as it is."

Heat flared in my chest, but instead of giving him the satisfaction of anger, I lifted my hands and mimicked a scale, pretending to weigh my options. "Learn from a goddess or get browbeaten for my attire." Folding one arm across my chest, I rested my other elbow on it and tapped my chin as if pondering an impossible decision. "Tough choice, but the goddess won."

I pulled my hand down and flashed Alden a sweet smile, knowing it would piss him off.

"Enough." Seraphina smacked her hands together. "You've made your point, Mahlia. Now, tell us—will Ereshkigal help us? What did she say?"

While I told the council everything that I'd learned at Taras Mor, I stared at Schmendrick, curled in the shadow of the dais. "I don't know where Nox is…" My voice wobbled, just enough to sound desperate.

Seraphina waved her hand in a dismissive gesture. "Nor do you need to."

"But…" I pouted, hoping I looked like a lovesick school-girl, but not sure if I could pull it off.

She smiled, saccharine sweet in appearance, but I knew it was laced with arsenic.

Dipping my head, I blinked a couple of times, playing the part and keeping them from seeing my reaction. Because I didn't know if I could hide the fact that on the inside, I was giving myself a high five and doing a happy dance.

After an overly dramatic sigh, I looked back up. "But I will find Kur alone if I need to."

"Ya don't need to." Storm stepped forward, hands tucked in his pockets, voice firm. "I'm with ya, Molly."

"Count me in." Nahvienne lifted her hand without hesitation. "You're not going alone."

Caius lifted halfway out of his chair. "The council decides on assignments, not you."

"I'd like to go, too." Thorn tapped his chest with three fingers. "We're stronger together."

Lorelei took a step toward the dais. "I was left out last time. I won't be this time."

Caelan scoffed, swaying slightly. "Of course. Everyone wants to follow Molly." His words were thickened by the alcohol in his body. He spread his arms unsteadily, stumbling forward. "But *I'm* the leader. Why aren't you all lining up to follow me?"

Schmendrick lifted his head off his paws, his voice as dry as a desert wind. "Because everyone here can find the liquor cabinet on their own. But how many people have sat with a goddess of death and lived to tell the tale?"

Caius's jaw clenched, and he sprang to his feet, stabbing his finger through the air, aiming it at me. "This is not a democracy. You don't *volunteer* for assignments." He turned his glare on Schmendrick. "And why the hell is *that cat* here again? How many times must you be told he's not allowed in here?"

"He is here because I was told not to go anywhere without him." Pressing my palm to my forehead, I sucked in several long breaths through my nose. "Didn't you listen to anything I said?"

"Enough!"

The word, low and firm, cut through the room like a blade, stopping everyone.

We all turned.

Thaddeus stood, calm and unwavering. And in him, I saw what this cabal could be.

He was everything Seraphina and Caius would never be. Neither of them would ever set aside their hunger for power.

Thaddeus strode to the front of the dais and turned toward the council members. "The world is unraveling. Kur is awake, and the person who might be able to do something about that threat is standing right in front of us." He waved his hand at me. "We can argue over protocol and clothes and timeliness later. Right now, we *need* to stop the Primordial Waters. We *need* to find Kur. Let Molly go—with those she trusts."

Alden muttered under his breath but didn't object.

Seraphina folded her hands tightly in front of her. "Fine. But if this ends in disaster, your blood is not on the Council's hands."

"No, you've never been good at taking the blame for anything." Lifting my chin, I held her icy gaze for several tense seconds. With a shooing motion toward her, I faced the guardians who'd volunteered to accompany me. "Meet me in the arena at dawn tomorrow."

Schmendrick yawned, baring his teeth. "Lovely. Now that we've had the customary power struggle, can we get on with the actual apocalypse?"

## Chapter 42

*"Those who'll play with cats must expect to be scratched."*
*—Miguel de Cervantes*

**R**estlessness prickled underneath my skin, urging me to continue pacing behind my couch. With each pass, I dragged my fingers along Schmendrick's back, grounding myself in the silky feel of his fur. "I don't think anyone should go with me."

"Where you go, I go." He nipped at my fingers as they brushed his fur.

Jerking back, I glanced down at the puncture marks before shaking my hand like it would ease the sting. "Ow. What the hell, Buddy? I meant besides you." When I resumed pacing, my steps hit the floor with more force. "What if the song captivates them? What if it tries to lure them back?"

Schmendrick stood and stretched a paw out to me, gently patting the air until I paused. When I did, he butted his head against my hand, and I scratched behind his ears, earning a rumbling purr. "Lorelei is the only volunteer who could return on her own, but if you ever want to bridge the gap between the two of you, you must allow her to go."

Cocking my head to the side, my lips parted, and my eyebrows pinched together without conscious thought. "Why could she return and not the others?"

"Whether she has realized it or not, her necromancy gives her the ability to shadow walk."

His green eyes tracked me as I started pacing again, slower this time. Something in his expression—hesitation edged with concern—made the hairs on my arms lift, giving me the impression that he wanted to add something else.

"What, Schmendrick?" Stopping mid-step, I turned to face him fully, wrapping my arms around myself. "You know you can say anything to me, don't you?"

He walked in three circles before curling into a furry ball. He fixed me with a look too knowing for an ordinary house cat. "What are you going to do if you find the overgrown lizard?"

Rubbing the back of my neck, I licked my lips. "I'll think of something."

The morning was still sheathed in darkness when I drove to Ravenwood Estates. (Yeah, I could've shadow walked, but I'd hoped music would help settle my nerves and make my decision easier.) The road hummed beneath my tires. The cold morning air whipped my hair around my face, and Schmendrick slept on the passenger seat, softly snoring.

But nothing came to me. I had no idea what to do once I reached Ravenwood. No idea who should go with me to the Primordial Waters, and absolutely no idea what to do if I encountered Kur.

My song was interrupted when my phone rang. With a sigh, I rolled up my windows and pressed the green button. "Hello."

"Molly." Jayden's voice came through the car's speakers, husky with sleep. "Schmendrick came to me in my dream. He said you were going to the Primordial Waters."

Soft snores emanated from the curled-up kitty. His magic was a mystery to me, but dream walking seemed like something he would be able to do. The real question was, did he? Or was Jayden's dream some strange coincidence?

"You there, Molly?"

"Yeah." Fog hovered above the empty fields on the sides of the interstate and diffused the headlights coming toward me. "I'm here, and I'm going."

"Let me come with you." The grogginess was gone, replaced with a desperate edge.

A sharp pang stabbed my chest, taking my breath away. Every part of me wanted to say yes. The word sat on my tongue, but I swallowed it down, unwilling to put him in danger. "I'm sorry, Jayden. I can't let you go near Seraphina. She can't see that we're still together. I don't know what she'd do to us… to you."

Silence filled the car.

It was louder than my music had been. Louder than the wind rushing in through the open window. Louder than the crack that fractured my heart.

"I can meet you somewhere." His voice startled me. "She doesn't need to know."

My grip on the steering wheel tightened until my knuckles ached. Words failed me, my thoughts tangling together, uncertain what I wanted to say.

Glancing at Schmendrick, I willed him to wake up. If he had initiated this—sent that dream—he had a reason.

"I want that." My eyes pinched shut for a moment too long, and the rumble strip grumbled beneath my tires. The vibration reverberated through the steering wheel and into my hands. "More than anything."

"But…" Disappointment laced his voice.

"She can't find out we're still together." My chest tightened as I sucked in a shaky breath through my nose, trying to hold my ground, trying to steel myself.

The sky lightened in the East, the soft gray that signaled dawn was nearing.

Jayden growled, not at me, but at the situation. "I'm not afraid of her."

"I know." The steering wheel squeaked beneath my twisting hands. The movement helped me think, helped me try to find my words. "But…"

But what?

But I was afraid for him?

But I'd been fighting since I was born, and I didn't know how long I wanted to keep fighting.

The silence stretched while I tried to breathe.

"I can't—" My eyes stung with unshed tears. "I can't let her use you against me."

He sighed, deep, heavy, weighted with all the things he wasn't saying. "I hate this."

"I'm sorry." An ache ignited in my chest, burning, throbbing. My palm pressed against it, trying to smother the fire within.

"Molly…" His voice cracked just a little. "Promise me you'll come back."

Could I? What if I didn't? What if I found Kur and couldn't convince him to guard the Waters?

What if he ate me? Squashed me like a bug?

"Molly?"

"I promise I'll do everything I can."

## Chapter 43



*H*olt stood across from me, his sword held loosely at his side. Relaxed. Confident.

I'd expected to train with Nahvienne again, but he'd been waiting for me. Sunlight caught the silver streaks in his brown hair. He was older than the others, sterner too, and I couldn't help but wonder—why wasn't he the one leading the Ancestral Guardians? Why Caelan?

Holt flipped his sword up, the steel flashing in the light. The movement was smooth, and even though I'd been watching him, I hadn't seen it coming. Before I could draw a breath, the blade was slashing down. I blocked. The clash rang through my arm, the sound filling the arena.

I pressed back, hoping to drive him off balance, but he held his ground.

Then he pushed forward, forcing me to retreat. His blue eyes sparkled. He was having fun.

He swung again. The blade came dangerously close to cutting through my ribs, but I parried in time.

I stumbled back, and he advanced. Relentless. His blade slashing. His feet gliding over the ground.

Each step made me retreat farther. My muscles burned. Sweat dripped down my face.

The shadows stretched long across the ground as the morning sun inched higher in the sky.

I shuffled to the side, blocking. Striking when I could. Fighting a battle I couldn't win.

Holt had years of experience, years of training that I didn't have. His blade flashed faster, harder. Driving me back.

I swung, and he blocked. Instantly, he was back on the offensive. He lunged. His sword slammed against mine with a force that rattled my teeth.

I gasped and staggered sideways, my boots scuffing against the ground.

He didn't stop. Another step. Another strike. Another tremor. My fingers strained to keep the sword from being wrenched from my grasp.

My chest heaved. My lungs burned.

Holt stared down at me. His eyes steady, calm, merciless.

I edged farther to the side. Holt followed, and the sun shone in his eyes. Blinding him.

Instinct flared.

I gritted my teeth and shoved forward.

He twisted, parrying easily. My blade slid off his. Too quickly, he struck again.

I dropped low, narrowly ducking beneath the steel aimed at me. My sword swept out at his knees. A desperate attack that was far from elegant, but he jerked back to avoid it, his rhythm broken.

I lunged upward, driving my blade toward his chest. Surprise flickered in his blue eyes as he raised his sword.

Steel rang against steel as he blocked my blow.

His face returned to its impassive mask.

He swung again. His sword crashed against mine hard enough to rattle my bones.

My breath sawed in and out. Sweat stung my eyes. My arms trembled as I lifted them, letting him know I was done.

Holt lowered his blade, and a slight smile lifted his lips. His chest rose and fell faster than I'd realized while fighting off his attacks. "Nahvienne taught you well." The words snuck out between heavy breaths.

I knelt in front of him, using my sword to help hold me up. "I'm taking a team to the Primordial Waters to search for Kur." I shifted my grip on the hilt, the blade's tip tracing a line in the dirt. "You're welcome to join us."

He reached his hand out to me, and when I took it, I saw his magic. The knowledge of what he could do—of how easily he could twist my thoughts—sent a cold shiver rushing up my spine.

# Chapter 44



*"My relationships with my cats have saved me from a deadly, pervasive ignorance." -William S. Burroughs*

"**B**loody hell! Have you ever seen anything like this?" Storm's mouth hung open.

Holt stood next to him. He nudged one of the floating rocks and watched as it drifted away. "Nah, man. Never."

The Primordial Waters stretched out in front of us. Deeper. Darker. Deadlier.

They'd swallowed all but the very tops of the ancient bones. Their waves crashed against the jagged rocks that had stood sentinel but were now at risk of drowning.

Lightning forked across the purple sky, reflecting both life and death on the Waters' surface.

The rich scent of petrichor filled the air. But something else was mixed in. Something that brought to mind beginnings and endings, creation and collapse.

The song danced on the breeze. Calling to me.

Closing my eyes, I swayed to the rhythm. The notes wrapped around me, settling deep inside of me.

Soothing.

Mournful.

Dangerous.

Teeth sank into the back of my leg.

Jumping away, I snapped my eyes open. Schmendrick stared at me. "Do not be seduced by its call, Molly. Only madness lies that way." He brushed his head against my knee, an apology of sorts. "Tune it out."

The words were a command. Filled with power that broke through the music's spell, jerking me back to the present where chaos loomed.

Thorn and Storm were locked in a brutal dance with Nahvienne. Their swords crashed against hers as they drove her away from the Waters' edge.

Cobalt strands of hair whipped about her face, drawn toward the Waters. Her eyes were wild and fierce. "It needs me!" Her voice crashed like waves upon the shore.

And, I realized the mistake I'd made. Bringing a water sorceress to the Primordial Waters had been stupid. The magic that saturated the air and the ground, that swelled on the waves, would be like a siren's call to her, beckoning her with its vast knowledge and irresistible power.

In my peripheral vision, I caught sight of a ghostly image. Lorelei.

Her light-colored clothes and white, billowing hair stood in stark contrast to the stormy palette surrounding her. She glided as if in a trance, her gaze fixed on the bones jutting from the Waters. Her face ashen, devoid of emotion.

Until a tear trailed down her cheek.

What did she see in the Waters? For the first time, I wondered what it would be like to be a necromancer, to deal in death, what type of toll it would take.

"Lorelei." Sharp stones stabbed through my boots into the soles of my feet as I bolted toward her.

She didn't seem to notice me. She stepped closer to the Waters. It lapped at her toes, then rose higher.

When she moved to take another step, I grabbed her arm and yanked her back.

The Waters surged, reaching for her.

Schmendrick leapt onto a boulder, narrowly avoiding the rising tide, and sat on its jagged tip. His tail flicked, and his green eyes glowed. He grew, becoming sleeker—more regal, a feline god.

Power hissed from him, slamming into the Waters. It recoiled in a crackling wave.

"I've only bought you a moment, Molly." Schmendrick jumped down, landing beside me and nodding at the others. "Kur is not here, and neither should you be."

Wrapping my arm around Lorelei's waist, I guided her away from the Waters and certain death. "I need your help."

"Me?" She blinked up at me as if waking from a daze. Disbelief swam in her honey-colored eyes.

"Yeah." Leaning in, I whispered my plan to her while we crossed the rocky ground to the others. As we closed in on them, we separated.

Nahvienne whirled and hacked. Her blade a blur, keeping both Thorn and Storm on constant guard. Their sword strokes slowed, but with the Waters fueling her, Nahvienne was as energized as if she'd just begun the fight.

Holt stood on the edge of their battle, staring at Nahvienne. "Stop!" His voice drowned out the song. It drowned out the breaking waves. It drowned out the rumbling thunder. He'd poured his magic into the command, and I doubted I could move if I'd wanted to.

All three swords stopped. Strikes frozen in mid-air.

The guardians' chests rose and fell, ragged breaths tearing out of them. Their shadows stretched, growing darker, thicker.

Holt focused on them, releasing me from his hold.

Hoping she was free from Holt's magic, I nodded at Lorelei. She rushed to Nahvienne, grabbing her around the waist. One moment, they were there, and the next, they were gone.

Hopefully, safe in Ravenwood.

Keeping my distance from Storm and Thorn, I rested my hand on the hilt of my sword. "Are the two of you in control of yourselves?"

Lightning sparked in Storm's eyes, but he sheathed his blade. "The tempest beckons me, but it does not control me." He held his hands up, letting me know I had nothing to fear from him.

Thorn followed suit. "I'm good. This place is as creepy as all get out, but it holds no sway over me."

I nodded. It made perfect sense. His power was Earth. He was grounded, steady.

Turning my back on them, I pointed. "Over that rise is where Kur broke free." My feet sank into the muddy ground as I climbed the hill. Each step added more weight to my boots. Magic would have been so much easier, but I wanted to see what I was walking into. "Let's check it out, then go back to check on the others."

We crested the ridge, and Schmendrick stopped. The fur on his back bristled, every strand standing on end. A deep, menacing growl rumbled through his body.

"What is it, Buddy?"

"He was here." Schmendrick stood on his back legs and surveyed the area. "Presently. He probably watched us emerge from the shadows." He dropped back down and let out a quiet hiss. "But he is gone now."

True to my word, as soon as I shadow walked Holt, Thorn, and Storm back to Ravenwood, I stepped into the nearest patch of darkness and back out to Castle Unicorn with Schmendrick draped across my shoulders like a furry scarf.

After the balmy air near the Primordial Waters, Iowa felt frigid. The sun hung lower in the Western sky than seemed possible, a pink glow kissing the clouds, promising a spectacular sunset.

Jayden rounded the castle, strolling along the curved pathway as if drawn by my presence. "Molly." The tension in his shoulders instantly released. He picked up his pace, his gaze roving over every inch of me. His booted feet stopped when they were a breath from mine. "Didn't find him?"

"He was there, but…"

"He escaped."

My gaze drifted from his. "Before we even saw him." My shoulders sagged, and Schmendrick jumped down, padding toward the moat. He crouched next to it, butt wiggling as he prepared to snatch a fish.

Watching him act like a normal house cat, I recalled how he'd appeared at the Waters' edge. The power that had pushed the waves back.

"And what would I have done with him anyway? Two sorceresses enthralled by the Waters, two fighting to keep one from heeding its call, and one controlling everybody. Some band of warriors we turned out to be."

Bowing my head, I tucked my hands into my pouch. "The world's going to end because I'm not enough."

"No, Molly." His voice was thick with grief. "It may end for a thousand different reasons, but that isn't one of them."

My eyes rolled, and I shook my head, but he lifted his hand, cupping my cheek. His rough calluses brushed against my skin. His fingers were warm and gentle. "I mean it, Molly. You are enough. You always have been."

Clutching his tee in my fists, I stepped into him. His woodsy scent enveloped me, soothing me in ways I couldn't remember anyone else doing.

He cradled my head in one hand, the other anchoring me against him. "You're more than enough." His breath ghosted over my ear. "You're everything."

# Chapter 45

*"Having a bunch of cats around is good. If you're feeling bad, you just look at the cats, you'll feel better because they know that everything is just as it is. There's nothing to get excited about. They just know. They're saviours." ~Charles Bukowski*

*You're more than enough.* Jayden's words echoed through my head as I stepped into Ravenwood Arena, Schmendrick sleeping soundly in my arms, his body warm and heavy.

My crew sat slumped on the benches. Shoulders hunched in defeat, and I doubted any of them agreed with him.

"Hey." Stopping in front of them, I ran my fingers through Schmendrick's silky fur and rocked back on my heels.

Nahvienne dropped her head into her hands. "I am so sorry, Molly. I—"

"Stop." I held my hand up. "I'm sorry. I knew the Waters had power. I know yours is water. I should have realized."

She looked up at me, her blue eyes rimmed in red. "I would've killed them if it meant reaching the Waters."

"I would've let you." Thorn draped his arm over her shoulders, pulling her closer.

Storm shrugged. "I wouldn't've." He lifted his hand, sparks crackling over his fingers. "Was just about ta let the magic fly when Holt an' Lore jumped in."

"I would've watched everyone die—" Lorelei's voice sounded haunted, hollow. "No... I did." She shivered, then crossed her arms, rubbing them for warmth. "It felt so real. Too real." She looked up, but her gaze was on something distant, something only she could see. "The Waters whispered to me. They told me I could rest. Find comfort in their depths."

When her eyes finally met mine, they carried that same haunted look her voice held. And for the first time, I felt sorry for the girl who had terrorized me until I'd fled. Finally, I understood her a little.

If she'd had these visions since childhood, no wonder she'd felt the need to control—bullying was most likely her only outlet.

And that was where I'd come in. An easy target with my horns and tail. And someone who she'd thought had been given everything.

She looked up at me with a smile that didn't reach her eyes, a thin mask that barely covered her pain. "Where did you disappear to?"

Staring at her, I debated whether I trusted her enough to tell her about Jayden.

"I mean, you were there." Lorelei's voice faltered. "But… you obviously weren't."

The tension in my shoulders eased as relief spread through me. "The music calls to me." My voice drifted off as I tried to grasp the song again.

Everyone stared at me. Their faces filled with confusion.

"Music?" Storm's brow furrowed, and he looked at the others as if for confirmation. "All I heard was waves crashing."

The rest of the team nodded in agreement, very obviously not looking directly at me.

"The song sings for the few, not the many." Schmendrick's voice was low and drowsy, his eyes half-lidded as if he hovered on the verge of sleep. His tail flicked, sharp as a metronome. "It chooses its audience… and there is always a price for hearing its song."

"I didn't hear a song." Holt stared at the ground in front of him. "But I felt its consciousness. How can the Waters be sentient?"

"As easily as you." Schmendrick lifted his head and looked at Holt like he was dumber than a box of rocks. "They are older than time. They hold the memories of the world, of each of its beginnings, and each of its ends."

Thorn frowned. "So I was the only one not affected by the Primordial Waters?"

"Water may cover the land. It may try with all its might to drown the world, but Earth remains, ready to rise above the tide. Steadfast, eternal." Schmendrick curled into a tighter ball and flipped his tail over his eyes. "Now, let me rest."

Wondering if he was really sleeping or just pretending to be, I stared at him for a few seconds. When he didn't move except for the steady rise and fall of his chest, I turned to Lorelei. "Do you feel its call?"

"How do you mean?" She tipped her head to the side.

"The song—" I faltered, searching for words. How did I explain what it did to me? "It's like a niggling feeling that I can't let go of. An itch that I can't scratch. But when I go back… I finally feel whole again."

"You don't have to worry about me." Lorelei's voice was steady, but her hands trembled as she folded them tight against her chest. "I am *never* returning."

## Chapter 46



The Primordial Waters stretched out in front of me, whitecaps dancing on their roiling surface. Deeper and angrier than even the last time I'd stood on their shores.

Nahvienne and Lorelei stared at me from the Waters.

Waves crashed over them, drowning their images.

Sacrifices.

That was what the Waters had intended them to be.

And somehow I knew that the Waters' anger was directed at me for freeing them.

The melody that haunted me floated through the air. Each wave a rising crescendo.

Lightning spiderwebbed across the twilight sky. Distant thunder rolled over the Waters' surface like the rumble of timpani.

Notes rose and fell like the tide.

They surged—ancient and wild.

Powerful.

As mournful as a dirge. As deadly as the undertow.

The tune called to me. Pulling me toward its depths. Toward something vast and sacred.

The chorus swelled, then crashed over me like a tsunami. Gasping, I bolted upright, my heart thundering like I'd surfaced from the depths.

Schmendrick yowled, nearly thrown from the bed. Hissing, his claws sank into my comforter. His fur stood on end, making him appear twice his normal size. His ears swiveled as he scanned the room for danger. When there was none to be found, he casually licked his paw and stared at me through narrowed green eyes. "What's got your fur ruffled?"

The song vibrated through my body, drowning out Schmendrick's words. Its notes thrummed in my chest, mirroring my beating heart. Its echoes lingered, and I was determined to hold onto them.

"I have to go." Kicking off the covers, I dashed to my dresser, pulling on the first pair of leggings I found. "They're calling me."

"Who's calling you?" Schmendrick's eyes darted to my nightstand, where I kept my phone. "Can they call back after I've had my beauty sleep?"

"The Primordial Waters." My hands shook as I yanked my hoodie over my head. "I need to go. Now!"

The pull was unbearable—a fire that ignited in my chest and crawled through my veins, promising no relief until I stood on the Waters' shores. They stirred, drawing me to them, and my magic surged in response, slamming against my ribs like a tidal wave. It took all that I had in me to tug my boots on and tie their laces.

Schmendrick jumped off my bed and trotted over to me. "Fine. Let's go. But bring the dog."

"I don't have time—"

"Molly." His voice grew sharper than his claws. "Bring. The. Dog."

The world tilted as if a riptide had me in its grasp, dragging beneath its icy currents, and I needed to reach the surface before it was too late.

Schmendrick tipped his head toward the corner of the room. "See that shadow?"

My eyes tracked his gaze, following it to the corner. The darkness there was absolute, indistinguishable from every other shadow in the room.

"It'll take you to Jayden." He nodded his head again. "So will that one or that one." His gaze danced around the room. "One step, Molly. Then one more, and you'll be standing in front of the Waters."

Grabbing my phone, I shot off a quick text to Jayden. I'd go to him, but if he wasn't ready, I didn't know if I could wait. With each passing second, the Waters' call intensified.

My feet stilled at the edge of the shadow. Swords. I needed my swords. While I strapped them on, Schmendrick moved to my side. His tone softened—unusually gentle, stripped of all snark. "Let's not keep the Waters waiting. They expect to be answered when they call."

Jayden waited on the other side of the shadow. His dark blond hair was tousled from sleep, his amber eyes alert. "What is it, Molly?"

"Be a good dog and heel." Schmendrick's whiskers tickled my cheek.

Jayden's lip twitched as he glanced at Schmendrick, just for a second. Then he pulled on his socks and shoes. "Let's go." He slipped his fingers through mine—steady, certain.

No questions, no hesitation, no doubts.

Just trust.

The three of us turned toward the nearest shadow.

One step and the world we knew was left behind.

One step and we emerged where gods and monsters had fallen.

The jagged ground jutted through the soles of my boots, crumbling at the edges with each step I took. Warmth radiated from it, and I wondered if, like the Waters, it too was awakening.

Lightning flashed across the bruised and battered sky. The air buzzed with power, thick with the scent of ozone.

The melody that had awoken me rose from the Waters. Each note touched my soul, calling to my magic, pulling at its threads.

Trying to rouse it.

We crested the ridge. Before us lay the ruins where Kur had been held captive.

But he wasn't there.

Only the three of us and the song.

"What?" Throwing my hands into the air, I stomped my foot like a spoiled child. "What do you want from me?"

Lightning streaked across the sky. Its jagged forks reflected on the Waters' surface. It had to have been a trick.

Or magic.

The Waters rose and fell. Too choppy, too rough to reflect anything.

The song faded. Straining my ears, I fought to hear it, but the notes were too faint.

As the melody disappeared, the Waters stilled until the surface was as smooth as glass.

Then, as if someone had skipped a rock, ripples formed. When they settled, a large black dragon looked up at me from the depths. The beast's eyes were haunted.

"They want Kur back."

Jayden's voice made me jump. A reminder that I wasn't there by myself.

But without Kur, the Primordial Waters were alone.

And, apparently, they didn't want to be. Didn't want to destroy everything.

"I'm trying to find him. To return him to you."

Jayden squeezed my shoulder. "You will, Molly. You will."

## Chapter 47

*"Cats choose us; we don't own them." –Kristin Cast*

With Schmendrick cradled in my arms, I took Jayden home. Then I stood on the porch and pulled my phone out of my pocket. Selecting Viv's text string, I stared down at the screen. Guilt clawed at my insides. I'd never lied about being sick before, never called in, but this Ancestral Guardian gig was overstepping into other parts of my life. "I'm not going to make it in today. Sorry."

Swallowing the lump that blocked my throat, I tucked the phone into my pouch. Then, I shadow walked onto the porch of Ravenwood Manor. The early morning sunlight couldn't pierce the darkness beneath the slanting roof.

Standing in front of the door, I reached for the knob, then drew my hand back.

Yeah, Seraphina wanted me to move in (so she could have total control of my life), and Schmendrick declared it was more mine than Caius'. But I couldn't bring myself to just show up. Maybe if I felt welcome at all…

"Molly." Schmendrick's green eyes rolled. "You are giving them power by showing weakness. Act like a cat."

I huffed a laugh. "How's that?"

"Act like everyone is beneath you and you own the place." He jumped down, swishing his tail as he walked through the closed door. No shimmer of magic, no ripple in the air—just gone.

My skin prickled. Schmendrick had done plenty of strange things, but walking through solid wood wasn't one of them. A nervous snicker escaped me, betraying my disbelief. "Okay. Sure. Why not add ghost cat to the list?"

Wiping my hands on my leggings, I grasped the knocker attached to the raven's head, slammed it against the door twice, and followed my slippery cat into the entryway without waiting for an answer. My eyes slowly adjusted to the dim lighting.

Shadows slithered up the stairs, making the house feel abandoned, haunted.

Lifting my hand, I lit all the candles in the room with a thought. Immediately, the manor felt more loved. With a silent command, I drew the curtains back. Sunlight streamed through the windows, pouring into every nook and cranny.

"Now, that's acting like a cat." Satisfaction filled Schmendrick's voice.

My heart thrummed as I braced myself for Seraphina or Caius to storm the entryway. For them to scream at me for making their house feel like a home. But their thunderous cries didn't rumble down the stairway. And neither did they.

My eyebrows pinched together, and I shook my head before climbing the steps.

The burgundy runner that had always seemed so dark and depressing actually complemented the wood floors, bringing warmth to the room.

Why Seraphina would want to live in a house that felt like a tomb instead of enjoying the rich warmth light brought to it was beyond me.

I turned into the office, fully expecting to find her behind her desk, but she was nowhere to be seen.

Schmendrick stepped into the room. His tail low and still, his steps cautious. He lifted his nose, inhaling deeply, then opened his mouth to get a better whiff. "This room will always smell of brimstone and lizard, but the scent is diminished."

"Brimstone and lizard." A startled chuckle slipped from me at the unexpected comment.

"What else would a dragon smell like?" His tail snapped through the air behind him, agitation clear in his tone.

"One that old?" I rubbed my chin in thought. "Stale, musty bonfires?"

Schmendrick vanished—without a snarky comment or haughty look. I spun in a circle looking for him.

Something on the bookshelf caught my attention—a small, heart-shaped container, black as midnight, with a thin dagger plunged straight through its center. Veins etched along its surface pulsed faintly, a thrumming heartbeat with a steady rhythm of its own. Enthralled by the subtle, life-like movement, I leaned in.

Inside the dark crystal surface, the dagger's tip rested against a tiny, humanoid skull, topped with horns. Its eye sockets glowed red, giving me the distinct impression that it was watching me. Everything about the ampule screamed danger—and curiosity made it impossible to look away.

The echo of a scream drifted from the container, barely audible, like the wind hissing through a graveyard. I froze, my hand hovering above it. Shadows stretched and twisted around the heart, concealing the skull within. One of them reached toward me, nearly grazing my outstretched fingers. A chill ran down my spine, and I snatched my hand back, staggering away.

My hip slammed into the desk. The drawers rattled, and I remembered the photograph of Malachai—how I'd held it, staring at his likeness until Schmendrick told me that demons could see through their images. I remembered Seraphina talking to Malachai, like the picture was a phone of sorts.

But now… now that I knew him, I wasn't afraid of him seeing me.

Opening the bottom drawer, I pulled out his photo. "Malachai, I need your help."

His eyes in the photo seemed to come alive, too real to merely be a picture. "What is it, Molly?" Concern filled his voice.

"What do you make of this?"

The photo warbled, like ripples over water. Then I saw Malachai in the throne room at Taras Mor as if I were there, standing right in front of him. "Someone is dabbling in forbidden magic. *MaunDagnir* was bad enough, but with that vessel to contain the blood the blade spills, immortality can be obtained."

"So Caius not only wants my power but to live forever?" The shock hit me like a punch in the chest, and I slumped into Seraphina's chair, unable to stay on my feet. "What a douche."

Anger radiated off Malachai—hot wrath that made the air shimmer around him. "If your mother hadn't bound me, I'd tear that cretin limb from limb."

"If you trust me with your true name, I could break every chain she's wrapped around you."

His stoic expression made it impossible for me to tell what he was thinking, but the flare in his red eyes revealed the storm beneath. "No matter how much I trust you, that is a lot to ask of me."

"I'm not asking for my benefit—but for yours."

"I hate to break up this touching father/daughter moment, but he'll never freely hand you his name." Schmendrick plopped onto the desk in front of me, his tail curling through the air behind him.

"And, you would, *cat*."

"Really, Malachai?" He lifted his paw to his mouth, unsheathing his claws, dipping his head to lick their sharp tips. "I am no dog. I don't play fetch. I don't beg. And I don't come when called."

I shook my head. "Why don't you two get along?"

"You may as well ask why the sun shines." Schmendrick lifted his other paw. "No one is lurking about. The house is as empty as your mother's heart."

"Watch your back, Molly." Malachai's voice dropped into a deep, rumbling growl. "Neither of them can be trusted."

## Chapter 48

*"If that cat could talk, what tales he'd tell about Della and the Dealer and the dog as well, but the cat was cool, and he never said a mumblin' word." ~Hoyt Axton*

"Molly, you are magic." Schmendrick gave me a disapproving look that most house cats had perfected. "Shadow walk. Create a portal."

I trotted down the steps. "I'll walk." Stepping onto the front porch, I breathed in the magically enhanced air. It didn't have quite the same effect as the real stuff, but it was better than the stagnant air inside Ravenwood Manor. "I'm not anxious to deal with Seraphina."

"You won't find her here." Vak's voice rasped low and gravelly—rocks tumbling over each other as they skittered down a mountainside—a jarring contrast to the first time I'd met him. Then, it had been high-pitched like someone who'd sucked the helium out of a balloon.

Striding to the railing, I looked down at the kobold standing on the bright green lawn. His hat was planted firmly on his head instead of clutched in his hands, and he didn't bow the way he usually did. He just stared up at me, eyes shifting color with every blink.

"Seraphina has gone to the Primordial Waters with Kur."

My fingers tightened around the railing, a chill running through me. "How did she know where to find him?"

Vak glanced at Schmendrick, and something danced through his eyes. Fear maybe. It was quickly masked by a steely edge. He lifted his chin, defiance radiating from his stance. "I told her."

"You knew Molly was looking for him." Schmendrick's voice was a low growl that lifted the hair on the back of my neck.

"Why would you tell her?" My fingers curled around the railing, clutching it like a lifeline. I'd found out the hard way that Vak was a fae who liked to make bargains, but I'd still counted him as an ally. "Why not come to me?"

"Because, my dear Molly—" Vak's jaw tightened. His hands pressed against his hips, his claws flexing ever so slightly. "She and Caius held the strings, but with that bit of information, I was able to cut them. This Kobold Clan is no longer beholden to the Ravenwood line. We are free."

Schmendrick grew until he towered over the kobold. "How did you find him?"

"He's been slinking around here in human form long enough with none of you realizing who—or what—he truly is." A faint smirk curved the corner of his lips, like his species was far superior to my own.

"Nox." The name slipped out of my mouth on a breath. He was the only person who'd come to the cabal since Kur was awakened.

My fingers pressed against my lips, and I stared over Vak's head at the impeccable lawn while I processed the thought.

Could Nox really be Kur? He'd been helping me search for the dragon. He'd given me so much knowledge and insight into the beast.

He couldn't really be Kur.

Could he?

"Yes." Vak's voice was calm, unwavering. His chest lifted, shoulders squared—a picture of absolute certainty. "Nox is the guardian of the Primordial Waters."

My eyes narrowed, and I wondered what he would gain by misleading me. He seemed to be telling me the truth—but how could I trust him?

"You and I, we're even." Vak tilted his head as though challenging me to object. "Each of us is indebted to the other, and so our debts have been canceled, unless there is something else I can help you with."

"No." I shook my head and took an unconscious step back. "No, as much as I appreciate your help, I like being free from debt."

"In that case, may our paths cross again someday." He bowed before scurrying off through the grass.

"You need allies." Shrinking to his normal size, Schmendrick jumped onto the railing, and his tail flicked as he watched Vak disappear.

Hoping the other guardians would be training, I snatched him up, walked into the inky shadows crouched on the floorboards, and stepped into the arena.

The crash of steel against steel rang across the grounds, echoing off the archways.

Willa's blade swung through the air. Nahvienne blocked it with practiced ease. Then Willa's leg kicked out as fast as a viper striking. Her foot connected with Nahvienne's side.

Nahvienne stumbled back. Her sword slipped from her hand, landing on the grass right before she did.

Willa stood over Nahvienne, and the smile that crossed her face was so warm and friendly that it was difficult to believe she'd ever raise a weapon to protect herself, let alone to attack.

"I've been working on that move." Willa sheathed her sword, then reached her hand down and helped Nahvienne to her feet.

Nahvienne brushed the dirt off her pants, then pulled blades of grass out of her hair. "It worked. I never saw it coming."

Ember bounded over. The shaved half of her head had been dyed bright pink since the last time I'd seen her. She seized Willa by the shoulders and shook her, bouncing up and down as she did. "You did it! You beat her." Laughter bubbled in her voice.

Her enthusiasm cut through the funk that I'd found myself in since talking to Vak. Hope sparked in my chest—small but bright. Maybe we could actually find Kur and guide him back to the Waters where he belonged.

Ember bounced around and patted Willa on the back. "The student has become the master."

"No." Willa chuckled, fidgeting with her French braid pigtails. "Let's not go that far."

Nahvienne bent down to pick up her sword. Her eyes met mine as she straightened. "Hey, Molly, did you come to train?"

"No." I lowered Schmendrick to the ground. "I came to recruit."

Nahvienne whistled, a shrill, piercing sound that made me want to plug my ears.

While Nahvienne tried to get everybody's attention, Willa turned to me, her smile still brightening her face. "Any luck finding Kur?"

Ember's face was suddenly serious. She stood with her hands behind her back and her shoulders squared, a soldier at attention.

"I have a lead." Growing up, I hadn't really known either of them. They hadn't tormented me the way Lorelei had, but neither had they befriended me. Each other's company had been all they'd needed.

I'd longed for a friendship like theirs, but I'd had Caelan. Until I didn't.

Willa rocked back on her heel, then a look of determination settled on her face, hardening her blue-green eyes. "I want to go with you."

"Me, too." Ember stepped forward. "I can fight. I can follow orders. I'm good in a pinch."

Trying to remember what her element was, I stared at Ember for a moment. "You're fire?" I waited for her nod. "The Primordial Waters might douse your magic, but they shouldn't be able to control you."

Then I turned toward Willa. "And you're nature?"

Willa's chin dipped down to her chest, then snapped back up in a quick nod. A grin tugged at her lips, but she fought it.

Rubbing my hand along my jaw, I tried to decide whether they would be advantages or liabilities. "The Primordial Waters are dangerous." My eyes held each of theirs for several seconds, making sure they realized how serious this was. "Even without Kur in the equation."

"Is that a yes then?" Willa's hand tightened ever so slightly on the grip of her sword, causing the tip to bounce.

My gaze traveled over the guardians striding toward us. Two of them couldn't go with me, no matter how badly they wanted to, and another of them shouldn't. I turned back to Willa and Ember, focusing on them, forcing myself to ignore the others. "There's more that you need to hear before you decide to come along, but if you still want to, I'd be glad to have your help."

## Chapter 49

*"I have lived with several Zen masters — all of them cats."*
*-Eckhart Tolle*

The guardians stood in front of me. All nine of them. It was the first time I could remember all of us being together.

Caelan glowered at me, not liking that I had the information. "If my source is correct, Nox is Kur, and Seraphina took him to the Primordial Waters."

"Why would she do that?" Caelan narrowed his bloodshot, hazel eyes at me and turned as if to walk away.

"Because she's a power-hungry bitch." Schmendrick shrugged (an odd move for a cat, but I'd seen him do weirder things, like walk through closed doors).

"The Waters want Kur back." Nine sets of eyes stared at me, making my heart pound against my ribcage. I hated being the center of attention. Hated being watched, being judged. But

I had to set my discomfort aside to stop Seraphina, to save the world.

Sweat coated my palms, but I didn't let my gaze drop, didn't let them see my fear. "But I have no idea if he'll willingly be bound to them again. If he won't…"

Caelan shook his head and stumbled with the movement. "You have no plan. Do you?"

"No." I dropped my gaze. "Nobody has given me any clues about how to stop him. All I can do is talk to him, see if he'll listen."

Caelan staggered forward. "Everyone who wants to follow Molly to their death step forward."

Everyone but Caelan and Lorelei stepped toward me. Lorelei's shoulders slumped. "I'm sorry. I can't go back there."

Tears pricked at my eyes, but I refused to let them fall. Hoped nobody could see them glistening there.

Storm lifted his sword in the air, and the others followed.

I walked to Nahvienne. "The Waters—"

"How can I stay behind when everyone else is going?" The question broke from Nahvienne in a tight whisper, her words thick with shame.

Lorelei settled her hand on Nahvienne's shoulder. "Not everyone. We would be liabilities. Distractions that they don't need." She squeezed gently before letting go. Her words seemed to be a reminder for her as much as for Nahvienne. "They can't watch us and save the world at the same time."

"I know…" Her chin dropped to her chest as she crumpled in on herself. "I just—" She swallowed hard. "I just feel so useless." Her gaze drifted, unfocused. "I mean, what good does it do to train and practice if you can never use it?"

After a moment of awkward silence, I stepped forward, uncertain how to comfort Nahvienne. My hand hovered in the air, trembling, before I reached out and caught her arm, my grip tighter than I meant for it to be. "You, Nahvienne, are not useless." I eased my hold on her. "And you will get a chance to show it—but not today."

"Fine. Okay." Her smile was thin, wavering. "Thanks."

While the others prepared to go to the Primordial Waters, I clutched Schmendrick to my chest and stepped into a shadow. Castle Unicorn sprawled out in front of me, a sentinel standing guard over the Missouri River Basin. Most of the leaves had fallen from the trees, leaving their bare, twisted branches ready to carry their winter loads.

Schmendrick climbed onto my shoulders, draping himself across them. I strode along the sidewalk to the back patio. When nobody was there, I knocked on the sliding glass door.

"What the hell?" The voice was unfamiliar to me. "How did somebody get up here?"

A guy about my age pulled the blinds to the side and stared out at me. His wolf was near the surface, making his eyes appear more canine than human. His gaze trailed from me to Schmendrick, and for a second, I wondered if I'd need to break up a fight between the two of them.

Schmendrick's tail flicked, smacking me across the face. I snatched it, holding it still. "Is Jayden here?"

"How did you get up here? Nobody was let through the gate." The man's eyes moved to meet mine.

"Magic." I lifted my shoulders, and Schmendrick teetered, fighting for balance.

The man only held my gaze for an instant before looking beyond me. "I'll get him." He didn't move, didn't say a word, just stared off in the distance. "Give him a few minutes. Do you want to come in?"

"No." I pointed behind me at the tables dotting the patio. "I'll wait out here." I turned to walk away. "Thank you."

Pulling Schmendrick off my shoulder, I set him on the table. He immediately adjusted each paw, placing it just so, until he was perfectly situated. Then he flicked his tail and glared at me.

"Sorry, Buddy." I pulled out a chair but didn't sit. Instead, I stared into the timber lining the property, sensing Jayden running toward me. Urgency propelled his steps across the forest floor, the wind carrying the rhythm of his strides to me.

Flattening my hands on the table, I leaned forward, my body angling instinctively toward the place I knew he'd break through the trees, anxious to see him bound across the lawn.

Schmendrick's tail swept over the wooden surface. "You're vibrating more than an attention-starved kitten getting belly rubs. Is everything okay, or should I fetch a sedative?"

"Really, Schmen?" Tilting my head to the side, I pressed my lips together. "As soon as he gets here, we can figure out what's going on."

He lifted a paw and ran his tongue over it with slow precision, never breaking eye contact—as if daring me to flinch first. "Yes. I'm sure that's all it is."

Jayden erupted from the forest like the devil was on his tail. His tan fur rippled with every powerful stride, each step pounding against the earth. His amber eyes never left me.

The door opened behind me, and Jayden darted inside. A heartbeat later, he was standing outside in black sweatpants and nothing else. His chest heaved. The wind blew his hair back, reminiscent of his wolf. "You okay?"

There was too much space between us. Without thinking about it, I closed the distance, needing to be closer to him. "Nox is Kur." I settled my hands on his forearms. "Seraphina has him at the Primordial Waters, and I have this feeling…" Wanting his comfort and support, I moved even closer. "I don't think it's good."

## Chapter 50



*"What greater gift than the love of a cat?" -Charles Dickens*

With Jayden's hand in mine and Schmendrick cradled in my other arm, I stepped into Ravenwood Arena. The other nine guardians turned toward me all at once like a dance team that had perfected a choreographed move.

"So, the wolf's going, too." Caelan's hazel eyes rolled back (so far that I kinda hoped they'd get stuck there). "Shocker."

Jayden's grip tightened on my fingers, but he didn't respond to Caelan.

"Who's coming?" I silently prayed that Nahvienne decided to stay behind. I knew it was hard for her, but it was also the right thing to do.

Seven guardians stepped forward. My jaw dropped when I met Caelan's gaze. His was defiant, waiting for me to challenge his decision.

"I don't know what we'll be walking into." My teeth dug into my bottom lip, pulling it into my mouth. "Last time I went to the Waters, they were deeper and darker." I rubbed my arm. "When we find Seraphina and Nox, I need you all to surround them—but not too close. We don't want to scare him, but we don't want him to get away either."

"And then you'll talk him into submission." Caelan's laugh was rough, half-drowned in the burn of whatever alcohol he'd had to drink for breakfast. "Because words always work on monsters, don't they?"

Jayden's growl brushed against my neck, quiet enough that I doubted anyone else heard it. Sucking in a deep breath, I hoped I wouldn't have to deal with the two of them arguing the entire time. Convincing Kur—Nox—to resume his post guarding the Waters was going to be hard enough without them turning it into a pissing contest.

"We're going to shadow walk, so form a line and hold hands." With Schmendrick draped over my arm, I grasped Jayden's hand and called on the darkness that clung to the edges of the arena, extending it. It slithered over the ground, growing darker, thicker until it was large enough for nine of us to fit inside it.

We stepped out of the shadows beyond Kur's altar. The ground squished beneath my boots, cold and saturated. Each step drew out a wet, sucking sound that made my toes curl.

The song blared all around me, its notes a feverish dance, rising with each breath I took. No longer subtle, the melody pulsed and thrummed. Urgent.

Beneath Kur's symbol, Seraphina stood on the rocky ground with Nox. The half-lidded eye stared at them as she forced Nox to his knees. His hands were bound, and strange runes flickered across his bare chest, pulsing faintly like embers.

My gaze slid from her to Nox and back again, shaking my head.

"No." The word came out as barely a breath. The world tilted, and I staggered with it. "That's not—"

Realization sank like a boulder thrown into the Waters.

The way he looked at me.

Ancient.

And endless.

And sad.

Kur.

Nox was Kur.

I'd known it. I really had. But until that moment, I hadn't believed it.

He'd brought me here. Shown me. Given me truths he shouldn't have known, but I'd refused to see.

His nose wiggled as if he'd scented something. Then his gaze fell on us.

His eyes pleaded with me. For what? Understanding? Help?

Staring at him, I didn't know how to react, how to help him.

He bowed his head against his chest as if the lies had weighed it down, and he didn't have the strength to deny them anymore.

My heart clenched. Whatever else he was, he appeared… broken. For just a breath, I wanted to reach for him. But I couldn't. Not now. Not with the Waters stirring and not until I knew what Seraphina was doing here… with him.

Lifting my fist in the air, I brought my companions to a stop. "Circle around them, not too close." I looked at the others, hoping they would listen to me, follow my orders. "We can't let Kur get away."

Jayden stayed by my side as the others spread out, boots squelching across the sodden earth, water splashing up their legs.

Stepping forward, I cleared my throat.

Seraphina's head snapped in my direction. Her gaze trailed over me, then slid to Jayden. "The wolf." Venom dripped from those words. "I gave you this one." She waved her hand toward Nox. "Power immeasurable, and you chose a slavering, savage beast."

Jayden growled and strode toward her, but I threw my hand out, stopping him as he walked into it.

"Power immeasurable." Huffing a laugh, I tried to appear unaffected, but my heart went out to Nox. "Yet, he can't even lift his head." I took a step toward her.

Seraphina raised *MaunDagnir*. "That's close enough." With her other hand, she clutched Nox's hair and jerked his head back. She pressed the blade to his throat. "It seems Nox led us to Kur after all." Her laughter—normally the twinkling of wind chimes—twisted into something sharp and cruel, as corrupted as the blade she held.

## Chapter 51

*"Curiosity killed the cat." -Ben Johnson*

The runes that had flickered on Nox's skin flared to life, deep red.

Blood runes.

Dark, forbidden magic.

Nox's skin was paler than ever. His dark hair hung limply, and his body trembled as if he were fighting her hold, but the strength had been drained out of him.

My eyes darted to my fellow guardians, making sure they were in place.

Seraphina's gaze followed mine. "Well, look at you, thinking of your mother for once." She smiled, and chills raced through me.

Tipping my head to the side, I tried to figure out what she meant by that.

She raised her hands, and the guardians encircling her went still. Magic shimmered in the air like a mirage rising above the asphalt in the heat of summer. Then flames raced across the ground, drawing a perfect pentagram with a guardian at each point. "All their power—" she inhaled deeply "—at my command."

Ember and Holt stood on the outside, pounding their fists against a barrier that I couldn't see.

My gaze traveled to each point of the pentagram. Caelan, Willa, Thorn, Storm, and Lane stood with their hands lifted toward Seraphina. Unmoving, unblinking, their faces like porcelain masks, devoid of emotion.

Power slammed into me, infiltrating my body, rushing through my veins, carried by my blood. I stumbled back.

Jayden caught my arms, grasping me until I steadied.

Seraphina cackled, the sound reminding me of the stereotypical witch in cartoons and movies. "Didn't I teach you better than that?" Her eyes glinted. She was enjoying this. "You should know not to turn your back on the one wielding the power."

My magic surged through me, a tidal wave desperate to wash away her taint.

But, it recoiled from her hate-filled, vile threads. I yanked it back, using it to erect barriers in my mind, building each one stronger than the last.

Her magic smashed through the first one.

Then the next.

*Molly.* It crawled through my body and my mind, oozing into me, spreading darkness and despair. *Join me. Together, we will be unstoppable.* It burrowed deeper inside of me, holding me immobile, a prisoner in my own body.

Panic lanced me. Sudden. Sharp. It spread through me like frost coating the ground.

My magic flared, lashing out in retaliation, but it splintered against hers.

I was powerful but virtually untrained. She smothered my strike as easily as someone snuffing a candle.

My stomach twisted, and I swayed, one hand reaching out for balance. My fingers brushed Jayden's arm. He didn't move. Didn't reach for me.

Schmendrick yowled as he sprang from my grasp, landing on the boulder with a soft thud. His green eyes blazed. Static rippled along his fur, each strand lifting until it stood at attention. "You cannot have her." His voice boomed.

The words reverberated across the Waters, echoed off the stones, and thrummed inside my skull. They shoved Seraphina's power back, and she staggered.

Nox lifted his head, muscles trembling as he fought the oppressive weight bearing down on him. His gaze locked on my cat, and the corner of his mouth twisted up as if he'd been waiting for this moment.

"Stay out of this, cat." Seraphina flicked her hand, and inky, black vines entangled him. Her eyes narrowed on me, her jaw clenching tighter. "She is mine."

"No!" Falling to my knees, I ignored Seraphina while I clawed at the slimy cords binding Schmendrick.

The deep bass of the music thumped. My pulse rose, keeping time with its beat. The song was all I could hear. All I could feel. The rhythm consumed me, and I dropped my hands.

*Power. Eternity.* The silken voice of Seraphina's power promised as it wrapped around me, slithering forward. It smashed another wall. *It can all be yours.*

The Waters' song pushed the words away, and images of Kur danced in my vision, drawing my attention back to the man kneeling in front of Seraphina.

"What have you done to him?" Grinding out the words, I pushed them through the song and past the magic's coaxing voice.

The look she shot me was sweet innocence. "Who?"

My thoughts flashed to Jayden. The way he hadn't moved when I'd touched him. But I didn't want her attention on him. "Nox." I tossed my hands out in front of me in an oh-my-gods-I-can't-believe-you're-so-stupid gesture.

"Oh, him. Nothing he'll live to regret." She lifted one shoulder, like this was something she did every day. (And maybe it was.) "I can't have him shifting into a dragon before I sacrifice him."

## Chapter 52



*"The problem with cats is that they get the same exact look whether they see a moth or an ax murderer."* ~Paula Poundstone

Schmendrick's claws shredded the last of the vines. He stood and shook them off. "Oh, goody. The evil villain monologue I've been waiting for." He sat, wrapping his tail around his paws. His whiskers curled forward, green eyes glimmering. "Somebody fetch me a bowl of popcorn."

Seraphina didn't bother glancing at Schmendrick, but his comments—dry, familiar, *normal*—snapped me out of her hold.

A moment of clarity.

My magic roared to life. I poured all of my strength into it. A bright wave of power crashed into the dank darkness of Seraphina's.

Attacking. Fighting against her hold on me. Pushing her magic back. Shoving it out.

Then I slammed the doors to my mind shut. A steel fortress she couldn't infiltrate.

As if she didn't notice, Seraphina began chanting. The words were like the distant rumble of thunder. But they were lost to me, hidden behind the Waters' song.

Winds rose, whipping Seraphina's gown around her legs. Jewels sewn into the black silk reflected the lightning, sparkling like the night sky.

The Waters surged, white-capped and furious, battering the pentagram's magical barrier. It held the waves back, but spray showered over me, plastering my hair to my head.

Ember and Holt collided against the barrier. Their faces smashed against it with a sickening *crack*. The current yanked them away. Their arms and legs flailed. Their eyes bulged, filled with terror.

"Stop." I lifted my hand, but my magic struck the barrier and bounced back. I ducked under the spell.

When I straightened, Ember and Holt were gone. Nothing remained but the churning Waters. Their lives snuffed out, ended before they even had a chance to live.

My heart clenched, and a lump blocked my throat. Anger, guilt, and helplessness swirled inside of me, a maelstrom of emotions fiercer than the storm surrounding me. I wanted to scream, to cry, to fall to my knees and beg the gods to take me instead.

But I forced it all down. I needed to stop Seraphina. To put an end to this. Or we would all end up drowned by the Waters' wrath.

Seraphina's chant continued, and the song grew more frenzied. Each chord pounded against me.

I needed time to think of a plan, to come up with a way out of this, a way to keep the Waters from destroying the world, a way to free Kur and stop Seraphina. "You don't have the vial." The words came out of me drenched in sorrow and guilt.

She pointed *MaunDagnir* at me, and a crazed smile lifted her lips. "The vial was necessary to contain your blood. Your sacrifice." She waved the dagger at Nox. The tip of the knife nicked his ear, and a drop of blood soaked into it.

*MaunDagnir* glowed. Darkness thrummed over the blade, and I could sense its hunger.

"I don't need it for Kur's blood." The eerie glow from the dagger lit her face from below, casting long shadows across it, changing her beautiful features into a haunting image of cruelty. "Where your life force would have sustained me for decades, Kur's will sustain me for eternity." She waved the knife lazily through the air. "You should thank him for infiltrating our cabal and leading you astray." She brought *MaunDagnir* down again, slow, deliberate, resting it against his collarbone. "But do make it quick. The ritual must be performed soon."

The truth hit me like a blow to the chest.

It had been her all along.

Not Malachai.

Not Caius.

My mother.

The woman who used to hold my hand. The one who told me how strong I would be. How I would lead the cabal into the future.

The person who was supposed to love me more than anyone else in the world.

How could a mother plan to sacrifice her only child?

Caius I could have understood. He'd always hated me. Always tormented me.

And even though Seraphina and I had a difficult relationship, I thought she loved me. I thought she wanted to see me
succeed.

Bile rose in my throat as hot tears pressed against my eyes.

But I couldn't cry.

I couldn't break.

I needed to be strong, to figure out a way out of this mess.

To save us all and hold the Waters at bay.

As if to emphasize that thought, the Waters swelled, rising
higher, thrashing against the barrier. They wanted Kur, and it
seemed they would stop at nothing to reach him.

But the Waters weren't my main concern. Not at that moment.

Seraphina was.

I wanted to tell her to release Nox, to stop being a sadistic
bitch, but those weren't the words that spilled out of my mouth.
The ones that did shocked me, and her betrayal slammed into
me. "How could you?" The weight of her treachery crashed over
me, knocking me back. My body slumped against Jayden's, but
he didn't reach for me, didn't try to comfort me. Trapped beneath her spell, he was unable to move.

Clutching his hand, I sent my magic into him. The power sought out Seraphina's energy, purging it from him, freeing
him from her hold.

Jayden wrapped his arm around me. His claws snagged on my hoodie, and I looked up into his wolf's eyes.

"He wants out." Jayden's canines were elongated, biting into his lower lip. "But we are not bonded, so we can't communicate if I transform."

"You, Mahlia—" Seraphina waved *MaunDagnir* through the air, her other hand clenched around Nox's shoulder "—you have infinite power, and you serve coffee to *humans*." She practically spat the last word. "And you gave your heart to a mongrel." Her eyes darted to Jayden, and her lip curled with disgust. "That kind of power should belong to someone who would use it. Someone who would cherish it and know its value."

Jayden stepped in front of me, shielding me with his body. "Say what you want about me." His voice was a growl, low and dangerous. "But Molly is worth more than you will ever be."

"Ritual sacrifice. Black magic. And speciesism." Schmendrick's tail flicked from side to side as he stepped beside Jayden. "With parenting like this, it's amazing there are still any sorcerers alive."

Nox's gaze met mine, unblinking.

The endless chasms I found within them made sense.

Kur was ancient. Eternal.

Waves crashed against the shore, pounded the barrier. Furious and feral. With each splash, the melody grew louder, more pressing.

The song called to me, begging me to use it, but I didn't know how.

## Chapter 53



*H*olt and Ember were gone. The other guardians were batteries, powering Seraphina's stupidity. (I mean, what good is immortality if the world ends?) Jayden wasn't planning to shift. Though I was certain he would if he needed to protect me.

Schmendrick had powers I couldn't comprehend. I glanced at him, licking his paw as if this were just another normal, boring day. If things got too out of hand, there was a chance he would step in, but he'd always left me to my resources, made me figure things out.

So… that left me.

And I had been pretending to be normal for far too long. Even though I'd started training again when Seraphina had been kidnapped, my magic was nowhere near as strong as it should have been.

"What's your plan, Molly?" Jayden lifted his hand, cupping my cheek. He stared into my eyes.

Lightning crackled across the sky. Thunder boomed so loud that it shook the ground. Rocks floated up from the sodden terrain, fleeing the death and destruction that was heading for us all.

My gaze was pulled back to Nox, to the knife at his throat.

And though I found no fear in him, I knew I had to save him.

If I didn't, the world would end.

But I didn't have a plan. I didn't know what to do with the song.

Jayden's thumb brushed my cheek.

And I didn't know how to tell him that I didn't have a plan, that I didn't have a clue how to stop Seraphina, how to save Nox, or how to stop the Waters, that we were all about to die.

"I'll let you know when I come up with one." I tried to smile, to comfort him, but really, there was nothing to smile about. The world was about to end, and all it had was me.

Not very promising.

Seraphina's voice rose. Malice filled the ancient words of her chant.

Death and destruction rode the howling wind.

The Waters showed Earth dying. Plants withered and faded. Animals wasted away. Their carcasses covered the dry, barren land.

Then the Waters surged, flowing red as they destroyed all life that remained, covering the planet in a vast, angry ocean.

Jayden leaned toward me. "You are enough." His words brushed across my ear, raising goosebumps on my skin. He squeezed my fingers, and I felt his confidence pour into me.

"Do not let the tide turn red." Nox's voice was deeper than the Primordial Waters, filled with ancient wisdom. "End it, Molly. Let me return to sleep."

The Waters calmed at the sound of his voice. The song paused. Though its hum still echoed through the air.

Seraphina continued her chant, tightening her grip on *MaunDagnir* as she glared at me. The blade bit into Nox's skin. A thin line of blood soaked into the corrupted unicorn horn.

"Are you sure this is what you want?" I stared into his eyes, seeing the weariness he'd hidden in them. "Is there no one else who could take your burden?"

"I am the guardian, the protector." He winced as the dagger scraped against his throat with each word. "I have neglected my duties long enough."

Seraphina's chant grew into a frenzied call. She pulled her arm back, giving Nox a slight reprieve from the dagger's bite.

I'd never been part of a ritual like this, but I knew it was drawing to a conclusion.

I couldn't wait to see what would happen.

I had to stop this.

Somehow.

# Chapter 54



Shadows stretched across the ground. I backed into the darkness and stepped out behind Seraphina, pressing my stiletto into her lower back and wrapping my sword around her neck. "Drop *MaunDagnir*."

"It's too late." She laughed, the laugh of a crazed woman drunk on power. "It's already tasted the dragon's blood."

The melody grew louder. Its rhythm pulsed inside me, syncing with my heartbeat. It tugged at my memories, plucking them like harp strings.

Suddenly, I pictured myself sitting with Malachai in Taras Mor. His voice echoed in my mind, as clear as if he stood beside me. *"…which was why she sang him to sleep."*

"Sang him to sleep," I murmured. The song flared in response, as if it understood. Certainty settled in my gut like a stone sinking to the bottom of the Primordial Waters that surged and writhed, inching ever higher. I knew what I had to do.

"What on earth are you talking about, Mahlia?" Seraphina twisted in my grasp. A strand of blonde hair slipped from her chignon, trailing over my arm like a thread of spider's silk.

I pressed the dagger into her back—not enough to pierce, but enough to make her think twice.

She didn't even flinch, just continued berating me. "And what have I told you about mumbling?"

The heavy bass of the song pounded against the earth, and it trembled in response. I widened my stance to stay upright. Magic erupted around us—violet shafts racing across the ground before bolting into the sky. Each drop of Nox's blood that hit the earth sent another burst of power into the clouds above.

The sky darkened—deep purple and black, fractured by lightning like veins of violet fire. Thunder rolled. The storm churned, unnatural and wild.

And the song crescendoed.

Waves crashed against the bones of fallen gods, splintering them. Mist filled the air—thick, ancient, but somehow still clean, smelling of beginnings and endings.

Another surge of magic bolted for the heavens, and the Waters answered, rising higher than they should have, impossible in their fury.

Over Seraphina's shoulder, I stared at Nox, silently pleading. *Please let her be wrong. Please let him survive MaunDagnir's bite. Don't let this be the end.*

"Do it, Molly." His voice was barely more than a whisper, but it cut through everything—the storm, the song, the fear.

His body trembled where he knelt, blood dark and endless, saturating the mud beneath him. His shoulders sagged, head bowed as if it weighed too much for his neck to hold it up, yet he still managed to lift his gaze to mine.

His eyes, once the black of a bottomless chasm, were now a washed-out gray, like coals fading into ash. But they held.

Somehow, even in death's grip, he was the stronger one.

"But why? You've done so much." My throat tightened, barely allowing the words through. "You've already played your part."

A faint smile ghosted across his lips. A goodbye. "Because you can't, Molly. And there's no one else. No other way out of this."

"You're too late." Magic streaked from Nox's body into Seraphina's—a jagged bolt of violet and black that split the air with a thunderous crack. It struck like lightning, lifting her from the ground and throwing me back. My body slammed against the rocks. The air whooshed out of my lungs.

Seraphina laughed—high and wild. Her eyes glowed as Nox's power lifted her beyond my reach. Golden strands of hair whipped free, haloed in stolen magic.

Wind howled around us, and the song crescendoed in response, refusing to be drowned out. Lightning spiderwebbed across the sky before blasting against the ground. The waves surged, their spray drenching me, cold and stinging.

And Nox's magic fueled the chaos.

My lungs finally accepted a breath of air. Sucking it in greedily, I scanned the ground for my weapons and for *Maun-Dagnir*.

Amongst the chaos, a sound caught my attention. Pure and radiant. As I sat up, I tipped my head to the side.

The melody.

No longer the violent chords.

This was pure, untainted.

It touched my soul.

Faint at first.

But as I listened, it pulsed within me like a heartbeat. Steady. Strong. Impossible to ignore.

Staggering to my feet, I fought the gale and followed the song to Nox.

The roar of the storm dimmed as I sank beside him. The rocky ground was slick beneath my knees. His blood floated on top of the rainwater, reflecting the lightning strikes and shimmering with flecks of purple and silver.

It was mesmerizing, hypnotic. Fighting the urge to stare at it, I closed my eyes and let the song fill me.

Words slipped from my lips on a breath, curling into the air, wrapped in magic. I didn't know where they came from or how I knew them.

*"Kur the dragon.*

*Kur the man.*

*Guardian of the Waters.*

*Protector of the Land."*

They were barely audible to even me, but they pulsed with power and intent. Opening my eyes, I met Nox's. He nodded before letting his head drop to his chest again.

Silent and steady, as if not wanting to disrupt the spell, Jayden approached. With each of his steps, my racing heart calmed. He placed a hand on my shoulder, grounding me. His touch said, *I'm here. Keep going.*

Schmendrick padded through the chaos like he was born of it, settling beside Nox with his tail curled neatly around his paws. His green eyes glowed, reflecting the magic in the air.

The lullaby continued, the notes shaping in the mist.

*"Rest your weary body in the deep once more,*

*Let the waves silence upon the shore."*

The storm shifted, thunder pulling back like a breath held in reverence. Lightning stilled above us, frozen mid-strike, suspended in the sky like a shattered crown.

Seraphina writhed in the magic that had lifted her. It twisted, faltering. She screamed, a shrill, piercing screech that was not a cry of triumph, but of fury and disbelief as the power slipped from her grasp.

I didn't stop singing.

*"Kur the dragon.*

*Kur the man.*

*Bound to the Waters.*

*Bound to the Land.*

*Dragon heart, pure of soul.*
*Harken back to days of old.*
*Dream in serenity.*
*Hold back the Waters for eternity."*

As the verse rose, the wound in Nox's chest pulsed with a silver gleam—moonlight glimmering on still water. His breath hitched.

*"Kur the dragon.*
*Kur the man.*
*Savior of life.*
*Savior of the Land.*

*Protect the Waters.*
*Protect its shores.*
*Dream in peace, forevermore."*

And then… he exhaled.

Not in pain.

In peace.

*"Kur the dragon.*
*Kur the man.*
*Still the Waters.*
*Still the Land."*

As the final syllables left my mouth, I swayed.

## Chapter 55



Jayden's arms were around me at once. His warm breath brushed against my cheek, and I shivered in his embrace.

"Your singing usually makes me pass out, not you." Schmendrick shook the water from his fur.

Not having the energy to come up with a witty retort, I smiled at him.

The storm stilled.

Waves that had towered and thrashed moments before bowed, cresting and rolling back in reverence. The wind dropped to a hush. Lightning vanished into the clouds like serpents retreating to their dens.

The magic that clung to Seraphina cracked.

Her body seized mid-air. Her mouth opened wide in a scream that never escaped. Violet tendrils of Nox's power snapped back from her, severing the stolen bond.

She dropped to the ground, hitting it hard. Coughing and pale, her power leaked like smoke between her fingers.

The flames of the pentagram hissed like a campfire that had been doused by water. As soon as they were extinguished, the guardians stepped free and surrounded Seraphina.

And for a single moment, there was silence.

I strained, listening for the song, but the only sound was the steady lapping of waves.

"You killed them." Willa's blue-green eyes narrowed. She slid her sword from its sheath, her hand trembling with rage and anguish, and rested the point over Seraphina's heart. "They vowed to protect you, and you killed them."

Seraphina's eyes darted from face to face, stopping on Caelan's. "You can't let her hurt me." Panic filled her voice, making it high-pitched. "I am your archon."

For the first time in weeks, Caelan appeared to be sober. "Not anymore, you're not." He pulled magic-blocking cuffs from his back pocket and snapped them on her wrists. "Seraphina Morgana Ravenwood, you are being apprehended for dabbling in dark magic, for attempting to kill the immortal dragon, Kur, thereby releasing the Primordial Waters to destroy Earth, for plotting to kill your daughter, and for anything else I can think of before we get back to Ravenwood Estates."

"I only did what was best for the cabal." Her chest heaved, each breath sharp and ragged as she stumbled back, pulling at the cuffs until her wrists reddened.

Willa clutched her hilt tighter, and I could tell that it was taking everything she had not to plunge the blade through Seraphina's chest.

Storm settled his hand on her shoulder. "Give it a rest, Willa." His normal jovial brogue was weighed down, heavier than I'd ever heard it. "It won't bring 'em back."

My heart went out to them. They'd had to stand there—unable to move, unable to help—and watch their friends get taken by the Waters. It had gutted me, and I hadn't known Ember and Holt like they had.

The ground rumbled beneath Nox, drawing my focus back to him.

A thin line of silver traced from his wound outward, fanning across the stones like veins through marble. Where it touched water, the surface shimmered—not with violence, but with purpose. The tide calmed further. A soft rain began to fall. Warm and clean.

Nox's body no longer bled. The air around him shimmered. Light and mist wove into a cocoon that pulsed as it wrapped around his body.

The beams expanded, pushing outward until they were too bright to look at directly.

## Chapter 56



*"A cat can be trusted to purr when she is pleased, which is more than can be said for human beings." -William Ralph Inge*

"Take us home, Molly." Caelan dragged Seraphina to her feet. Rain dripped from his hair, trailing down his face. His hazel eyes were clear, but a deep sadness filled them.

Seraphina looked like she'd been fished out of the sea. Her tattered dress clung to her body, dull and lifeless. Most of her hair had fallen out of her chignon. Her makeup was smudged, and the haughty expression had been wiped from her face. "Molly." She lifted her cuffed hands, reaching for me.

Taking a step back, I turned from her to the cocoon pulsating around Nox's body. It seemed to be growing with each throb. "I can't, Caelan, not until I know that Kur will guard the Waters."

"It wasn't a request." The Caelan that had entered Harvest Moon a few weeks ago was back. The hard, callous version of the man I'd once cared for so deeply, but even that version was better than the drunkard. "It was an order."

"What if this isn't the end?" I waved my hand at our surroundings. Even though the Waters were no longer churning, they hadn't receded.

A muscle ticked in his jaw. "I have to get her back before her magic replenishes."

"I can portal us home." Lane stepped forward. "Whoever wants to go, and Molly can make sure this is over."

I lowered my head. "You can't." I tugged my hand through my hair. "You can't portal between realms."

"Two steps." I held my hands out and looked at Jayden. "Two steps, and I'll be back."

He nodded. "Stay safe."

Caelan and Lane slid their hands into mine. "Anyone else." Sweeping my gaze over their faces, I tried not to feel their pain.

"No one else?" Caelan looked around the group.

Willa shook her head. "I need to cool off a bit before I'm in her presence again." Her hands tightened into fists. "Right now, I can't promise my sword wouldn't accidentally slip and pierce her cold heart."

"Nahvienne told me to stay by Molly's side since she can't be here." Thorn rubbed the back of his neck, and his gaze met mine. "I haven't done a very good job so far, but I'd like to make her proud of me."

"Sorry, mate." Storm shrugged. "Not leavin'. Not 'til the bloody end."

I tried to suppress the shiver that crept up my spine. "I know what you mean, but I hope this end doesn't get any bloodier."

Lane grabbed one of Seraphina's arms, and I backed into the shadow that would take us to Ravenwood.

"Be safe." Lane looked at the cocoon that had been Nox once more and shuddered.

I stepped into the shadows beneath the archways in the great hall and dropped Lane's and Caelan's hands.

Caelan nodded at me, a grim expression on his face. "I expect a full report when you return."

Then the three of them walked away. Seraphina's steps were off-balance, and I huffed out a laugh when I realized one of her heels had broken off in the tumult.

I stepped into the shadows again. When I returned to the Waters, I faced the guardians who'd stayed behind. Grief etched their faces, but I knew they wouldn't give in to it until Kur was guarding the Waters again.

"Any ideas?" Storm nodded to the cocoon.

Light flickered over its surface, making it shimmer, reminding me of an opal, its colors ever changing.

I shrugged. "All we can do is wait."

It stopped sprinkling, and a rainbow stretched across the lilac sky, reflecting in the Waters, appearing to be a perfect circle.

Staring at it, a sense of peace spread through me.

Then the cocoon shivered.

And again.

A sickening rip split the air, wet and stringy. It tore through the fibrous strands. A vein of darkness glimmered beneath the opalescent exterior.

My stomach dropped, my throat tightening until I couldn't draw in a full breath. Every instinct screamed for me to run, but I pulled my sword from its sheath and inched forward, stretching my neck to see what was about to emerge.

Storm's hand twitched. Sparks danced across his fingers as he edged closer.

Willa dropped into a fighting stance.

Thorn cursed under his breath. His jaw tightened, but resolve hardened his eyes.

Fur rippled across the backs of Jayden's hands. His body trembled as he strained against the change.

Their fear mirrored mine, but they stood with me. That steadied me more than my blade.

The cocoon ripped apart with a wet, tearing sound.

My heart raced, and my legs seemed to turn to stone, locking me in place, preventing me from moving.

Obsidian claws punched through the shell, hooked and dripping, each scrape echoing across the Waters.

My grip tightened on my sword until my knuckles ached.

A snout forced its way out, black scales glistening like oil on water.

Terror clenched my gut, but I willed myself to hope—hope that Nox was somewhere inside Kur, that he would recognize me and remember his plea to return him to his role as guardian.

The cocoon shivered violently, and dread gnawed at me.

*What if he didn't?*

Then the dragon's head surged free, its copper eyes blazing with intelligence. For a heartbeat, a shadow of recognition seemed to flash through them.

My chest leapt with hope.

Then they locked on our weapons. A low, desperate growl, raw and ragged like an animal backed into a corner, tore from him.

His lips curled, revealing jagged teeth, and my heart slammed against my ribs as I staggered backward.

# Chapter 57



Not taking my eyes off the dragon, I lowered my sword. My hands shook, and the blade scraped against leather when I sheathed it. There was a finality to the sound that stole my breath.

Out of the corner of my eye, I saw the others follow my lead, and I prayed I wasn't making a mistake we'd all regret.

Slowly, I lifted my hands, showing the beast that I wasn't armed. "I mean you no harm."

"Dragon." Schmendrick trotted up next to me and sat by my feet.

The dragon's top lip lifted on one side, and I wasn't sure if it was a smile or a snarl. "Cat."

"Forgive me for waking you." Schmendrick bowed low. When he lifted his head, a mischievous glimmer lit his eyes. "But 5,000 years." He raised his paw and licked it with deliberate nonchalance, but his gaze remained locked on the dragon. "That's excessive even by cat standards."

Lowering my hands, I stepped forward. "I don't know if you're Kur or Nox or something in between, but the Waters missed you."

He climbed out of the cocoon, growing larger with each movement. Shards of shell tumbled from his onyx scales, littering the muddy ground. His wings snapped open with the booming crack of thunder, a gust slamming into me and knocking me back a step.

Jayden's hands clamped around my arms, steadying me before I fell. His grip was firm, but a tremor of fear ran through them.

The dragon's tail lashed the air, splattering all of us with mud. "I am."

"You are what?" Willa's voice was soft, coaxing.

"I am beginnings and endings. Protector and destroyer."

While I wiped the grime from my face, the dragon lifted his head. A plume of fire erupted from his maw, billowing outward in a wave of blistering heat. The air reeked of sulfur and smoke, and the cracked altar glowed as if the stone itself might combust.

Silence followed.

Broken by the crackle of fire dying on his tongue.

Other than the twitching of Schmendrick's ears, none of us moved. "Ooh, shall we get some marshmallows and roast them over the fire while singing Kumbaya?"

"Oh, how I've missed your catty comments Tha'—"

"It's Schmendrick." Schmendrick's ears flattened against his head, and his green eyes narrowed on the dragon.

A sound like rocks crashing down a mountainside rolled from the dragon's throat. The air itself seemed to shake. My pulse hammered, catching in my throat.

*What kind of hell was he about to unleash?*

"Would ya look at that?" Storm's rugged Australian drawl cut through the chaos. "The overgrown lizard's havin' a laugh."

The sound of tumbling rocks rolled to a halt, and the dragon's gaze settled on Schmendrick. "Fool." Smoke puffed from his nostrils. Adding to the harsh, acrid scent in the air. "Your name these days is Fool? Oh, how the mighty have fallen."

Schmendrick narrowed his green eyes on the wyrm. "And yours is Kur. Guardian of the Waters. Protector of the Land." He curled his tail around his legs. His voice was silk layered over steel. "Will you honor your name?"

Breath catching, I flinched and prayed Kur wouldn't take offense. Reaching behind me, I slipped my hand into Jayden's. Even through his fear, he was a steady, comforting presence.

Willa's gaze darted from Schmendrick to Kur, and her fingers twitched above her sheathed sword, hovering there, ready to draw her blade. But what good would it be against a dragon?

A wave crashed against the bones, splashing all of us. Schmendrick hissed, shaking his paw.

As the tide rolled out, silence pressed in, thick and suffocating.

Dread crept up my spine.

Then a single note cleaved the peace. It danced over my skin before being joined by another and another until the air thrummed with Kur's song. Rich and resonant, the tune vibrated through my chest.

Words poured from my mouth without my consent, and I swayed to the melody.

> *"Kur the dragon.*
> *Kur the man.*
> *Guardian of the Waters.*
> *Protector of the Land."*

The great dragon bowed his head. His eyes—Nox's eyes—locked with mine. They were filled with the echoes of eternity. With beginnings and endings.

Storm shifted his weight from foot to foot. "Bloody hell." His voice was low, almost reverent. "Did ya see that?"

Thorn took a step forward, and the ground shuddered beneath his feet.

"Get ahold of your magic." Schmendrick's tail thumped against the sodden ground, curling and uncurling in time to the music.

While singing the next verse, I stared into Kur's eyes.

> *"Kur the dragon.*
> *Kur the man.*
> *Savior of life.*
> *Savior of the Land."*

Kur sank to the ground, immense wings folding against his body, massive claws stirring up floating rocks like a conductor guiding an orchestra. The Waters receded, unveiling the skeletal remains of long-dead gods, white and gleaming under the pale light.

The melody thrummed softly, guiding the last of my words.

*"Protect the Waters.*

*Protect its shores.*

*Dream in peace, forevermore."*

Kur's body grew, rising like the mountains the Mesopotamians named him for. His tail lengthened, wrapping around the Waters, cradling them in his soothing embrace.

His eyes drifted closed, and soft snores rumbled across the land.

## Chapter 58



Kur's symbol blazed the same purple as the sky. Pieces of the altar rose into the air, spinning like they were caught in a cyclone. They joined together. The seams glowed with the same violet light that had strung from Nox to Seraphina.

The altar settled on the ground in front of Kur's symbol. It pulsed, a steady throb like a heartbeat.

The wind carried the melody to me, softer than it had been. My hips swayed to the rhythm.

"You must leave an offering." Schmendrick jumped onto my shoulders, his claws catching on my sweatshirt as he settled around my neck.

I scratched beneath his chin. "What? All I have are my weapons."

"MaunDagnir."

As if called by its name, the dagger throbbed. Dark waves of energy rolled off it. The ground blackened beneath the blade.

"How?" I swallowed my fear. "You told me I couldn't touch it, that Jayden couldn't touch it." Not wanting them to be corrupted by its power either, I glanced at the others.

He swished his tail, whacking me in the face with it. I grasped it, keeping him from flicking it at me again. "You cannot, but your magic can."

*My magic.* When would it feel natural to call upon it again? As a child, it had been, but for the last several years, it was an afterthought.

I focused on the weapon. Malevolence radiated from it. Hatred imbued the blade with a taint that my magic recoiled from. But if Schmendrick was telling me to do it, I needed to trust him.

The dagger rose into the air. *Together, we can rule.*

When *MaunDagnir* spoke to me, I nearly dropped it. The words pressed against my mind, the voice as soft as silk. Warm and seductive.

My magic faltered, its hold on the blade loosening. But then Schmendrick began purring. The sound so pure, so comforting. It reminded me of a thousand nights spent with him curled beside me, protecting me while I dreamt, holding the boogeyman at bay.

My power's grip tightened, and the blade floated toward the altar.

*No one will terrorize you again. You will have nothing, no one to fear.*

This time, the words sounded like an empty promise. Desperate and hollow.

*MaunDagnir* hovered above the altar. "Are you sure, Schmendrick? Are you sure it won't corrupt Kur?"

"The dragon will keep it safe." His body vibrated against my shoulders, his rumbling purrs calming the panic that threatened to rise in me.

*Whatever you want, Molly. I will give you whatever you want.*

That promise was enough for me to know that leaving the blade as an offering was what needed to be done.

I settled the dagger on the onyx altar. The pulsating stopped as the blade was swallowed by the rock. The symbol dimmed, and light shone through the clouds for the first time since I'd discovered the Primordial Waters.

The glassy reflection showed stars being born.

## Chapter 59

*"If you want to write, keep cats." —Aldous Huxley*

Willa, Thorn, Storm, Jayden, Schmendrick, and I stepped into a shadow and out into Ravenwood Citadel, bypassing the runes that would show me images that made no sense until it was too late.

Shouts echoed through the corridors, bouncing off the walls before disappearing high above us. "The great hall." Thorn stepped around me, leading the way.

My shoulders slumped as I followed behind him. We all looked like drowned rats, and we were about to stand in front of an already enraged council.

Jayden took my hand in his, gently rubbing his thumb along mine. That simple gesture gave me the strength to continue putting one foot in front of the other until we pushed through the heavy doors.

The council members, minus Seraphina and Caius, stood on the dais. Alden's voice boomed over the others'. "This would've never happened if we had competent guardians."

Caelan's fists clenched at his sides. "I put Seraphina in her cell myself."

"Before or after you drank a bottle of scotch?" Isadora smirked, and I could almost see her lick a finger and mark a point for herself on her mental scoreboard.

"Seeing your archon try to sacrifice a man with a cursed blade is quite sobering." His fists tightened and relaxed several times. "Not to mention watching two of my friends being swept away by the Primordial Waters and not being able to lift a finger to help them."

Thaddeus stuck two fingers in his mouth, and a sharp, piercing whistle filled the great hall, silencing everyone in the room. "This is not the time for infighting. We need to find Seraphina and Caius and bring them to justice. We need to appoint a new archon and find new guardians. Then we will rise from the ashes like the mighty phoenix."

"She escaped." My feet stuttered to a stop, and I fought the urge to sink to the floor and curl into the fetal position.

My words drew the council's attention.

Alden turned his sour glare on us. "Get your zoo out of here, Mahlia. This hall is for sorcerers, not their" —he focused on Jayden—"*pets.*"

A low growl rumbled out of Jayden. "Until you can guarantee her safety, I'll—"

"We'll," Schmendrick corrected.

Jayden inclined his head, never breaking Alden's stare. "We won't be leaving her side."

"And why, pray tell, do you believe her safety is in jeopardy?" Alden stroked his beard like a beloved pet.

Caelan shook his head and pinched the bridge of his nose. "Like we already told you, Seraphina planned to sacrifice *Molly* until she figured out that Nox was really Kur."

"Now that she can't sacrifice Kur, Molly is in danger." Willa strode forward and took her place in front of the dais. Her red hair clung to her face in sodden strands. Her clothes were torn, soaked, and mud-splattered. But she stood before the council members with her back straight, her chin lifted, and her eyes defiant. "We won't lose another guardian, especially not because of your supposed superiority."

Siobhan settled her hand on Thaddeus' arm and spoke too quietly for me to hear what she said. He nodded and took his seat. Most of the other council members followed his lead. Siobhan glared at Leonora and Darian until they sat.

"Molly, can you tell us what became of Kur?" She twisted her ring around her finger, appearing insecure and maybe a bit lost. "Are the Primordial Waters contained?"

Holding Jayden's hand in mine, I strode forward, refusing to be cowed by Alden or any of the council members. "Kur is protecting us once more. The Waters have calmed."

Her hand fluttered to her chest, and relief loosened her shoulders. "You are a Ravenwood."

"No." Alden slammed his hand down on his armrest, the sound like a gunshot aimed straight at my heart.

"Yes." Schmendrick, who had been on my shoulders a blink of an eye before, appeared on Seraphina's throne. His tail flicked. "She actually *is*."

Alden's jaw tightened so much that I wondered if he would crack a tooth. "I will not allow her to be the next archon."

"I'm afraid that decision isn't yours to make." Siobhan's lips curled into a thin smile, daring him to argue with her. "Molly, step forward and take your place."

# A Note from Schmendrick

(Yes, me. I get the last word.)

So, you've reached the end, devoured every page, gasped at all the twists, and fallen hopelessly in love with me. Don't worry, it happens all the time.

Now, before you scurry off to your next book, I have one teensy, tiny favor to ask. It would be the cat's meow if you'd leave a review. Just use those opposable thumbs and type up a few words, click five stars, and voilà! By doing so, you give this book a chance to shine.

Why should you?

Because reviews tell my author that her sleepless nights were worth it. They help other readers find her story (and meet me, obviously). Plus, the more reviews we get, the more chances I have to appear in sequels, spin-offs, plush toys… Schmendrick everywhere. World domination at my paws.

So log on, say what you loved, who your favorite cat was, what made you yell at the page, or which part you think I should've had more lines in. (The answer is all of them.)

Go on. Shoo. I'll wait here, basking in the warm glow of your future five stars.

With infinite charm and just enough cattitude,

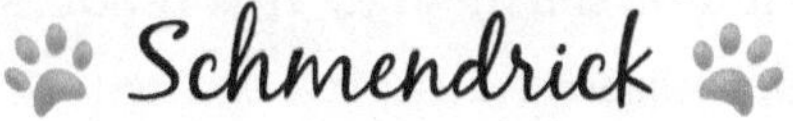

# Acknowledgments

In case you haven't figured it out from my previous books, my husband, Jeff, is the greatest. He supports me. He cheers me on. He loves me unconditionally. And in this book, he helped me come up with Seraphina's spell, helped me get through my writer's block, and helped talk me through scenarios. When I'm feeling down, he reminds me that all I wanted was to be a published author and that I need to enjoy the journey because sometimes, the little moments really are the big ones.

My children, Jami and Jesse, inspire me every day. I am so proud of them, and even if I sell a million copies of a novel, they will always be my greatest achievements.

When Shadowborn Secrets decided it needed a dragon, my brothers, Jason and Zach, let me toss ideas at them and helped me figure out which dragon I wanted to include.

My dad, Jim, is one of my biggest cheerleaders. He's always telling people about my books. His support means everything to me.

Miri Cosette, LA McBride, Jenny Sandiford, MH Woodscourt, Sophia Alessandrini, and Emilie Ocean are not only fantastic authors, they're also amazing people who have all given me a pat on the back when I needed it and helped me along the way.

Mariruth and Dana are my stars. They're always there, even when I can't see them.

Bella, Galadriel, Merida, and Westley are cats with so much purr-sonality and the inspiration behind Schmendrick.

And last but not least, you, my readers, thank you for picking up this book and giving it a chance.

# *A Special Thank You For Your Coffee Orders*

Less time was spent at Harvest Moon Coffee Shop in this novel than in the first one, but even so, your orders were extremely helpful. I don't drink coffee, so I didn't know where to begin with coffee orders.

Nalani Titcomb & Ashley W. Slaughter
(Gray-haired woman's drink)
Sophia Alessandrini (Molly's drink)
Mary Ford (Mary's drink)
Dana Firkins (the last coffee Molly served for the day)

I'm planning one more book in this series,
so your order might still show up in one of them.

If you liked this story, you can join my mailing list.
Drop by my website <u>MandiOyster.com</u>
or if you have any comments,
shoot me a note at mandi@mandioyster.com.
I am always happy to hear from people who've read my work.
I try to answer every email I receive.


Facebook – <u>https://www.facebook.com/MandiOysterAuthor</u>
Instagram  –  <u>https://www.instagram.com/mandioyster/</u>
My web page – MandiOyster.com

# About the Author

Mandi Oyster lives in Southwest Iowa in the middle of an enchanted forest where unicorns, fairies, and dragons abound. At least, that's what she assumes when she looks out into the trees. Her husband, two kids (when they're not away at college), four cats, and two chinchillas share the house with her. 

Besides being an author, she also runs her own editing business and works full-time as a digital prepress technician for a local printshop.

You can find her online at:
https://www.MandiOyster.com
https://www.facebook.com/MandiOysterAuthor
https://instagram.com/MandiOyster/

www.ingramcontent.com/pod-product-compliance
Lightning Source LLC
Chambersburg PA
CBHW061635190726
48289CB00006B/1611